Heart's Revenge

Heart's Revenge

Julia C. Porter

Five Star • Waterville, Maine

First Edition
First Printing: May 2006

Published in 2006 in conjunction with Tekno Books.

Set in 11 pt. Plantin by Carleen Stearns.

Printed in the United States on permanent paper.

Library of Congress Cataloging-in-Publication Data

Porter, Julia C.
    Heart's revenge / Julia C. Porter.—1st ed.
        p. cm.
    ISBN 1-59414-447-8 (hc : alk. paper)
    1. College teachers—Fiction.   2. Divers—Fiction.
3. Shipwrecks—Fiction.   4. Ocracoke Island (N.C.)—
Fiction.   5. Teach, Edward, d. 1718 (Spirit)—Fiction.
I. Title.
PS3616.O782H43 2006
    813'.6—dc22   2005033740

For E.J., of course. And D.J., too,
who came along a wee bit later.

Acknowledgments

Huge thanks to Elizabeth Jasper, Carolyn Jasper, Andrew Jasper, Rachel Heslin, Jon Hansen, Jim C. Hines, Kathy Sedia, Jenn Reese, Mary Madewell, Marie Savoy, Stephen Francis Murphy, John Helfers, Mary Smith, Kathleen Stowers, and Brittiany Koren.

Chapter One

Ella Simon was not the kind of person who saw things that weren't there. So when it happened for the second time on her drive south, she hit the brakes and pulled off the road. She'd seen something out in the dark waters of the sound, on top of one of the submerged houses. Was that a *person* up there?

She'd been driving all day, hoping to get free from the ghosts she'd left behind in Boston. Her father. Steven. Her cold, empty apartment. Her stalled career. She needed to leave all those bad feelings and haunting memories back in the city, far from the strip of two-lane highway bordered by wind-blown sand that she was traveling on now.

Traveling, and seeing things that weren't really there.

The sun had come out again, and she was on her way past the black-and-white Hatteras lighthouse that still lit up the North Carolina coast. She'd just driven onto the rebuilt section of the highway that had been washed out in the hurricane when she saw the movement on top of one of the flooded houses in the sound.

I'm letting my imagination get away from me, she thought, *and that's not like me. My nerves are shot from driving all day, and it's making me see things that aren't there.*

The first time it had happened, she'd been crossing over the Oregon Inlet Bridge. The cold March wind had slammed into her car as she reached the highest section of the bridge. For an awful moment—a moment that seemed to last *forever*—she thought she was going to go over the side.

The dark waters of the Croatan Sound were on her right, far below her, and the whitecaps of the Atlantic Ocean were marching off in the distance on her left. The sun came out of the clouds just in time to nearly blind her with its brilliance.

The sudden blasts of wind against her car windows made her think of broken glass. When she regained control of her car a second later, she risked another look down at the water off to her left.

Flashing just under the surface of the choppy waves were faint lights, flickering orange and white. They looked like emergency beacons, or tiny explosions.

Impossible, she'd decided. *It's just the sun, reflecting off the water. Playing tricks on my fatigued eyes.*

And now, half an hour later, it was happening again.

Feeling like a tightrope walker on this narrow slip of land surrounded by water, Ella left her car. Tall and slender, she wore a faded pair of jeans and a Boston University sweatshirt that hid her figure in a way that she always liked. Holding her breath, she stepped onto the sandy shoulder of the new patch of highway.

She kept her gaze locked on the drowned house surrounded by driftwood and tree limbs, and then she saw the movement again. It looked just like a shadowy outline of a person.

The person—if that's what it was—moved in a strange, irregular fashion, like a beat-up flag or a tree limb blowing in the wind. But the wind had died, and none of the trees in the area were left standing.

Still squinting across the dark blue waters of the sound, she reached into the back seat and felt around for her binoculars. She found them after a few seconds of searching around her suitcases, computers, scuba gear, and other equipment. She didn't dare take her eyes off the battered roof 300 yards out in the sound.

There has to be a reasonable, logical explanation for this, she told herself. But that didn't stop her heart from pounding out of control. She still held her breath, as if she were afraid to let the air out of her lungs.

She brought the binoculars up to her eyes in one quick movement. Even when she focused the binoculars, she still couldn't see the figure clearly.

But it was a person, without a doubt. Whoever it was, the person was big, and covered in shadows like a robe.

The figure seemed to almost float through the air as it leapt and spun to some silent melody. Ella could barely keep up with its movements as the dark figure danced to the edge of the roof, and then danced back.

He was *dancing* on the roof of the drowned house. The blurry man—she was pretty sure it was a man, not a woman—looked deformed somehow, but she couldn't focus on him long enough to figure out what was wrong with him.

And then she realized that the person out there was missing his head.

She blew out the breath that she'd been holding and almost dropped her binoculars.

"Come on," she muttered, turning the dial on the binoculars to try to get a better look at him. She blinked to refocus her own eyes.

When she opened them again and looked back at the house, the man was gone.

Ella scanned the rest of the newly made sound, paying close attention to the pieces of wood and roofing floating in the choppy water. She saw nothing. The dancing, headless shadow was gone.

As she took one last long look at the cluttered mess of

the flooded town, she heard a deep, rolling laugh. She would have run back to her car if she thought she could have kept herself from turning around and heading back to Boston.

Instead, she held her ground, determined not to be rattled for the second time that day. She sucked in a quick breath and caught a whiff of sulphur in the air, as if someone had just blown out a match.

When her pulse had gone back to normal, just as she was about to go back to her Escort, a car horn blasted at her from the highway. This time she did drop her binoculars, and she almost pitched forward into the murky water of the new inlet.

Swearing in a shaky voice, she turned as the car roared past her, its horn still blaring but fading now like a siren. It was a boxy blue Mercedes with rusty New Jersey plates. Three white-haired people sat in the car, two in front and one in the back.

"Friendly folks," she said as she picked up the binoculars and walked back to her car. "At least I'll have some company on the island after all."

With her back to the drowned house, her face felt hot with embarrassment, even though she was all alone. She wasn't normally so easily spooked like this; she prided herself on her independence and her emphasis on the facts, not fiction.

If I can't prove it with facts, she'd always thought, *I don't believe in it.*

"Prove it to me," she told her students every time one of them shared a wild theory or far-fetched idea about history or the world. "Prove it to me, and I'll believe it."

And that determined need for the facts had always ruined the stories her father had told her as she was growing up.

12

Tales about ghosts, water sprites, will-o'-the-wisps, fairies, and angels. Ella knew, even as a child, that such stories were just a naïve diversion, a foolish waste of time. And they were certainly not something for a professor of Maritime History to enjoy.

As she looked up and down the highway behind her, watching out for more speeding senior citizens, she couldn't dispel the image of the headless, shadowy figure she'd seen so far out in the sound. Surely it had all been a trick of the shadows.

With a half-hearted laugh, she scanned the dark waters of the sound one last time before climbing back in her car. After one last glance back at the ruined house out in the sound, she drove to the southern tip of Hatteras Island to meet the ferry that would take her to Ocracoke and the start of her expedition.

Over an hour later, Ella's car was the last to clatter down the short metal bridge leading from the ferry that had carried her from Hatteras to Ocracoke Island. She followed four other cars, a minivan, and two couples on Harleys. The first car off the ferry was the old blue Mercedes.

She parked her car in the small lot next to the deserted ferry landing to wait for Mitch. Drumming her fingers on the steering wheel, she listened to the fading engine of the ferry on its way back to Hatteras, abandoning her here on this tiny island.

Apparently her dive master was running late today. She bit down a wave of impatience, wondering if they should've agreed to meet in town instead of here. At first she thought it was quaint, almost old-fashioned, that Mitch wanted to meet her at the ferry landing so he could welcome her and show her around town. Now it just looked like a bad idea.

Ten minutes later, she was still waiting.

"Where are you, Mitch?" she muttered.

Needing to stretch her legs, she got out of her car at last, letting her light brown hair out of its ponytail and shaking it loose onto her shoulders. After being in motion all day, she didn't feel like stopping now. Stopping made her think of all those things left behind in Boston.

She'd been in such a funk since her father's sickness and her breakup with Steven that she'd been in a mad rush to get away from the city. Away from the snow and the cold and everything else up there. Away from her apartment, which was starting to feel like someone else's home, full of broken glass.

She stifled the urge to pull out her cell phone and call the number of Mitch's diving company. She glanced at the sun and then looked back at all the diving gear and computer equipment in the back seat of her car. Unpacking and getting set up in her rented house was going to take forever.

I'm giving this Mitch guy ten more minutes, she thought, *before I go find someone else with a boat. Someone reliable.*

A familiar voice spoke up inside her head like a life preserver thrown to a tired swimmer fighting the deadly pull of a riptide.

"Relax," the voice said with a hint of laughter in it. "Quit rushing things."

She felt a sharp pain in her chest when she recognized the voice. Dad's voice.

"Relax, and listen to the surf," he'd always said.

She smiled a bittersweet smile at Dad's memory. She had to remember that life out here was going to be much slower than city life. She'd have to learn all over again how to slow down and not rush so much. Dad had always reminded her that everything fell into place on its own. She didn't need to force it.

If only that were true, she thought.

She leaned against the passenger side of her car and took a deep breath of salty air. She stretched like a cat and felt the fatigue and edginess from her drive begin to melt away. As she stared out at the breakers on the ocean side of the island, she thought about the swirl of events in the past week that had brought her here.

It was all about the shipwreck, of course.

Less than a week ago, she'd gotten the call. Boston had been suffering under a cold snap, and she stared out of the ice-rimmed window of her apartment, listening to her department head. She remembered wishing for winter to hurry up and end.

"What would you say," Dr. Bramlett had said, "to a couple weeks on an island off the Outer Banks?"

Suddenly alert, Ella had felt her blues begin to melt at the prospect of going south and getting away from the cold. Outside her window, all she could see was a gray city filled with dirty snow clogging the streets.

"When do I leave?" she said. "I can be packed in an hour."

A low chuckle came from the other end of the line.

"Don't you even want to know what the project is going to be about?"

"If it gets me out of here for a while, I'll do whatever research you need me to do. Even if it's as dull as looking up tide charts."

"Oh, I think this will be *better* than tide charts."

As department head of Maritime Studies at the university, Dr. Bramlett always came through with the best research ideas and leads for her. Hopefully, this one would be another winner.

"I'm sure you've heard of this fellow," he said. "Goes by the name of . . . Blackbeard."

The howling wind outside suddenly picked up, throwing hard pellets of snow against the window, as if trying to get inside.

"Oh no," she said, "don't even joke about that. Not *The Queen Anne's Revenge*? I thought they found the *QAR* already."

"You're right—they're pretty sure the *QAR*'s down in Beaufort, North Carolina. But what my contact person down in Ocracoke found may be even better."

"Better?"

"Yes. You know how legend has it that Blackbeard sank the *QAR* so nobody else could take her treasure? Well, we've found what may be the remains of the actual ship that Blackbeard used after the *QAR* sank. The ship Blackbeard moved all his treasure onto. This ship once belonged to Stede Bonnet, who called it *The Revenge*. If it's *The Revenge*, the historical significance would be unbelievable. Let me give you the details . . ."

Pacing around her apartment as Dr. Bramlett talked, she turned too quickly and knocked a framed photograph off an end table. The glass in the frame broke, leaving her ex-boyfriend Steven's brown, puppy-dog eyes obscured by the shards. She'd been meaning to get rid of that photo anyway.

"Okay, I get it," Ella said. She'd found the cloud in his silver lining. "You're going to make me fly down there, aren't you, so I can start checking out Blackbeard's lost ship right away, huh? You know how I feel about flying."

A harsh buzz of static ran through the connection. She winced, holding the phone away from her ear. After a few seconds, the fuzz disappeared as quickly as it had started. Dr. Bramlett was already talking.

". . . Trust me, Ella, please. I know how you are about flying. But this assignment is perfect for you. You can drive down there, catch the ferry, and spend all spring putting your scuba gear to good use once you get to the island."

There *had* to be a catch. Ella stopped pacing. The late winter wind continued to rattle her windowpanes.

There was always a catch. Just like Dad's sudden illness last year that had taken his life a month after his fiftieth birthday. Or that look in Steven's eyes on their last date, the look that told Ella he was getting too serious, too fast. So she'd ended it. She'd been in a funk ever since.

"So," Dr. Bramlett had said at last. "Are you interested? Or should I find someone else to go?"

Mitch's time was up.

Still standing outside her car next to the ferry landing, Ella pushed herself away from it, surprised at how relaxed she'd been, just sitting there, not moving or doing anything.

When was the last time I'd done that? she wondered. *Just sat and did nothing?*

As she inhaled the tang of salt and the slightly fishy scent of the ocean, she looked up in time to see a jagged line of pelicans fly silently past overhead, heading east into the great unknown. They were soon tiny dots against the cloudy sky.

In spite of being annoyed at this Mitch guy, she smiled, thinking of her father. Even if Dad was gone, she'd always have the gifts of the ocean and sailing that he'd given her all those years ago. Every year on her birthday he'd take her out to sea on a rented boat with her choice of half a dozen friends. Most years she'd chosen to go alone with Dad, so they could talk and watch the waves make the land disappear behind them.

Just as she was about to get back in her car and find her way around on her own, Ella heard the distant mutter of an engine.

Seconds later, a sky-blue pickup at least thirty years old flew onto the circle drive leading to the ferry landing. The truck made the turn, but just barely. She watched, waiting for it to go up on two wheels, but instead the truck turned toward her. It screeched to a stop and deposited someone from the passenger side onto the road before leaving in a puff of black smoke.

When the dark cloud of exhaust had cleared, Ella got a good look at the man who had suddenly appeared in front of her.

She certainly wasn't expecting to see anyone like this lanky, dark-haired man wearing a form-fitting blue T-shirt and jeans. She caught herself admiring his tousled brown hair and the solid muscles under the cotton of his shirt. He walked over to her, a question on his handsome face and a glimmer of mischief in his eyes. This was definitely not the salty old dog Ella had been expecting to be her dive master.

To her utter surprise, her heart was beating faster than it had in months, and she'd completely forgotten the name of the dive company. All she remembered was a first name.

"Mitch?"

She cleared her throat, her face red-hot.

"Um. Your name wouldn't happen to be Mitch, would it?"

"Dr. *Simon?*" His low voice had a slight Southern accent.

"Yes. I'm Dr. Simon. Why do you look so surprised?"

"Oh."

His tanned face turned red and his eyes widened. Those eyes were a fascinating shade of light blue, as if all his time spent in the sun—or maybe all his time spent underwater—had faded the color. Offset by his tanned skin, they were quite striking.

"Oh," he said again. "I'd just thought you were—"

He cleared his throat and stood a little straighter.

"I mean, I thought maybe you were a tour—Um. Right."

Ella waited, unsure if she was smiling or grimacing at him.

"I'm Mitch Thompson," he said at last, holding out his hand. He gave her a big, genuine smile that dispelled a good bit of her doubts about him. But not all of them. "From Thompson Deep Sea Diving. Nice to meet you, uh, doctor."

Ella shook his hand, feeling the calluses there and trying to ignore the tingling sensation his touch sent up her arm.

"Tell me, Mitch," she said once she had control of her voice. "Did you get lost on the way here?"

"No," he said with a sheepish look that may have been quite charming in other circumstances. If she hadn't been so annoyed, it may have even worked on her. "Just running late. My truck's in the shop, so I had to get my buddy Ben to drop me off."

Behind his smile, Ella sensed disappointment. With a sinking heart, she realized why he looked so confused.

Mitch had been expecting a *he*, not a *she*, to lead on their dives over the next few weeks. Ella hadn't signed her first name on the two E-mails she'd exchanged with him. She'd simply ended them with: "Sincerely, Dr. Simon."

He'd probably been expecting a new drinking buddy at best, or a stuffed shirt at worst. Definitely not a woman.

"We should get going, I guess," she said, and Mitch nodded, heading over to the passenger side of her car.

Back in the driver's seat, Ella glanced at Mitch as he sat

down next to her. He had a smudge of what looked like black caulking on the knuckles of his right hand, and four small scratches on the back of his left that seemed relatively fresh. She caught a whiff of his scent—a mix of salt, soap, and a hint of motor oil.

Mitch sat in silence next to her, staring out the window at the jagged sand dunes with a strange intensity. Ella wondered what was running through that head of his.

She was about to say something to him about the upcoming dive, but the wind suddenly came up, throwing sand against the car windows and reminding her of the booming laugh she'd heard from the headless figure she'd seen—*thought* she'd seen—over in Hatteras, dancing and leaping on top of the drowned house.

Without another word, Ella put the car in gear and aimed it toward the road leading into town.

These next few weeks, she thought, *are going to be* quite *interesting.*

Chapter Two

As they picked up speed on Highway 12, Ella kept looking for something—*anything*—outside her window to look at besides sand.

A mile from the ferry landing, all she saw were silent gray-white dunes on either side of the road, with the dark blue ocean dangerously close on her left. The hurricane had hit this stretch of the island hard, and in many places the sand dunes protecting the road from the incoming tides had been washed away.

With the windows down, the salty smell of the ocean filled the car. Just as it had been for her last few hours of driving down the coast, the only car on the road was hers.

Mitch sat next to her with his right elbow out his open window. He was staring out at the passing waves of sand as if trying to find some hidden message there. The wind ruffled his dark brown hair, mussing it up even further, if that was possible.

"So," she began. "What's the plan for tomorrow, Mitch?"

He blinked and sat up straight. "Thought we'd start early tomorrow," he said. "Get out early and miss the tourons, you know?"

"The who?"

"*Tourons,*" Mitch said, and gave a quick laugh. "Sorry. That's sort of a nickname we have for the tourists. At least for the annoying ones. My buddy Ben and I passed some of 'em driving into town from the ferry, like those old folks in that beat-up blue Mercedes with the Jersey plates. They were doing about eighty, I swear."

Ella nodded.

"We get them in Boston, too. We just call them tourists."

Mitch gave her a quizzical look, his head slightly cocked to one side, as if he was trying to figure out if she was joking or not. He shrugged.

"So, anyway. I figured we'd do some surveying and check out the wreck site bright and early tomorrow," he said, watching her with his faded blue eyes. "I can give you a wake-up call around four-thirty a.m. If that's not too early, that is."

"Sounds good to me," Ella said, hoping he didn't see her wince. She hadn't gotten up that early in a long, long time.

She watched the road continue to unfurl in front of her. Off to the right was a clump of tall bushes half-buried in sand. The bushes surrounded a fenced-in pasture where she caught a glimpse of half a dozen black and white horses.

Where was the town? she began to wonder. Was *there a town?*

They approached the third beach access on the road. This one had only three cars parked at it, all pickups. The locals, she guessed, out fishing. They passed the parking lot, and then once again they were surrounded by nothing but sand, road, and ocean.

"So how long have you been diving, Mitch?" she asked, glancing at him and the wind-blown bushes and trees on his side of the road.

Mitch's eyes had gained a surprising level of intensity when he looked over at her this time. She felt something deep inside her chest give a tiny lurch.

"My dad," he said with a crooked grin. "He got me

diving when I was barely a teenager. I think the happiest day of his life was when I was finally able to afford my own boat. It was one of *my* favorite days, that's for sure—the day I bought *Cassiopeia*. The name was my sister's idea. I just call her *Cassie*. My boat, not my sister. Her name's Melissa."

The sudden change in Mitch, from sleepy and stoic to focused and chatty and even a tiny bit funny, threatened to take Ella's breath away. His light blue eyes were almost burning into her skin from their sudden passion. This was someone who loved what he did for a living, someone who was always happy to talk about it, if asked.

I used to be like that, Ella thought. *Whenever someone got me talking about history.*

"What I really want to do," Mitch continued, "is take folks out on *Cassie* to dive and sightsee. Especially people who can't afford a trip on the big, expensive boats sitting out in Silver Lake Harbor. I want to work with regular people, not hoity-toity rich folks. People I can take out, and help them find new places the ocean and the wind and the sand have created, on the islands and underwater. It'd just be . . . awesome."

Ella could feel her own smile forming to match Mitch's, though it was tinged with a bittersweet feeling at the mention of Mitch's father. She remembered her own father's love of sailing and swallowed a lump in her throat.

"But don't get me wrong, I'm happy running dives, like what we'll be doing." Mitch's eyes had lost some of their fervor, as if he'd realized what he was saying and who he was talking to. Ella was a customer again, nothing more.

He glanced through the windshield toward the town, rubbing the stubble on his chin.

"My dreams, well, they're . . . they're a long, long way

off. Just . . ." He trailed off and turned to gaze out his window. Just like that, his enthusiasm had burned away.

"Mitch," she said, nodding at the road in front of them. "Any chance we'll get to town before it's dark?"

"Hey, it's not the big city, y'know. We're not *quite* as congested as Boston," he said with a chuckle. " 'Bout four more miles," he added when she didn't share in his laughter.

Ella wasn't laughing, because it had happened again.

Out of the corner of her eye, she saw something dark dart past her on the other side of a sand dune. She forgot about Mitch for a moment and touched the brakes.

It could have been a truck, she thought, *or maybe a fisherman on a four-wheeler. Surely I'm not seeing things again.*

But the shape she'd glimpsed had seemed all wrong for a car or truck, and she imagined that the beach had probably been closed to vehicles since the hurricane.

"Look out!" Mitch shouted.

She slammed on the brakes, while Mitch grabbed the wheel and turned it hard to the right.

All Ella saw in that frozen instant, as her seat belt locked her in place and the car swerved toward the shoulder, were two rows of yellowed teeth and a pair of red, panicked eyes inches away from the windshield.

For a split second the windshield turned black, and then there was a sharp double-thump from the front of the car.

The horse hit the hood.

Ella stood on the brake, and the car spun.

Neither Ella nor Mitch had time to even shout as the front tires hit the sandy shoulder with a crunching sound.

The rear tires swung around on the highway, and the Escort came to a rest perfectly parallel to Highway 12, but pointing the wrong way.

It took her ten long seconds to catch her breath, and when she finally did she felt a sharp pain in her chest. The seat belt was tight against her, holding her in place but also keeping the air from her lungs. She relaxed and the seat belt loosened.

We just hit a horse, she thought.

"Red-Eye," Mitch muttered, and then he turned to her. "Are you—" he began, but she slipped out of her seat belt and was out of the car before Mitch could finish his sentence.

Now that she had her breath back, Ella couldn't stay in the car. The horse was going to be hurt, badly, and she had to see the damage. She didn't know much about giving first aid to large animals, but that double-thump she'd heard on her car hood echoed in her mind. It was going to be bad, she could tell.

"Dr. Simon?" Mitch said from behind her.

She ignored him, scanning up and down the road and the beach next to them.

"Where is it?" she whispered. Her hands were shaking as badly as her voice was.

Mitch came up to her, with a concerned look on his face. He wasn't looking for the horse, but only at her.

"Dr. Simon, are you okay?"

"I'm fine," she said, crossing her arms in front of her chest. She could still feel her hands shaking, and she tried to tell herself to stop it. "But where's the horse we just hit?"

"Pony," Mitch said.

Ella glared at him, not understanding.

"I mean . . . That wasn't a horse. That was one of the wild ponies from the island. He looked just like the one we call Red-Eye. Remember the pens we just passed?"

"Pony, horse, whatever, Mr. Science. Where did it *go?*"

As Mitch shrugged again, she looked one more time at her surroundings. Except for a pickup coming down the road from town a few miles away, they were all alone on the highway. Just the two of them and her car, sitting backwards on the sandy shoulder.

She walked on unsteady legs toward the front of her car. There were no traces of the black pony either—no body, no tracks in the sand, no blood on the road. She searched for dents in the hood of the Escort, but the hood was untouched.

"I don't know *where* it went," Mitch said at last.

She was still staring at the hood when Mitch walked up next to her.

This is impossible, she thought. *I heard the pony hit the hood. Twice.*

"Look, I'm sorry about the pony-horse thing," he said. "Want me to drive the rest of the way to town?" He reached a hand toward her as if to console her, but stopped himself halfway there.

She stepped away from the hood with a sudden movement and shook her head.

"No. I'm okay."

"Well," he said, his deep voice calming her a tiny bit, "I don't see any tracks on the dunes on the other side of the road, so I'm just going to assume our pony went back to where he came from. I'll tell the sheriff about it when we get to town. Must have a hole in the fence back at the pony pens."

She nodded and got back into her car. After she gunned the little engine, the car shot off the shoulder, kicking up sand. Her U-turn was accompanied by more squealing tires.

As she turned, Ella barely missed running into a pickup coming at them from the direction of town. She heard

Mitch suck in his breath and mutter something under his breath, and then he waved at the driver of the truck.

"Charlie Midgett," he said with a nervous laugh. "Old buddy of my dad's. Probably going fishing or something."

Charlie gave them a quick honk on the horn on his way past.

"Um-hmm," Ella said. "Right."

Her hands were still shaking, and she was thinking she was going to need a drink to get the image of flying black ponies out of her head.

Red-Eye, Mitch had called the wild pony.

"And here we are," Mitch said.

At last, the town of Ocracoke appeared. It was made up of just one main road, with old, slightly weathered stores and shops lining each side. She'd been expecting piles of sand and debris left over from the hurricane, but she was pleasantly surprised to see that the town itself was neat and orderly, as if 100-mile-an-hour winds hadn't blown through these streets just a few months earlier. Pickups and bikes seemed to be the favored form of transportation, but even that traffic was light.

To her surprise, everyone waved at them on their way past.

"Welcome to Ocracoke, Dr. Simon," Mitch said with pride as they drove by the tall wooden storefront of Howard's Pub.

"Thanks," she said in a soft voice. She pressed the brakes as a sand-covered Bronco pulled out in front of her. "It's . . . nice. Really. And please, call me Ella."

The truck in front of her carried half a dozen fishing poles wedged vertically into its front bumper, and a blue cooler whip-corded to the rear bumper. They crept down the road after the truck at less than fifteen miles an hour.

"So where are you staying?" Mitch said.

Her hands relaxed on the wheel as she glanced over at her passenger. He still looked a bit out of sorts from their run-in with the pony. She was feeling jumpy as well, thinking about the incredible disappearing pony. They should've plowed right into that poor critter. She had no idea how the injured creature had gotten away, and now that the adrenaline had melted away, their near-miss was starting to seriously spook her.

"I'm renting a house somewhere close to the lake. Two-oh-two Silver Lake Drive is the address." She took a breath and swallowed a tiny bit of pride. "Look, Mitch, don't mind me if I've been a little snappy. I've just been in the car for too long today."

"You can drop me off here," he said, pointing at the nearly empty parking lot of the Creekside Café. She wasn't sure if he'd even heard her attempt at an apology. "Just take a left up here on Silver Lake Drive, and your place is three blocks away."

Ella stopped the car outside the café.

"Mitch . . ." she began, "I just want to let you know that I'm really looking forward to this project. Even if it's gotten off to kind of a . . . *weird* start."

Mitch nodded before he slipped out of the car. He closed the door and bent down to peer into the open window. His pale blue eyes were sparkling again with some inner fire, as if he'd enjoyed their near-miss with Red-Eye.

Or maybe . . . Ella looked closer at him. Maybe the guy really *was* just as shaken up as she was. The thought made her like him a tiny bit more, bad first impression and all.

"Thanks for the ride, Ella," he said. "Sorry about Red-Eye messing with you. He does that sometimes, with new people in town. You can't take it personally. He's like the town watchdog. I'll see you tomorrow, bright and early."

"See you," she said and watched him walk off into town, thinking about the feel of the calluses on his hands and his clean smell, with just a touch of salt to it.

She sat there for a moment in the small parking lot, listening for the sounds of honking horns, sirens, and screeching tires she was used to on the streets of Boston. Nothing but the wind and the soft hum of two kids riding by on their bikes.

As she drove the last three blocks toward the small rented house that would be her home for the next few weeks, she remembered the light that had filled Mitch's eyes as he talked about his boat and his dreams. That, at least, had been a nice surprise on a day full of bizarre sightings.

She pulled up in front of her lakefront house and killed the engine to her car. She looked at the back seat and gave a heavy sigh at all the equipment and luggage and other junk crammed in there. With a groan, she pulled herself out of the car.

"Red-Eye," she muttered, "if you'd like to come help haul this stuff in for me, I'd forget all about you scaring me."

After waiting a few seconds for a response she knew wasn't coming, Ella began the slow process of emptying her car.

Maybe next time, Red-Eye, she thought. *Maybe next time.*

Chapter Three

Like most nights before a new project, Ella was too excited about the upcoming day to get a good night's sleep. She kept worrying she'd oversleep, so she ended up waking every hour or so to check her clock. When she did, she'd feel a moment of panic in the unfamiliar bed and the strange, darkened room until she got her bearings.

And every time she managed to get back to sleep, she was hounded by strange dreams.

The first one had been about Dad. He was showing her how to work the sails on their boat just off Boston Harbor. His big hands maneuvered the ropes and pulleys like second nature, sometimes moving so fast his fingers and hands blurred together. Just seeing him, if only in her dreams, made Ella's chest ache, and she wanted to hug him.

But Dad was too busy with the sailboat and his lessons about the sails and the rigging to give her an opening. When he finally stopped, it was to give the ropes to her. She could barely hang onto them, and then, with a sudden gust of wind, the ropes jerked her off her feet. She saw her own tiny hands, digging into the thick ropes and holding on with all her strength, but her grip was slipping away already.

For a mad dream-second she was suddenly trying to stay on the back of a red-eyed black horse—"Pony," a man's deep voice said, "a wild pony"—and she was trying to grasp reins that kept slipping from her fingers as the spooked creature bucked her.

In the blink of an eye, she was back on the sailboat

again, just long enough to get thrown overboard. Her body was as light and helpless as a child as she flipped end over end and crashed into the icy water. The world went black.

And then she was no longer a child, but a grown woman. What felt like a cold, dead hand was pushing her under with a deliberate, crushing strength. Now her chest ached, not with longing or sorrow, but with deep, lung-searing pain.

She ripped herself free from the nightmare just before the water stole her last bit of oxygen. Rubbing her chest and gasping for air, she glanced at her clock again. It was five minutes to eleven.

"Crap," she said, dropping her head back onto her pillow. She let out a shuddering breath and immediately sucked in more air before closing her eyes again.

Four a.m. was going to come way too soon, she thought. *I've got to get some sleep.*

The small, two-story house on the lakefront creaked and rattled as it settled in on itself. A soft breeze made the branches of the tree outside patter against her bedroom window. Ella focused on the relaxing sounds, and she was back asleep within minutes.

The next dream took place on a plane. Planes, unlike boats out on the ocean, horrified Ella. Flying in them was something she avoided as much as a maritime researcher and traveling professor could. Coasting thousands of feet above the world had never felt natural to her, not like diving or being out on the water did. She had no foundation under her up in the air, nothing as reassuring as the steady pulse of ocean waves drumming on a ship.

In the dream, she'd been stuck in a hard, unforgiving airplane seat as the craft dipped and danced its way through a bad patch of turbulence. The only part of her body she could move were her eyes, and they were locked on the seatback in front of her. She didn't dare look out through the small window next to the seat. Once again, her lungs began to ache for lack of air.

From behind her she could hear the voice of Steven, her ex-boyfriend, floating into her dream like a forgotten piece of driftwood. He was arguing with someone else, a man with a deep voice. The voices of both men were raised in anger. They were fighting about what was more important—proving something was true without a doubt, or simply trusting in the unknown.

She tried to take a deep breath so she could turn around and tell them both to shut up, but the air in her dream tasted stale and made her want to cough.

Her hands ached from gripping the armrests of her chair too tightly. Just as she feared would happen, the plane encountered more turbulence.

The plane seemed suddenly smaller now, and the little craft shook, followed by a stomach-lurching drop.

This is it, she thought. *We're going down.*

She bit back a scream while someone on the plane began to laugh with a low, hissing sound. The two men continued to argue about scientific fact and superstition even as the plane began to plummet downwards. Her ears popped and the world shrunk down to the tiny little plane and the dark sky outside her window, swirling and churning like the leading edge of a hurricane.

"You've got to have faith," the deep voice said from behind her, ending the argument. "Just *believe*, Ella."

Ella opened her mouth to scream as they dropped faster and faster, but all that came out was a tiny, pathetic squeak.

Right before her dream-plane crashed into a white-capped ocean, Ella woke.

The clock read half past midnight this time, and the only

sound in the house was her own breathing, fast and shallow.

Twenty minutes passed before she was able to fall asleep again. The house had quieted its settling, but the wind continued to rattle the windows. She closed her eyes and eventually fell back to sleep.

And dropped into a dream of snow. The gray, dirty stuff surrounded her, muffling all sound except for a low thumping. At first she thought it was distant footsteps, drawing closer, but then she realized the sounds were both bigger and farther away. She shivered, but not from the cold. The sounds were alien, something she'd never heard before.

She was standing, almost floating, in the middle of the snowy nothingness when she realized what she was hearing was the distant roar of cannons. Real ones, not fake recreations shooting blanks.

The explosions rocked the gray twilight. She wondered if she had dropped into some sort of Revolutionary War reenactment outside Boston somewhere. Her entire body was numb, and her ears had started to ring. Just standing up was becoming a challenge.

The cannons came closer, growing louder quickly, until they were almost deafening.

Mixed in with the blasts of the cannons was a voice, calling out to her. A female voice, one she couldn't recognize. Somehow the person knew her name. The youthful voice had a trace of a British accent, and it was filled with suffering. The thin voice was scared and scary at the same time, the syllables of each word stretching out and echoing in counterpoint to the cannons.

"Ella . . . Help me . . . Ella . . ."

A dark shape flickered in her dream-vision, heavy footsteps crunching through the dirty snow. The steps were accompanied by the hissing sizzle of a wick burning down before exploding from its contact with gunpowder. She could smell something burning, along with the stink of something dead. The huge figure blotted out all the light in the snowy field, and Ella fell backwards, kicking out as if she were underwater. She had to get away from that shadow, feeling a biting cold cover her now.

The shadowy figure standing over her seemed to be missing its head.

She kicked again, but in spite of all her efforts, she wasn't moving anywhere. The figure was reaching down for her.

In the instant before contact was made, Ella realized she couldn't hear the young voice calling her name anymore. That sudden silence stung her more than the cold or the helplessness overtaking her body. She'd let that person down.

After one final, ear-shattering explosion, Ella rolled onto her side and opened her eyes.

She had thrown off her comforter, kicking it to the floor in her restlessness, and her right foot was caught in the twisted sheet like a noose around her ankle. She was freezing, just like in her dream. The clock read one minute to four.

"Okay, okay," she muttered, pulling her foot free. "I'm getting up, already."

At five a.m., the harbor at the center of town was dark and silent. In the weak glow of her car's parking lights, Ella loaded her equipment into Mitch's boat. She set her box of gear down softly onto the floor of the small, slightly worn Sea Cat, afraid to disturb the peace so early in the morning.

Boston was never quiet like this. She could almost hear

the clouds moving overhead in the purplish-blue sky, covering the stars like a blanket.

Part of her was annoyed that Mitch didn't help her load her stuff onto the boat; the scuba gear was heavy, and she was out of shape from a winter of teaching and skipping workouts. He *was* the dive master, after all.

But he had his own equipment to load, and she knew that she wouldn't have allowed him to be a gentleman and do her heavy lifting for her anyway. At least Mitch had offered to let her use his tanks and diving gear today, so that was one less thing she'd have to haul around this morning.

Today's goal was to simply get a preliminary look at the wreck site off the southern tip of Ocracoke Island. She'd take lots of pictures with the department's pricey underwater camera, and she'd try to get an idea of how long it would take a crew to uncover the ship.

She felt honored by the gift that Dr. Bramlett had given her with this trip. He had wanted *her* to be the one to start the investigation. She hadn't really thought about that until now, away from the distractions of school, Steven, and the city. Dr. Bramlett's friends from East Carolina University would eventually arrive at the site to help out, but she got first crack at uncovering the site and making the first guess as to the identity of the ship.

Ella had her doubts about this shipwreck actually turning out to be a lost pirate ship. She didn't even want to get her hopes up, even though Ocracoke *had* been a favorite haunt of Blackbeard and his fellow pirates, back in the day.

Pulling her windbreaker tighter around her, she felt a thrill run through her as she remembered the history of the elusive Captain Teach, better known as Blackbeard. She had to grin at the wild and wooly legend of how the pirate was tracked down here in Ocracoke after years of terrorizing the coast. And then, after a bitter fight, a naval officer from Virginia had beheaded Blackbeard and ended the pirate's plundering ways. Of course, his ghost was rumored to still haunt the waters off Ocracoke.

Ella shook her head as she put the last piece of equipment on board Mitch's boat.

Everyone loves a good pirate story. But you can't base your entire career on a legend. Or a ghost, for crying out loud.

As soon as she sat down next to the piles of equipment and diving gear, Mitch fired up the engine of his Sea Cat, and they slipped away from the dock in the cold gray light of pre-dawn. The rumble of the engine was the only sound in the cold darkness of early morning.

So far they hadn't said more than ten words to one another. Ella didn't mind—she was too excited about her first dive of the year to care about making small talk with her dive master. The lack of chitchat actually made the peaceful morning even better for her. It gave the start of this expedition a nice sense of decorum. History was to be treated with respect, and Mitch seemed to agree with her on that.

They passed through the Ditch, the narrow waterway that connected Silver Lake with the Pamlico Sound, and Mitch handled the choppy waves and tricky waterway with ease. He turned them south as soon they were out of the harbor and into the sound.

Huddled in her coat and wishing she'd brought a Thermos full of coffee, Ella glanced back at the dark town. Only a few lights dotted the land as the island slept.

She smiled at the slow sweep of the light coming from the short white lighthouse off to her left. Years slipped away from her—the year could have been 1906 or 1806 instead of 2006, and she liked it that way. She felt like a part of history instead of someone standing at the end of it, looking back.

She could imagine greedy pirates and honest captains alike sailing these waters, using the lighthouse and the stars to guide them to safety on their ancient journeys.

"Teach's Hole Channel," Mitch murmured from behind the wheel.

"Where our old buddy Blackbeard was killed," she said. She hoped she hadn't jumped at the sound of his voice. She didn't want him to think he'd spooked her.

"Oh crow cock!" Mitch shouted in a hoarse voice that cut through the night like an alarm. This time Ella did jump. *"Oh crow cock!"*

"What the hell?"

She glared over at Mitch. His eyes glinted mischievously in the moonlight, like flashes of light blue fire in the darkness.

So much for treating history with respect, she thought, feeling like a stern schoolteacher with a precocious student as Mitch broke into an addictive laugh. Ella had to bite her lip so she wouldn't smile.

"Sorry," he said between laughs, wiping his eyes. "I couldn't resist. That's supposedly what you-know-who said the night before he was killed. And that's where the island got its name: *oh-crow-cock.* Ocracoke."

His face grew serious, and he looked at her as if he were divulging a family secret.

"Did you know," he whispered, "that after he lost his head, they tossed Blackbeard's body overboard? And it swam seven times 'round the ship of the Royal British Navy officer who killed him. Then the body sank, never to be seen again."

Ella blew out her breath and watched it cloud up in front of her in the cold air. "Is this all included as part of the tour, or do I have to pay extra for the ghost stories?"

She could see Mitch's face more clearly now that the sky had begun to lighten. His grin was wide, but she thought she caught something else mixed in with that cocky tone of voice and rakish smile. The guy looked nervous, almost.

But nervous of what? she wondered. *This was his territory. He was in charge of this dive. Wasn't he?*

"Sorry," he said. "My sister and I have been telling and retelling each other all the old ghost stories about Blackbeard for the past few weeks, ever since I came across the shipwreck. We especially like the ones that scare all the tourons."

"You didn't *tell* her about—" Ella stopped herself.

"Nah," Mitch said with a laugh. "I know the deal. Only my pop knows. We don't want the press coming here to cause a scene. Plus my dad has been friends with Dr. Bramlett from way back, and I wouldn't want to mess up the deal they have going."

"Right," Ella said, wondering what was involved in that "deal" between Mitch's dad and Dr. Bramlett. She guessed that she probably didn't want to know the details.

"So tell me what you know about the shipwreck site," she said, setting out the scuba gear Mitch had lent her. "And please," she added with a smile, "leave out all the gory details you'd tell one of your 'tourons,' please."

Thank God for insulated wetsuits, Ella thought half an hour later as she slowly sank into the dark depths of Ocracoke Inlet.

Through the skin of the suit she could feel only a fraction of the iciness of the water, and even that was enough to shock her into complete wakefulness. Mitch had said the water at this time of year was usually about fifty degrees, but it felt even colder than that.

With a light strapped to her head like a miner and the underwater camera in her hands, she sank through the murky water, searching for hints of the shipwreck. She wore her own face mask and had two of her dive bags attached to her belt, but she was using one of Mitch's tanks and regulators, along with one of his bright yellow buoyancy devices and his smallest weight belt.

It felt good, being back underwater.

She was in another world, a simpler world, one free from the general sense of hopelessness she'd been feeling all winter. Down here, she was weightless and unencumbered, focused only on her immediate surroundings and nothing else. She felt strong and sleek and confident as she dropped down toward the ocean floor.

Mitch was off to her left, a blurry figure in a dark blue body suit, his buoyancy control device the same bright shade of yellow as hers. His light cast a weak beam through the silty water. He was keeping close, but not so close that he would interfere with her, which was good.

She figured he was probably sulking a bit at the way she'd scoffed at his ghost stories and Ocracoke history lessons. She didn't know who he was trying to impress with those stories of headless pirates and fierce battles. *Maybe himself,* she thought, and swallowed a giddy laugh.

A rocky outcropping appeared in front of her, and she let herself continue to sink past it. She followed the outcropping all the way to the bottom. She'd descended about sixty, maybe sixty-five feet, deep enough so they'd have to go up in forty or forty-five minutes to avoid having to decompress.

The water here was also deep enough to hide a wrecked ship for almost three centuries.

She touched down on the ocean floor, which was equal

parts silt and sand. Her flippers kicked up a cloud of both when she took a step. She turned in a slow circle, scanning the nearly empty inlet as best she could. She kept wishing her visibility was better than the murky fifteen feet or so she had this morning.

Feeling frustrated, she waved a hand in front of her light, making it flicker to get Mitch's attention.

Please don't tell me he doesn't know where the wreck is anymore, she thought. Her confidence in her superstitious dive master had been low all morning, ever since he'd started the day off crowing like a rooster.

She swam closer to the rocky outcropping, the only detailed object she'd seen so far. After two kicks, a flashing light off to the right made her pull up short.

The dot of light looked like some sort of fire, orange in color, which was somehow burning in the water. The color of the light seemed vaguely familiar. But before she could look closer at the light, Mitch swam up to her, kicking his long legs and churning up more silt from the ocean bottom.

Maybe it had just been his headlamp, she decided as he came to a stop in front of her.

Mitch pointed off into the distance and then took her by the hand. His grip was both surprising and irresistible as he pulled her past the rocky outcropping. Ella squeezed his hand and held on.

They moved together across the ocean floor until they were hovering over a twelve-foot-long anchor covered in coral and rust. It was half-buried in the silt and sand.

Ella squeezed Mitch's hand harder.

Five feet beyond the anchor was the start of the "pile," wood and iron and coral and algae that had all grown together, fused as if by some insane welder to form a shapeless mass that once had been a mighty ship.

Brown timbers that had first been nailed together centuries ago—by hands long since dead and turned to dust—now jutted up from the ocean floor. The pile stretched out in front of them as far as the murky water would allow her to see.

Ella let go of Mitch's hand and swam toward the ruined piece of history. She'd come home.

For the next few hours, she forgot all about taking pictures and kept herself busy pulling treasures from the wrecked ship. She'd already found a bell the size of her fist, the rusted and broken hilt of a cutlass, and five links of a chain that had most likely come from a slave's irons. She was now inspecting what looked like part of the ship's outer hull.

This was kid-in-a-candy-store time for Dr. Ella Simon.

She felt like a space explorer, dropping onto another planet, the only sound the slow hiss of her own breathing. She'd kept Mitch out of her hair by having him haul each of her finds to the boat so she could look at them more closely later. He didn't look happy at all about leaving her on her own down here. She just hoped he was storing everything in the salt-water container they'd set up for the artifacts. If some of the treasures she'd found got too much air, they'd crumble away to nothing.

More than once while she was in contact with the ship, she'd felt like she was being watched, but she brushed off the feeling in her excitement at what she was finding down here.

In the past two hours, she'd already had to rise to the surface twice to keep from getting the bends. She was going to have to go up again soon, and she needed to start taking some photos of the ship. Some of the silt in the water had cleared, but still the visibility was no better than twenty-five feet or so.

Ella was getting ready to pull out her camera when she hit a patch of water that was completely icy.

Her breath froze in her lungs, making them burn immediately until she exhaled and sucked in more air through her mouthpiece.

An overwhelming feeling of wrongness filled this water, and it made her whole body tighten up. At the same time, she could almost *see* every molecule of water surrounding her, as if she'd been encased in ice. She'd hit bad patches like this before, but nothing so sudden and strong as this.

She was so surprised that she couldn't move to kick her way out of the cold spot. So she allowed herself to sink.

As she dropped, she focused on her breathing. In. Out. In. Out. Slowly.

Stay in control, she commanded herself. *You just hit some bad water, that's all. It happens on every dive.*

In. Out. In.

In counterpoint to the bubbling sounds of her breathing came a distant thumping.

At first she thought the sound was just the thrum of the air tank on her back, but the thumping sound kept growing closer and getting louder.

And, worse, it sounded like the laughter of a man with a deep voice, just like the thunderous laugh she'd heard coming from the drowned house yesterday. But this wasn't laughter; the sound was more distinct, with pauses between each blast.

Cannons, she thought. And they were drawing closer.

Where the hell was Mitch? she wondered, and then a shadow fell over her. The water turned even icier.

She lifted her head and pointed her light up at the

shadow, but she couldn't see anything there other than darkness. Off to the right she could now make out Mitch swimming slowly toward her, and that put her mind at ease.

Then the cannons sounded again, even closer this time.

Mitch was causing that shadow, she told herself, even though a voice in the back of her mind told her Mitch was too far away to cast such a big shadow.

Twenty feet from her, Mitch stopped in mid-kick. Even from this distance, she could see that his pale blue eyes were wide with some wild emotion. He lifted a gloved hand and pointed at something directly above her. He tried to swim closer, but it was as if he'd hit a wall, underwater, and couldn't move past it.

Ella looked up, and when she did the water cleared, as if the silt in it had simply dissolved.

Just a few feet above her, in the clear, icy water, floated a man.

Not a corpse or even a skeleton, but a fully-clothed human being. He gave off an unhealthy blue glow, like some sort of underwater lichen. Wild black hair fanned out around his head, and he wore a long, torn jacket that floated in the water like black wings. Underneath the jacket, Ella caught sight of what looked like a thin, striped shirt, something that could have been a pajama top.

The cannons exploded again in her ears.

I'm seeing things, she thought. Her mind reeled at the impossible vision floating above her, and she felt herself sinking farther.

Before she could do anything more, the man reached down and made a sudden pulling movement with his bony right hand. He disappeared in a flurry of bubbles just as Ella's world exploded from another cannon blast.

The air she'd just taken into her lungs was forced out of

her as the mouthpiece shot out of her mouth. She jammed her mouth shut and refused to let herself breathe.

Her lungs burning and her body shaking with the need for air, she inflated her BCD and shot straight up toward the surface.

Her ears ached from the pressure. Her lungs screamed for oxygen.

The moment before she broke through the surface of the water lasted an eternity. But at last, just before she inhaled salt water, she reached the surface and took a glorious breath of air.

After a dozen deep breaths, Ella began to piece together what had happened. The hose connected to her air tank had come unattached. Mitch's equipment had malfunctioned on her.

Her panic and desperation became frustration, and then rage that wiped the vision of the floating man and the sound of the cannons from her mind.

Mitch broke through the surface a few seconds after her, his eyes still wide with shock. Treading water next to him, she did her best not to grab his head and push him back under.

"You okay?" he said after spitting out his mouthpiece. "What happened? I couldn't get to you. You were there one second, then you were shooting up to the surface."

"My tank," she said as she swam to the boat. She pulled herself into the boat with shaking arms. "*Your* tank. The one you insisted I use. It came *apart*, Mitch."

Tearing off her goggles and peeling back the hood to her diving suit, she didn't give Mitch a second to catch his breath as he climbed aboard after her.

"What is *wrong* with you?" she shouted at him, making her sore lungs ache even more. "What the hell were you doing down there? Taking a smoke break while your equipment came apart on me? Good God. I can't believe you let me go down there with that tank. When's the last time you used this equipment—back when Reagan was president?"

"I did check the tanks," Mitch said in a surprisingly calm voice. "I checked everything this morning—"

"Look," she said, "I know accidents can happen, but damn, Mitch. You're the dive master. This is your *job!* Check your equipment, and then check it again! Don't they teach that to you here out in the sticks?"

His only answer was to glare back at her, his face bright red. She pulled back her damp hair and slumped to the floor of the boat. She couldn't stop shaking.

After nearly drowning under the water, she was in the mood for a good argument. Arguing would keep her from thinking about whatever it was down there she'd seen and heard before she lost her air.

"There's nothing that makes me angrier," she muttered, "than someone who doesn't do his job right."

Her final words did the trick. Mitch stopped biting back whatever he was trying to keep from saying, and he let her have it.

"Don't tell *me* how to run a dive off my own damn boat, *doctor!*" Mitch scrubbed his face angrily with a towel and moved closer to Ella. "I was right there, but you had to go off and do all your research on your own. I was just your hired help, bringing your stuff up to the surface. Don't they teach you the buddy system up there in the big city? If you want to run this dive by yourself, just let me know."

She was about to respond to his outburst when she took a closer look at him. They were barely two feet apart, and she could see that he was shaking just as badly as she was. His eyes were still full of shock, as if he'd seen a . . .

45

"I'm sorry," he said, taking a step away from her and interrupting her thoughts. "That was out of line. I shouldn't have yelled at you like that." He let out a long sigh. "Look. If you want to use some other diving company, I'd understand. I can take you back right now."

"It's okay," she said, her voice still shaking a little bit. "I'm not ready to jump ship just yet. No pun intended."

They sat together in silence for a long moment. She felt like she should argue more, but the defeated look on Mitch's face had taken all the therapeutic value out of it. The guy almost looked disappointed when she told him he wasn't fired. As if he'd *wanted* her to use someone else to organize her dives.

"So . . ." he began after another long moment.

"So?" She watched Mitch closely as she spoke. "What did *you* see down there?"

"Well, I saw . . . something," he said. He looked away, out at the waves rocking against his boat. "But I think it only makes sense if you know the whole story."

"Oh boy. Not some more ghost stories for the tourons."

"Humor me," he said, and turned back to look at her. His eyes flickered with the return of that intensity she'd seen yesterday, making Ella wonder if there really was more to this guy than met the eye. She suddenly wanted to reach out and touch his face, to soothe the tension in his jaw.

Before she could, Mitch moved away. He opened up his cooler and dug out sandwiches wrapped in plastic.

"I'll tell you a story or two over lunch," he said. "Then we'll see about going down there again. If you still want to, that is."

Ella rubbed her side. Her sore lungs were already recovering, and some *other* sensation was filling her chest instead. A pounding that felt stronger than the surf, faster than her breathing. She hadn't felt this way in a long time.

"Okay, it's a plan," she said, taking a sandwich from him. She felt another tingling sensation run up her hand and arm when their fingers met. "But I'm not going down there again until you get me another tank. One that *works* this time. Otherwise all bets are off, Mitch."

Chapter Four

Ella unwrapped the plastic from the thick sandwich Mitch had handed her and did her best to not lose her patience. The last thing she wanted to do was break for lunch and listen to more of Mitch's ghost stories about Blackbeard while they sat sixty feet above what could've been the pirate's long-lost ship.

But after she sat back and took the first bite of her turkey sandwich, she realized she was more than a little bit hungry. She was ravenous.

I guess, she thought, *having a near-drowning experience gives a person a hearty appetite.*

"Okay, let's get things straight," Mitch said. He sat across from her on the other side of his narrow boat. "You think that ship down there could be one of Blackbeard's ships, right?"

Ella nodded and looked at the sky over Mitch's shoulder. Dark clouds had started creeping toward them from the direction of Ocracoke. She squinted at the distant coastline to the north and wondered if they were getting rain on the island. The darkness reminded her of the shadow that had fallen over her in the cold patch of water where she'd had her accident.

"Well," Mitch continued, "I grew up here, and we've got all sorts of stories about him. Blackbeard. My sister Melissa and I would talk about him all the time. Actually, we'd talk about his ghost. He was usually headless in those stories, of course, us being kids. That made them better, you know."

A child-like look had come over Mitch as he began talking about Blackbeard. Even if she wasn't ready to forgive him for the whole broken tank incident, she felt herself warming to him again as her anger began to fade.

"You should stop by the Jolly Roger where Melissa works and talk to her. She has lots of good stories, and she may know something about Blackbeard that you can't find in a book."

Ella nodded and took another bite of the surprisingly good sandwich. "Sure, that might be a good idea. But you said something about me needing to hear the whole story . . ."

"Okay, okay," Mitch said, "Melissa once told me about old Edward Teach and his pirating buddies and one of their raiding runs up and down the coast. They stopped off at Charleston in South Carolina and kidnapped a bunch of folks. But here's the crazy bit—he didn't ask for gold or money or jewels. He wanted to get medicine for his men, who were sick, and some of them were dying. I always thought that was sort of noble of him, taking care of his men." Mitch chuckled softly. "Of course, it wasn't until I was in high school that I realized that most of the pirates on his ship had syphilis and were probably all out of their minds from it, but that's a whole 'nother story."

"Mitch," Ella said. "Why are you telling me this?"

"Sorry," he said, giving her a quick, sheepish grin. "Just trying to show you that I grew up on this stuff, and that all the stories you may have heard may not have been completely true. That there's more to Blackbeard—and Ocracoke—than meets the eye."

Ella stared at the remains of the tank she'd been wearing, at the broken hose that had nearly killed her. She was trying to keep from getting too irritated.

"I really don't see your point," she said.

"My point is this: if this ship is really *his* ship—Blackbeard's—then we're sort of walking on mythical ground. Or swimming in mythical water, I guess, to be more exact."

Ella had finished her sandwich and was dying for something to drink to clear the salt water from her mouth. "And . . . ?"

"I guess what I'm saying is that this is as close as I get to being religious. I think there are some serious spirits hanging around down here."

"Spirits," Ella said. The clouds were darkening above them even more now, promising a cold rain any minute.

"Yeah." Mitch glanced away from Ella, as if he were suddenly nervous. "They're part of the story, you see. Melissa is convinced the island is full of ghosts, because of all the shipwrecks that have happened around it. And," he took a deep breath, "it was Melissa's stories that kept me from freaking out when I went diving down here last week." Mitch looked back at Ella and exhaled. "By myself."

"What?" Ella nearly dropped her sandwich, and the sudden breeze turned her wet skin cold. "Surely you know better than to dive alone, Mitch. What—"

"I know. But hear me out. All three times—" he looked away again as Ella's mouth dropped open "—all three times I went down there alone, it had seemed like a good idea. I had this feeling that the ship was mine to find, and I got kind of greedy, I guess. I've never felt that way before, and I could kick myself now for being such a fool."

Ella could relate to that desire, to want to rush ahead and discover something while the opportunity was there. But she'd also heard of too many people drowning alone when they got over-confident, thinking they didn't need to use the buddy system. As a dive master, Mitch knew better.

"And there's one other thing," he said, crossing his arms tightly over his chest as if he were suddenly cold. "When it was just me and that wrecked ship, I *felt* someone else down there, Ella. Someone who touched me. I thought I could feel fingers creeping up and down my neck and shoulders."

"You've got to be kidding," Ella began, but she stopped herself when she saw the determined look on Mitch's face.

"Just hear me out," he said. "At first I thought, yeah, it's just my imagination. It's just like one of Mel's ghost stories. But then, when I came to the surface on my last dive, after feeling those hands on my neck and arms, I had *these* on my hand."

Mitch held out his left hand, showing her the four scratches on the back of it. Ella had seen them yesterday, but had thought nothing of them at the time.

"Whoever it was down there," Mitch said, "did this to me, I think."

Ella tried to think of something to say. There had to be a logical explanation; she was always getting banged up on her underwater dives. Scratches like that were common. Weren't they?

All she could think to say was, "Did you tell Melissa about this?"

"No." Mitch gave a weak smile. "Knowing her, she'd probably want to hold a séance underwater so she could talk to . . . whatever it was down there in the shipwreck."

Ella looked at the healing scratches on Mitch's hand. They were parallel to one another, barely half an inch apart, and the fourth was a bit smaller than the others, as if made by a pinky finger.

"Oh my God," she said in a low voice.

This was all too much. She closed her eyes for a long

moment, hoping she'd misunderstood him somehow. But with her eyes closed she could see the shadow she'd seen underwater fall on her again, followed by the sickly blue light. She opened her eyes again, not wanting to see any more.

Mitch inched closer to her, eyes focusing on her with their burning intensity. "You didn't *feel* something down there today? Right before your tank malfunctioned? Didn't you see something too? I thought I saw . . ."

Ella stared at him, and he left his sentence unfinished.

Great, she thought, putting the image of the ghostly man in black out of her mind, hopefully for good. *I've got to get a new dive master,* she decided. *This whole project may be completely shot. Just great.*

"Call me crazy," Mitch said when she didn't answer him, "but I saw something above you, right before the hose to your tank came loose. I'm pretty sure it wasn't another human."

"What was it then, Mitch?" Ella said, her voice almost a croak.

Come on, big guy, she thought. *Go ahead and say it.*

Mitch swallowed the last bite of his sandwich and balled up the plastic wrap from it. He wiped his face with his towel one final time.

"I think it was a ghost, Ella. One of the ghosts that haunt the island."

"A *ghost.*" Ella found herself using the voice she used with small children. "You're saying a ghost was down there with us today."

Mitch nodded, his head moving as if in slow motion. He never lowered his gaze from her face. He didn't even seem to blink.

"Mitch," Ella said. "I just don't know how . . ."

"Still want to go back down today?" Mitch's eyes were losing their intensity, and they told Ella what his answer would be. "It's getting late, you know."

"No," she said, shaking off the feelings of doubt she'd been feeling ever since she surfaced from the ocean floor, dying for a breath of air.

All of this was just a delusion caused by Mitch and his superstitions. There was nothing down there but a rotting ship.

"No," Ella said again as thunder rolled across the sky and the first drops of rain began to hit the water around them. "No, I don't want to go back down there with you. Actually, I think you'd better take me back to town. Right now, please."

By four o'clock that afternoon Ella was back in her rented house, showered and mostly recovered from her chaotic morning. Rain pattered against the windows like tiny fingertips. She wanted to curl up in her bed after her restless night of wakeful sleeping and her brush with death that morning, but she refused to give in to fatigue. She was still too mad to call it a night.

"Ghosts," she muttered, flipping open her laptop, then flipping it shut again. "I drove for fifteen straight hours for *ghosts?* Shit."

On the silent trip from the shipwreck back to Ocracoke, Ella had convinced herself that whatever had appeared above her in the water was just an illusion. Yet another fluke of the lighting and her imagination. She blamed Mitch for that. He hadn't said another word about it to her.

Ella glanced at her unpacked bags and the equipment she'd made Mitch help her unload from his boat. They sat in the front hall of her little two-bedroom house like abandoned pets. The house smelled of mothballs and the ocean, salty and bitter. She dropped onto an overstuffed red chair in the living room, creating a puff of dust. She had two choices: she could unpack everything and make the best of her summer with some other dive master, or she could leave her bags as they were and call Dr. Bramlett to cancel the whole deal.

Leaving would be stupid, she told herself. *That's the old Ella talking, the one that gave up too easily. The Ella who had stopped talking to Dad for a year after her parents' divorce.*

And that would be the same Ella who'd been treading water all winter. She winced as she thought about how she'd let her grad students teach her Maritime History classes at the university for her, and how she'd explained it away by claiming to be swamped with research on the latest artifacts from her last dive almost a year ago. She'd been treading water, doing nothing but feeling sorry for herself.

"No more," Ella said, surprised at the sound of her voice in the unfamiliar confines of the house. "No more crying in my beer."

She pried herself up out of her chair, struggling with the too-soft cushions until she nearly fell onto the floor. She went to the first of her five bags. This was the bag with her files and books about shipwrecks and her previous dives from up and down the Atlantic coast. After dusting off her jeans, she picked it up, along with the biggest suitcase, and lugged them into her bedroom.

An hour later, after unpacking all five bags in the bedroom and setting up all her laptops and equipment in the living room, Ella took a good look around her new home away from home. Her flurry of activity had taken her mind off the negative events of that day's dive and reminded her of why she was here—to search the shipwreck. For the first time since getting up that morning,

Ella felt good about being in Ocracoke.

She also realized that she was starving. Mitch's sandwich, as good as it was, had been hours ago. She always worked up an appetite diving. For the first time since returning to her rented house, Ella thought about the ship hidden just off the coast, and she knew she'd made the right decision about staying.

Tomorrow I'll find a new dive master, she told herself. *Tonight I want to be a tourist. Not a touron, though.*

Ella grabbed her Boston University sweatshirt, checked in the hall mirror to make sure her hair wasn't standing up, and went outside. She couldn't believe she was able to walk outside in late March without a heavy coat, and she gave the island bonus points for that.

The light rain had stopped, and the sky was clear and blue as if no storm had ever happened earlier that day. Ocracoke had no sidewalks, so Ella walked along the sandy shoulder, facing traffic. She walked down Silver Lake Drive toward the main part of town, with the lake itself on her left, and then took a detour down Creek Road. Traffic was light, even at a quarter past five, a shock to Ella. She imagined the gridlock that had to be happening up in Boston, and she nearly laughed out loud with relief.

"That's the brightest smile I seen all day," a gravelly voice called out from across the street.

Ella took three more steps before she realized the owner of that voice was talking to her.

On the other side of Creek Road sat a long wooden cart with metal wheels, and in a rocking chair next to the cart sat an elderly man with a tan so deep his skin was brown as leather. The man had a pencil-thin white mustache the same shade of white as his thick eyebrows and the cottony tufts of hair on his head.

A rectangular sign with "Owen's Fresh Produce" carefully lettered on it leaned against the cart, which was partially filled with cucumbers, onions, potatoes, and, strangely enough, ornately carved and painted blue birdhouses.

"Hi," Ella said, crossing the street. She pointed at a row of produce and birdhouses. "Quite a selection you have there."

"Spring's a slow time f'r me," the old man said in a thick accent that Ella couldn't place. The man lifted himself out of his rocker with a soft groan, giving Ella time to figure out just what he'd said.

"Got t' get by best I can with what I put together durin' winter. Interested in a birdhouse? Somethin' to take back north with ya?"

Ella had picked up a robin's-egg blue birdhouse with red shutters, holding it by the metal hook at the peak of the roof. She was admiring the details of the house, which reminded her of her own little rental house, when she realized what the man had just said. She set down the birdhouse with a thump.

"How did you know I was from the north?"

"I like to know things, that's all, miss." The old man gave her a bright white grin. "Some folks call me the town psychic, ya know?"

Ella gave the man a long look, eyes widening. Was everyone on the island obsessed with this goofy paranormal crap?

" 'Course," the man said, still grinning, "your Boston sweatshirt, not to mention your accent, sort of gave ya away, too." He held out his hand. "Owen Haley. Pleased to meet ya."

"Ella Simon," Ella said, shaking his hand with a smile. "You got me, Mr. Haley. I almost believed you about that psychic stuff. And I'm supposed to be a scientist."

"Call me Owen, please." Owen made his way back to his chair, but he didn't sit down in it. He rested his big hands on the back of it for support. "A scientist, huh? Don't get much of them 'round here, unless they're working for the government or researchers down from Raleigh on some erosion or conservation project."

He didn't say any more, but Ella could feel his unasked question about why *she* was there hanging in the air between them. The late-afternoon sky had grown darker in the last five minutes.

"Days're getting longer," Owen said as he eased himself into his chair. "But durned if it still gets dark too early. Didn't mean to trouble ya, Miss Ella. Just wanted to say hello. Welcome t' Ocracoke."

"It's no trouble," Ella said, picking up the birdhouse again and slowly turning it in her hand. "And please, it's just Ella. I'm actually glad for someone to talk to. I've had a crazy couple of days."

"Crazy? Tell me about it. Something's been brewing here in town. Hope ya don't get caught up in it, Ella. I see the signs everywhere. Started with these dark shadows on the new fruit, still hanging on the vine. Next thing I noticed were these tiny marks and bruises on the vegetables, what I call spirit fingerprints. Ponies running loose, dogs barking at strange hours at nothing, cats getting into fights."

"Ponies?" Ella was now paying complete attention to Owen. She set down the delicate birdhouse and moved closer to the older man. "We hit one yesterday on the way into town. I mean, I think I did. But the pony just . . . disappeared."

Owen ran a finger across his thin white mustache and his brow furrowed. "Wasn't a black one, was it?"

"It *was*. With sort of weird eyes. Why?"

"Oh," Owen said. "It's nothing."

"Come on, tell me."

"Listen," Owen said, shifting, uncomfortable in his chair, "I just pass along what I hear. And I say, don't worry none about old Red-Eye. He probably just wanted to say hello. I don't know much about ponies, especially ponies that disappear. My specialty's plants and fruits and veggies."

"Wait, don't tell me," Ella said, suddenly wanting the old man to relax and stop fidgeting. He looked like a little boy who'd spilled the beans about Santa Claus or the Tooth Fairy to an unsuspecting audience of kids. "Red-Eye's a ghost horse, right? I mean, pony."

Owen gave her a long, grave look that lasted almost five seconds. Then he burst into laughter.

"I'm sorry, Ella. I'm not laughing at ya. It's just that, well, the thought of Red-Eye bein' anything other than the most annoying, pain-in-the-butt pest of a wild pony is just too funny. He's sort of the town mascot. He's always gettin' loose and causing all kinds of trouble."

"Well, he certainly disappeared like a ghost," Ella said, chuckling along with Owen at last.

"That's Red-Eye all right. Always causing trouble." After casting a strange look at Ella, Owen leaned back in his chair. "Been strange stuff like that happening all winter and spring. Folks've been cancelin' their trips here in the past few weeks. And that means it's goin' to be a tough season for me and everyone else on the island."

As she nodded along with Owen's words of wisdom, Ella felt again the strange sensation of being watched that she'd felt while she was examining the hull of the wrecked ship.

I'd wanted to forget that, she thought. *I needed to forget that.*

That, and everything else that had happened down there when she started hearing the impossible sound of cannons underwater.

Maybe that's why I got so mad at Mitch after the tank accident, she thought. *Maybe his ghost stories were making my imagination get away from me. And scientists did* not *let their imaginations do that. Ever.*

"So," Owen was saying. "That's my opinion 'bout it all."

Ella blinked and came back to the present. The sky had filled with a dark red light, and Owen had packed up his cart while he'd been talking. He paused before pulling a lid over his cart, padlock in his left hand.

"Did ya want any vegetables, Ella? Or maybe a birdhouse for your place over yonder?"

"Maybe tomorrow," Ella said with a smile. "I don't have much cash on me. Sorry."

Owen pulled the lid down over his vegetables and birdhouses, and then lifted it again. With a wink in Ella's direction, he slipped a thick hand underneath the lid and came out with the light blue birdhouse that Ella had been admiring earlier.

"Here," he said, handing it to her. "Take it, please. For listenin' to an old man's crazy ramblin', and not callin' him crazy."

"But Owen," Ella began. "I can't. It's worth too much for you to just give it away."

After a few uncomfortable seconds, Owen cleared his throat and spoke in a soft voice. "Is it *common* for folks up north to not accept gifts from friends?"

Ella couldn't help herself. She leaned close and gave

59

Owen a kiss on the cheek.

"Thank you, Owen. I'll hang it up first thing when I get home. I have a feeling it'll bring me good luck."

"Better believe it," Owen said, snapping the lock on his cart. He put rocks behind both wheels and bowed his head slightly at Ella. "G'night, Ella. Thanks again for chatting. Enjoy your night out on the town."

He walked off in the opposite direction of the lake, whistling tunelessly and jangling a pocket full of change. Within ten seconds he had disappeared into the darkness.

"Good night," Ella said. She felt a goofy grin on her face as she looked first at Owen's departing figure and then down at her birdhouse.

"And thank *you*," she whispered.

She walked back home and had the birdhouse hanging from a hook on her front porch within a minute, and then she continued on into town to find a good meal. Whistling softly under her breath just like her new friend Owen, Ella told herself again that she was doing the right thing by staying. One bad dive didn't set the tone for a whole project.

She'd give Mitch one more chance, just like Owen had given her a chance.

Following the curve of the lake, with the street lights flickering on and the stars peeking out above her, she made her way up the road to the Jolly Roger restaurant. She'd heard good things about the place that morning from Mitch, before he'd started spouting off about ghosts and ruining her first dive of the trip with his crappy equipment.

Ella paused next to the lake and looked upward. Talking to Owen had lifted her spirits even more than she could have hoped. The stars were dazzling and bright out here, with so few lights to drown them out. Even if she started counting now, she wouldn't be able to count them all before dawn.

Maybe someday, she thought, grudgingly lowering her gaze, *I'll have time to sit back and do just that.*

Chapter Five

After she made her way down the dark, quiet streets of what made up Ocracoke's tiny downtown, Ella had her pick of tables at the Jolly Roger. Her only competition was the now-familiar group of elderly tourists, two women and a man. They sat outside the main restaurant on one of half a dozen picnic tables, and their bright white and yellow shirts and floppy hats branded them loudly as tourists. On her way up the three steps leading inside, Ella almost flinched when the old man nodded at her, and the two white-haired ladies smiled nervously in her direction. She returned the smiles and hurried into the main dining area.

She entered the covered part of the restaurant, leaving the trio shivering in the cool evening air and stirring their fruity drinks with their mini umbrellas. The smell of fried food and burgers mixed with the faint smell of fish. She took a lakeside seat and rested a hand on the rough, three-foot-high wall next to her that formed the only barrier between her and the dark water below.

A young girl in faded overalls and a pink satin shirt sat in the corner with an acoustic guitar, strumming it but not singing. A small, empty bar was tucked in the far corner of the cozy open-air building, and rows of bottles lined the wall behind it. The screen door leading into the kitchen closed with a soft bang, letting out the mixed aromas of burgers, fries, and boiled shrimp.

Ella leaned back in her chair and let the girl's guitar music flow over her. Her talk with Owen had cheered her up immensely, and with each passing second in the Jolly Roger she felt the tension from the day's dive slip away. The breeze coming in off the lake was just cold enough to invigorate her without giving her the chills.

So nice, she thought. *No smog, no traffic, no hustle and bustle of Boston. Just a bunch of fishermen and their boats. And the occasional misfit like me,* she thought as her waitress walked up.

"Hey there," the young woman said, giving Ella a quick smile. "Good to see a brave soul like you coming here so early in the season. What can I get you?"

Ella returned the smile, feeling like she already knew the slim woman with long blonde hair and light blue eyes standing next to her.

"I, uh, need a menu," she said. As her waitress stepped away to get a menu, Ella realized who the woman was. All it took was a good look at her eyes—she had her brother Mitch's pale eyes.

"Whoops. Here you go," the waitress said, giving Ella the laminated menu with a hand whose fingers were nearly covered in rings. "Sorry 'bout that. The owner's off shooting pool with the boys, so I'm sort of running the show by myself. Can I get you a beer, or maybe a martini? I make a mean one."

"How about a Killian's?" Ella said, admiring the other woman's silver dragonfly ring. "And I was wondering—your name isn't Melissa, is it?"

"Yep," the waitress said. "How'd you guess?"

"Your brother told me. He's taking me diving this season on a project I'm working on." Ella held her hand out. "I'm Ella Simon."

"Nice to meet you, Ella. Dr. Simon, right?" After shaking hands, Melissa pulled out a chair and took a seat in it, crossing her legs at the ankles and leaning forward.

"*Now* I get it," she said. "Mitch told me he had some big project going on this spring, but he's so damn secretive he never tells me any of the details. He's been a grumpy old man ever since his girlfriend dumped him right after New Year's. She was a real winner, that's for sure. A pretty girl, yeah, but in a fussy kind of way. And Julie *hated* being stuck here on the island. Though I think she hated going out with him in his boat even worse. Don't know what they ever saw in each other . . ."

Melissa paused for breath and gave Ella an almost comically shocked expression, as if she'd said too much. Way too much.

"Anyway," Melissa said, "what's your project? A shipwreck?"

Ella gave a quick laugh to cover her surprise at Melissa's guess. "Nah," she said. "Just some boring biology stuff about the water and soil off the coast. Nothing exciting, but it pays the bills, you know? Say, do you have Killian's on draft? I'll take that instead of a bottle, if you've got it."

"Oh yeah, your order." Melissa stood up. "Sure. Be right back."

Ella almost wanted to apologize to Melissa for being so abrupt, but she couldn't afford to tell anyone about the dive and end up with a bunch of tourists—*tourons*—hounding her while she carried out their project. People were fascinated by shipwrecks, and Ella couldn't blame them, especially when they had to do with pirates. But carrying out the preliminary stages of what could be a years-long process of exploration and excavation was a chore best done without spectators.

Ella was just thinking about what Melissa had said about Mitch's girlfriend breaking up with him when Melissa set a frosty mug in front of her. It had been a long time since she'd had an ice-cold brew. She drank almost half her beer in one long pull. It had been *too* long.

"I hope you haven't been taking drinking lessons from my brother," Melissa said, raising her eyebrows and following it with a wink. She took Ella's order for a shrimpburger and fries and hurried off to her other table outside.

Ella leaned back in her chair and looked at the twinkling lights on the other side of the harbor. She felt a relaxing sense of heaviness enter her limbs as she sipped her beer and enjoyed the solitude of the night. When Melissa brought out her food, Ella jumped as if she'd been dozing.

"Say, Melissa," she said, nodding at the rest of the restaurant. "I was wondering about something. Is it always this quiet around here?"

"No," Melissa said. She waved at the girl with the guitar, who had packed up her equipment and was on her way out of the restaurant. "It's really slow, for some reason. Has been all week. All month. Though it is early in the season, I guess."

Ella glanced behind her and saw that the three tourists eating outside were gone as well. She hoped they'd paid their bill. The place was empty except for her and Melissa. She thought about Owen's stories and barely stifled a shiver.

She gestured at the chair across from her, and Melissa sat. "Well, I think you have a nice little island here. Those other folks are missing out."

Melissa grinned. "It's not so bad. I like people, even if some of the folks I serve here can get a bit snippy. I've never figured out why some people allow themselves to get stressed out on *vacation,* but they do. It's like 'We've got to

65

see the lighthouse and walk on the beach and check out this shop and take this boat tour on the sound and eat here, all before noon.' People don't know how to relax."

"Ah," Ella said. "Tourons."

Melissa nodded and laughed, a sound more musical than the guitar girl's best strumming had been all night. "You got it."

"Well, call me a touron, then. It's always hard for me to relax." She'd devoured her shrimpburger, and her beer was gone. "Though it's pretty easy to do that here."

"Nah," Melissa said as she hopped up, flicked off the lights for the outdoor eating area and turned off the red OPEN sign. She came back with two more mugs of beer.

"You're not a touron," Melissa said as she sat down across from Ella. "I can tell that already. You'd fit in pretty well here, I'd say."

"Right," Ella said.

"I kid you not. I know about these things." They clinked their mugs together. "Cheers. And welcome to Ocracoke."

"Thanks." Ella sipped the beer this time instead of chugging it as she'd done with the first one. Already she was feeling a bit too chatty, but it felt great to finally unwind. She hadn't done that for months. "So don't you feel a bit cut off, living down here? I mean, you've got to take a ferry to get anywhere outside the island."

"Nah. Mitch has his pilot's license, and we can bop all over the place in the company plane. Plus I have fewer distractions, so I can get lots of work done."

"Waiting tables, you mean?"

"Oh hell no!" Melissa said with another hearty laugh. "This job here just pays the bills and buys the stuff I need for my real job—making pottery. Everyone's gotta have an obsession, you know. I've got pottery, my brother's got his boat, Ben has this bar, my dad . . . well, he used to have my mom to obsess over, but . . . she passed away last year."

Melissa stifled a cough with her hand and left it there for a moment. She again wore an awkward expression on her face that told Ella she'd said too much. The four earrings in each ear glittered in the light cast by the revolving lamp of the lighthouse on the other side of the lake.

"I'm sorry to hear that," Ella said.

"No, *I'm* sorry, Ella," Melissa said. "I'm babbling. Usually I get to chat a little with the customers, but most of the people who've been coming in lately are locals, and they've all heard my stories."

"Don't apologize," Ella said. "I like stories like yours. Actually, I've heard a couple good ones today from your brother. Not to mention a nice chat I had with Owen, the guy who sells fruits and vegetables over on Creek Road, close to the house where I'm staying."

Ella took a quick breath at the funny look Melissa was giving her. "Oh no. Don't tell me Owen's a ghost. That I was having a conversation with a ghost. This island's crawling with them, it seems."

Melissa's eyes went wide. "A ghost? Owen? Hell no. He's just a bit loopy, you know? I hope he wasn't rude or weird to you. Same goes for Mitch, now that I think about it. Sometimes those two get talking about stuff that spooks the tourists, and even some of us locals." She laughed softly, sounding just like her brother this time. "No, Owen's definitely not a ghost."

"That's a relief," Ella said.

"He didn't give you a birdhouse, did he?"

"Well, actually, he did." Ella drank the rest of her beer. "Why?"

"You'll just have a friend for life, that's all. He'll probably bring you flowers next. He's mostly harmless. Just don't let him get going on his opinions about the folks on the island, or the weird stuff that happens to his fruits and vegetables. He'll never shut up."

"Oh great," Ella said. She yawned before she could cover her mouth. "Well, I'd better get going. Here. Keep the change," she said, handing Melissa a twenty and ignoring her protesting. "Use what's left over to get some clay or glaze or whatever you may need for your pottery."

"If you say so. Thanks."

"No problem. It was nice talking to someone with her feet on the ground and not all obsessed with hauntings and spooks and the 'dark side.' You've given me hope for the rest of the folks of Ocracoke."

Melissa gave Ella another strange look before smiling at her.

"If you say so," she said at last. "Though I think my brother would say you've gotten it exactly wrong. But I'll take the compliment. And your change. I have my eye on a new wheel for my studio. See ya 'round, Ella."

"Good night," Ella called on her way out of the restaurant.

As she walked back to her rented house, breathing deeply of the cool, salty night air, Ella felt her enthusiasm for the shipwreck exploration return.

It was all a case of keeping things in perspective, she realized, something she'd been having trouble doing all winter. She was relying too much on first impressions. Ocracoke wasn't some backwater island, and the ship buried out there in the inlet wasn't some anonymous ship. Owen wasn't a ghost, and Mitch wasn't some superstitious lug with great shoulders and captivating eyes.

Well, Ella thought. *Maybe Mitch* does *have nice shoulders and hypnotic eyes.*

The superstitious lug part she'd have to prove for herself. Tomorrow morning, before the crack of dawn, Ella planned on putting her belief in Mitch to the test.

Chapter Six

Ella thought that Mitch looked more than a little bit surprised to find her waiting for him aboard *Cassiopeia* the next morning at 4:45 sharp. She sat on the dock, wrapped in her coat, sipping coffee from her Thermos and watching over her equipment in the boat. The pile of gear included her own tanks and hoses this time.

"Pardon me for saying so," Ella said when he moved into the glow of the light from the dock, "but you look like hell, Mitch."

"Gee, thanks," Mitch said. He dropped an armload of gear onto the floor of the boat. "Good to see you, too, doc."

"Let me guess, you and your buddy Ben were out late last night, drinking beer and shooting pool, right?"

Mitch stopped straightening his gear and stared at her. "Look who's become psychic," he said at last, rubbing his eyes and smiling. If there had been more light, Ella was convinced that they would have looked quite bloodshot. "Either that, or you've been talking to my sister. In any case, I really didn't think you'd be back, to be honest." Mitch grabbed the last box of equipment from the back of the same truck she'd seen at the ferry landing. "But it's good to see you here."

"Thanks," Ella said. She took a deep breath and chose her words carefully. She'd been going over what she was about to say all morning. "Look, Mitch, I really need your help to pull off this dive. Yesterday was just a fluke. An honest goof-up. Just promise me one thing."

"Sure. What?"

"No more ghost stories. Okay? Deal?"

Mitch looked at her for a long moment, his eyes narrowing slightly. His face seemed torn with indecision, as if there was something more he'd wanted to say, and then he nodded. "Deal."

After stowing the last of his equipment on board, Mitch slid easily behind the wheel, as if dropping into a favorite old chair. His movements had become confident and crisp, as if all of his fatigue had drained away from him now that he was back aboard his beloved boat.

"Now," he said before firing up *Cassie*'s engines, "what do you say we take another look at that pirate ship?"

"Sounds like a great plan," Ella said, hoping her voice didn't betray the sense of uncertainty Mitch's look of indecision had given her.

Don't make me regret my decision to stick with you, she thought. *We've got to make this work, skipper.*

Three hours later, Ella had a pretty good feeling that Mitch the dive master would never have imagined himself sitting out in the ocean in his anchored boat, alone, typing numbers into a laptop computer, while his diving client worked alone sixty feet underwater below him. But that was exactly what she'd had him doing all morning, under her orders to take a break every forty-five minutes to tug on a tether attached to her right arm to remind her to surface so she didn't get the bends. He had argued with her the whole trip out to the shipwreck site, but Ella wouldn't change her mind.

Her first task had been to get a reasonably accurate measurement of the downed ship, despite the fact that the hull was in a series of pieces. It had broken apart years ago, and it now spread across a stretch of the sandy ocean bottom that was half as long as a football field. She surfaced with the coordinates and measurements on her waterproof pad and showed Mitch how to enter them onto her laptop.

When she sank back down to the ship again, Ella passed over the great crack in the hull. She had discovered the opening that morning, another sign that this expedition was definitely looking up. She guessed that either water pressure or damage from an attack caused the crack that had just about split the vessel in two.

North of the split in the ship, the sand had been disturbed. Ella tried to see more details, but the rocky outcropping next to the ship had cast the entire area into shadows. Half-expecting the water to turn icy cold on her, Ella swam toward the marks in the sand.

What she saw there made her want to kick back toward the surface. Half-buried in the sand of the ocean floor next to the outline of the downed ship was a pair of tiny footprints.

What in the world? Ella thought, feeling her stomach tighten and her hands clench into fists. She looked at the tether on her arm leading to Mitch, as if it was all somehow his fault. She should have known something like this was going to happen.

The faint tracks led away on a course parallel to the wreck. Determined to disprove the nagging voice inside her head, the voice that insisted that these marks in the silt and sand had somehow been made by a human, Ella kicked out and followed the tracks. The voice in her head sounded distinctly like Mitch's.

The tracks in the sand became clearer when she hit a cold patch in the water, just like the water from yesterday.

The instant she felt the coldness assault her skin through her wetsuit, a distant thudding sound made her pull up short. It was the firing of a cannon.

No, she told herself. *It was no such thing. It was nothing.*

She swam ten feet farther, following the tracks as the imaginary cannon continued firing, each blast a little bit closer. She half-expected a dark, headless figure to emerge from the shadowy depths, but all she could see was a mound of sand and another rocky outcropping, like a cave, just ahead of her.

She felt almost hypnotized by the sight of the tiny impressions of toes and feet pressed into the sand under her. In spite of the cold water enveloping her, she let herself sink to the floor until her flippered feet straddled the tiny footprints leading into the small hole worn into the rock. She had to fight off the urge to simply drop to her hands and knees and start digging.

A hungry sensation of greed filled her, and she wanted to expose the treasure of the ship all at once—its gold along with its priceless knowledge and historical artifacts. The throbbing of the cannons stopped her just before she scooped up a handful of sand.

Ella looked up at the ear-numbing sound, shocked back to reality. When her gaze touched the tiny opening in the column of rock, she saw something *moving* inside the cave. She figured it was probably just a fish, but the movement made her jump, and her sense of being watched from yesterday's dive had returned.

Coming from the crack now was a barely visible, orangish glow. She needed to see what was in there.

She kicked away from the ocean floor and was about to swim toward the crack when something jerked at her right arm. The cannons sounded again, and Ella choked back a scream. When she was able to risk a panicked look at her upper arm, she saw that she'd reached the end of the tether tied to Mitch's boat. The rope had pulled tight on her.

Come on, girl, she scolded herself. *Quit spooking yourself.*

She slipped the tether off her arm without a second thought and swam into the faint light of the rocky cavern.

Inside the low-ceilinged cavern, Ella encountered two wonders. The first was a mostly intact piece of the ship. The second wonder was a young boy.

Both were so unexpected down here in the cold, silty water that Ella didn't know which one to look at first. The second object in the cave made no sense to Ella, so she focused on the first.

The piece of the ship was covered under almost half a foot of sand except for a three-foot section that jutted out. It was made of thick wooden beams connected with spikes. Amazingly, the structure was still intact, and the spikes had barely even rusted. A small metal plate had been pounded into a corner of the structure, and just before she was able to look away, Ella could have sworn she'd seen the numbers "1717" carved into the plate.

Unbelievable, she thought. *This really could be one of Blackbeard's ships. The pirate's last reported appearance had been back in 1718.*

Then she looked up and forgot about Blackbeard. Floating above the half-buried piece of the ship, on the far side of the cavern was a slender, delicate-looking boy who looked to be barely in his teens.

The boy wore a torn vest and old-fashioned knickers that had been patched together and held up with a rope belt. He looked at her, his eyes big and scared, and that was when Ella realized the boy was glowing.

Impossible, she wanted to say.

The boy's eyes were as round and blue as portholes as he shook his head as if to say "No."

Ella inched closer, surprised she was able to move at all.

The boy's skin gave off a faint orange light, and he wasn't wearing any sort of breathing apparatus, though he was over sixty feet from the surface. As Ella stared, forgetting to breathe, the boy reached out for her. Without even thinking, Ella lifted her left arm out to him. She took one step closer to the child, then another. She could almost feel the boy's tiny fingers, grabbing for her arm.

The cannons exploded again, but this time they sounded muffled and weak from inside the cavern.

The boy had been crying, Ella noticed, and then the scientific part of her brain reminded her that such a thing was impossible to see underwater. Still, in spite of the voice, she continued reaching out for the boy. Without needing to speak, she could tell he desperately needed her help.

When she was less than five feet from him, someone grabbed her. A pair of strong hands pulled her backwards out of the cave so fast she was unable to fight them off. When she finally managed to break free of the hands on her shoulders, Ella turned to the sound of cannons exploding all around her.

Mitch swam next to her in his damp shorts and T-shirt, a mask sitting crookedly on his face. He had a tank strapped to his shoulder and a mouthpiece jammed in his mouth. Ella realized she was tensed up, about to hit him. She unclenched her hand and winced at another cannon blast. He had to be freezing in this icy water.

He pointed up at the boat and reached out to her again, his eyes as wide as the boy's eyes inside the cavern had been. Ella shook her head and grabbed Mitch instead. Hanging onto the straps of his tank, she pulled him back into the cave with her. She wanted him to see the boy, if that's what she'd seen in there.

But of course, when they were back in the cave, with the cannons sounding more and more like laughter with each blast, all Ella could see was the piece of the ship. The glowing boy was gone.

It happened again, Ella thought, letting go of Mitch.

She stared at the perfectly preserved piece of the ancient ship, sitting safe and sound in this sandy cave for nearly 300 years, and tried to ignore the deep laughter echoing outside the cave. Mitch moved closer, and Ella could imagine him wanting to drag her back to the boat as fast as possible.

What's going on? she thought. Her legs felt weak as she searched the cave for any hint of the boy. *Am I losing it down here?*

Another thought hit her as hard as a cannonball to the stomach: *Why the hell did I try to dive alone after what happened yesterday?* She thought about Mitch diving by himself when he first found the ship and wondered if there wasn't some sort of curse on this site after all.

As if responding to her thoughts, the water inside the cavern turned frothy from another loud, laughing blast from the cannons. Mitch gave Ella a determined look and took her arm. He pointed outside the cave, and this time Ella nodded in agreement. It was time to get some air.

Ella could feel how badly Mitch was shaking as he reached for her hand, and he didn't let go of her until they left the cave. Ella wished he would have held onto her longer, because someone was waiting for them outside.

Floating above Ella and Mitch was a wild-haired man in a long black coat. Just like the boy in the cave, he was without diving gear, and his bearded face seemed to glow with a sickly drowned whitish-blue color. His mouth was open in an oval of silent rage, even as laughter bubbled up around them. His thin, striped shirt was open, revealing a pale, hairless chest, and around his purple neck he wore a gallows noose. The ten-foot-long rope was frayed and broken, and it floated around his head like a snake.

This is the same guy as yesterday, Ella thought, her ears aching with the pounding of the man's mad laughter.

The wild-eyed man floated toward them, his fingers spread wide as he reached out like a starving man grabbing at food.

Ella watched Mitch undo his weight belt and pull it free. Just before Mitch threw the belt at the man, Ella grabbed his other hand and hit the button to inflate her BCD for the second time in two days. In an instant she was flying upwards and dragging Mitch up after her. She didn't dare look back to see if they were being followed.

Her ears were aching with the sudden changes in pressure, but she held tight to Mitch's hand as they rushed up toward his boat. They burst up out of the water at the same time, and Ella's entire body was trembling with fear and adrenaline.

For a painful moment she didn't know where she was. She panicked. After she spit out her mouthpiece, she began punching and kicking at Mitch in a sudden fit of fear. She was convinced she was going to either lose her mind or drown until Mitch wrapped his arms around her. He held her tight until she calmed down.

Without speaking, Ella let Mitch pull her back to *Cassie.* After almost a minute of struggling to get back aboard the boat, she removed her tank and mask and set them on the deck. She sank to the floor herself, and closed her eyes. Something stung on her left arm, but she was too tired to look or to care. She was just glad to be out of that icy water.

When she finally opened her eyes, she saw Mitch struggling to take off his own mask. He looked like he was battling some invisible enemy, but it was just her and Mitch on the boat. He swore as he lost his balance and pitched forward. Somewhere in her fatigued and frightened mind she could hear the cracking sound of Mitch's forehead meeting something hard and unyielding on the hull of his ship.

Ella felt suddenly tired, and her eyelids wouldn't remain open. She let her exhaustion overtake her, and her world went darker than the ocean depths below her.

In the blackness behind her eyes, Ella Simon was no longer sitting in her wetsuit on Mitch's boat, the air cold on her wet skin and her heart beating frantically. Instead, she was thrust back into one of her bad dreams from her first night in Ocracoke. She was on the nightmare plane, heading down. Out of control. And the men behind her kept arguing with each other even as the icy sea approached.

She tried to cry out, to pry her fingers from her seat rest, to do anything to fight the inevitability of the coming crash. But they were going to hit—

The dream shifted, and Ella was hanging on for dear life on the back of the runaway black pony. The pony's eyes glowed a fiery red as it leaped over a narrow two-lane highway, narrowly avoiding a car packed full of diving equipment and suitcases. It was all Ella could do to hold on and brace for the impact. She was out of control.

But the impact never arrived. The dream shifted again, and Ella found herself alone in the middle of a cold black ocean, waiting for someone to come rescue her, even as laughter and the thunder of cannons filled the air. She was unable to move, helpless. The feeling filled her with rage;

she'd vowed to never let herself get into such a situation. She had to take care of herself, not rely on anyone else.

As she waited in the darkness, treading water, an invisible hand grabbed her by the hair and began pushing her down. With the water turning a sickly bluish-white color, cold water filled Ella's nostrils and mouth. Treading water wasn't enough.

Back on Mitch's boat, Ella opened her eyes and pinched herself, hard.

Enough of that garbage, she thought, the same feelings of anger and frustration filling her, heating up her blood. *No one's coming to rescue me—nobody can save me but me.*

Next to her, Mitch was breathing shallowly, his eyes closed and his pale face strangely peaceful. He had an angry red knot the size of a gumball on his forehead. Ella guessed that he'd smacked his head on the back of the wooden captain's seat when he'd fallen forward.

Worried that he might be seriously hurt, Ella reached out a shaky hand to wake him. But before she touched him, she froze. On the left sleeve of her wetsuit were four long rips, exposing her pink skin to the salty air. She hadn't even noticed them until now. Luckily they had torn only the thick hide of her diving suit, and not touched her skin underneath.

Staring at the four-inch-long gashes in her wetsuit, she thought of the strange glowing boy hovering above the ancient piece of the ship. Before the boy had slipped away, Ella could have sworn that she'd felt tiny fingers on her arm. The same arm which was now sporting four long tears in the fabric of her diving suit.

"My imagination," she murmured, glancing at Mitch as he shifted and groaned next to her.

There had to be some logical explanation for it all. For the boy and for the man-shaped thing standing outside the cavern. Surely that hadn't been a man, as she had at first thought. And surely that man hadn't had a purplish-black face, caused no doubt by the rotting noose still cinched tightly around his neck.

Ella blew out a sudden breath of air, as if trying to rid herself of a bad smell. The man had been reaching for her and Mitch, and she'd been unable to move. The man . . .

No, she told herself. *Both the man and the boy had to have been some sort of* illusion. *Probably caused by the bad lighting coming from my flashlight. Or I could've just mistaken some sort of underwater lichen or rocks for a boy and a man.* Ella knew all too well that the mind can play tricks on the eye, especially underwater.

And as for the rips in her suit, well, she probably hooked her arm on some rocks or a couple nails from the ship. Something like that. Everything could be explained, as soon as she was able to look at the situation logically.

Ella tried to put the illusory images of the glowing boy and the man in black out of her mind, but they were both too detailed and fresh in her memory to simply dismiss. She shivered.

She wondered if Mitch might have been right in all he'd seen and said. She remembered the water turning to ice around her, and the sound of laughter mixing with the thud of cannons. Maybe this area really *was* haunted.

Ella felt her fear turn once more into anger. *Believing in ghosts was no way to live life. There had to be a logical answer.*

"Mitch?" she asked at last, tired of waiting for him to wake. She slid closer, until she was sitting over him. She poked him in the shoulder with a cold finger. "Mitch. Wake up, Mitch."

Mitch's response was to reach up and grab Ella by the throat.

Chapter Seven

She couldn't breathe, and the pain made her want to black out again. Feeling the rush of adrenaline fill her again, Ella gripped Mitch's hand around her throat and pulled, but he wouldn't let go. His eyes were still clamped shut.

Ella threw herself backwards as hard as she could, out of her sitting position. Mitch followed her as she landed on her back. Before he could drop on top of her, though, she lifted both knees, catching him in the midsection as he fell forward. Mitch let go of her.

Mitch dropped back to the floor of his boat, holding his stomach, and Ella could breathe again.

"I'm sorry," Mitch gasped when he was able to speak again. His eyes were wide open now. His face looked pale and haunted, and Ella could see him shivering in his soaked shorts and T-shirt. She wasn't ready to give him much sympathy—or get too close to him—just yet.

"What's wrong with you?" she said, rubbing her throat.

"I was . . . dreaming, I guess. A nightmare, really. I thought I was fighting . . ." He shuddered and inched toward her. "I'm so sorry, Ella. Are you okay?"

"Yeah," she said, swallowing without too much pain in her throat. Thankfully, everything seemed to still be working.

"I'm sorry," he said again, holding his head in his hands as if he had a piercing headache.

"It's okay. I'm just glad I took that self-defense class at the university. I was just about to knee you another time, a little bit lower, but you woke up."

"Don't sound so disappointed," Mitch said with the hint of a smile. "You'll probably get another opportunity to kick me later. You sure you're okay?"

"I'm fine. So what were you dreaming about?" Ella asked.

"I don't want to talk about it."

"Come on, Mitch. Something's going on here, and we have to make sense of it."

"Okay. But you're making me break my promise about no ghost stories."

"Oh boy," Ella said. She heaved a long sigh and wrapped herself in a blanket. "Let's hear it, Mitch."

"Well," Mitch began, grabbing the other blanket, "I was dreaming, but it felt like it was really happening. I was up here, waiting for you to come back up for a break. I knew something was wrong the instant I felt the tether go slack. I don't know what we were thinking with that crazy plan."

Tell me about it, Ella wanted to say, but she bit her tongue.

"I knew, in my dream, I had to go down there, but I couldn't move. There was this light in the water, right over where you would've been. I had to go down after you, even though that light . . ." Mitch paused, as if trying to decide if he should say any more. He nodded, as if to himself. "That weird light was pure white, and looking at it made me feel *wrong.* I felt like I was nine years old again, scared to death after one of my dad's stories about headless ghosts haunting these waters."

"Um-hmm," Ella said.

"Then I got my courage up and reached down into the water. The second my hand touched the water, a hand grabbed me. And it *pulled.* I went headfirst into the water, and the hand still held tight to my hand." Mitch shuddered. "It dragged me down into that nasty white light. The water was cold as ice. And as I sank, another hand wrapped around my neck."

"But it was just a dream—" Ella said.

"I *know*," Mitch said, almost shouting. "I know," he said again, in a softer voice, "but it felt real. So real that my arms are sore from fighting those hands pulling me down. And that's when I reached out for the throat of the man who had grabbed me. 'If I'm going to die,' I thought, 'I'm not going alone.' "

"And that's when I tried to wake you," Ella said, swallowing again with less pain this time. "At the worst possible moment."

"You got it," Mitch said. "Have I said how sorry I am for that?"

With the pained look on Mitch's face, combined with his shaking voice as he told his nightmare story, Ella couldn't stay mad much longer. But she had one last question for him.

"Who were you fighting with, in your nightmare?"

"Well, this guy in the water—he was still glowing and, you see, he didn't have a *head*, Ella. Not even a neck. Just this black, empty space where a head should have been. In this dream, I kept trying to grab for a throat that wasn't there, all the way down to the bottom of the ocean."

Ella felt her body slump back onto the unforgiving tanks and diving equipment scattered on the deck of Mitch's boat as he finished his story. She felt a memory from the end of her drive two days ago break loose from where she'd been trying to suppress it. It floated to the surface like an ancient artifact: a dark, headless man dancing on the roof of a drowned house.

"Ella?" Mitch was next to her, a hand on her shoulder. That hand was still shaking as badly as it had been underwater, on their way out of the cavern, where another figment of her imagination had been waiting for her.

"Are you okay?" Mitch asked, calling out her name again.

Ella squeezed her eyes shut, sucked in air through her nose, and blew it out of her mouth.

This is ridiculous. I'm getting all spooked over nothing.

"I'm fine," she said.

She opened her eyes and looked from Mitch to the clear midday sky above her. Both his eyes and the sky were the same light blue color, and the clarity of each helped Ella clear her own mind.

"I'm fine," she continued, "but I *am* getting frustrated, Mitch. I've got work to do down there, but for whatever reason, I keep getting interrupted. And I can't stand that, not when—what are you doing?"

Mitch was now sitting next to her, and he had his hand on her left forearm. He touched one of the four scratches in her wetsuit.

"What happened here?" he asked.

"It's nothing," Ella said, trying to pull away, but Mitch held tight to her arm. "I just snagged it on something. I'm all right."

"Damn," he said. He flipped open one of the tears in her suit and touched her skin underneath. "You're lucky these didn't break the skin. You sure you're okay?"

"I'm okay, Mitch!" Ella pulled her arm away, her face red. She wasn't sure what was causing the blood to rush to her face. Surely it couldn't be due to Mitch's closeness, or his hand on her arm. "Just back off for a minute, okay? And for God's sake, quit asking me if I'm okay."

The look on Mitch's face was so shocked and hurt, reminding Ella for a sudden moment of Steven, who was so different from Mitch that the very idea of her ex-boyfriend out here in the ocean made Ella break out into laughter.

"I'm sorry," she began, but the more she tried to stop laughing, the faster it came. She knew it probably sounded hysterical after all that had just happened, but it also felt good.

"Are you sure you're okay?" Mitch said. When Ella gave him a scolding look, he realized he'd asked her the forbidden question again, and he threw his hands into the air.

"I give up!" he shouted at the sky as he began to laugh as well. "I can't do anything right on this dive! And my forehead's *killing* me!"

Ella crumpled to the floor of the boat, giggling harder than she'd even giggled since junior high. The sun broke through the clouds as they sat, laughing and recovering. Ella looked up at Mitch and heard him groan as he touched the red knot on his forehead. His agonized look set her off again into another round of cackling.

Ella realized that she preferred laughing her ass off to screaming her head off at the situation, and she liked the sound of Mitch's laughter in her ears, even if she could barely hear him over her own hysterical laughter.

"We're quite a sight, aren't we?" she said at last, rubbing her throat with her left hand and pointing at the scratches in her wetsuit. Mitch laughed again and winced. When he moved his hand from his forehead to the place in his midsection where she'd kneed him, Ella began laughing all over again.

"What a day," Mitch said a few seconds later. He laughed again, softer this time. "Some team we are."

"So," Ella said, wiping her eyes. She felt all of her fear

wiped away by their fits of laughing. She knew what had to be done. "I can guess what you're thinking. You're thinking that what we saw was actually a pair of ghosts down there."

"Ghosts? As in, more than *one?* Oh shit, Ella."

"What?"

"I just saw one . . . *thing* down there. Maybe it was a man, maybe just some sort of shadow. But that's all I saw. What did *you* see?"

Ella answered him by standing up and reaching for her mask. She was going back down there. She'd prove it to him, and herself, that there was nothing down there but a wrecked ship, some patches of bad water, and some over-active imaginations.

"Hold on," Mitch said. He pulled on his wetsuit and strapped on his tank and mask. When he was suited up, he grabbed a long black flashlight and his underwater camera. "I've got to be completely nuts. But if we're going to do this, we need to do it right."

Ella gave him a quick, nervous smile, and then nodded. She was hoping he'd come along. She needed him to. No more diving alone, no matter what happened.

"Thanks, Mitch," she said. "Now let's go see what's really down there. We'll be back up in ten minutes at the most."

The icy water tickled the skin of her arm, slipping through the four rips in her diving suit. The water was like cold, tiny fingers tickling her as they sank down toward the wreck site once more. Ella focused on her breathing, determined to stay calm and keep her head clear. Surely they'd imagined it all down here. Scratches or no scratches.

She flicked on the light attached to her forehead, and Mitch did the same, clicking on his flashlight as well. As they touched the bottom and their three lights brought the remains of the ship into sight, Ella glanced over at Mitch. He was slightly hunched over, somehow, as if waiting for something to creep up behind him.

She caught herself thinking about Mitch and his laugh and the way he'd examined the rips in her wetsuit. She'd liked the way he touched her arm, and the concerned look on his face had calmed her, for some reason. Too much time had passed since someone had looked at her like that, even if it had only been for a few seconds.

Stop it, Ella told herself as they began swimming toward the cave. *This is neither the time nor the place.*

The silt next to the shipwreck was undisturbed, even where Ella had stopped at different spots to inspect something on the wreck. In just a few seconds, the water covered any track or disturbance with what looked like a protective layer of dirt and sand.

She wasn't surprised nobody had found the ship until recently. She was impressed that Mitch had been able to find it at all. She thought again about the way both she and Mitch had felt compelled to dive alone around the ship, as if the shipwreck was something either of them could actually own and keep for themselves.

Mitch was right behind her, sticking close. As recently as this morning his proximity would have bothered and distracted her, but right now his presence calmed her.

A few seconds later they were back at the entrance to the cavern, and Ella forgot about Mitch, the moment they had shared on the boat, and everything else that had brought her here. The orange glow she'd seen earlier inside the cavern was back.

She flipped off the light on her forehead, and Mitch did the same. He turned off the flashlight and held it in his hand like a nightstick. Kicking softly, not even aware she was holding her breath, Ella peeked into the crack leading to the cavern containing the mostly intact chunk of the ship.

This time, along with the orange light, a whitish-blue glow burst into life inside the cavern. This new light circled around the edges of the orange light like an oversized firefly.

Softly lit by the strange orange and blue glows, the rect-angular chunk of the ancient ship sat half-buried in the sand. Alone. The cavern appeared to be otherwise empty.

Ella reached for Mitch, but he already had his camera out. Passing her his flashlight, he pointed the camera into the cavern and took quick aim. There were two silent flashes, and then the ocean was dark again. The pair of glowing lights had disappeared.

Ella heard what mostly likely was the burble of air coming from her mouthpiece as she exhaled. But the quiv-ering sound spooked her. For a moment she'd been con-vinced the sound was faraway laughter.

She looked over at Mitch, whose eyes had gone wide at the sound. He slowly shook his head as his face turned grim, and he pointed at his wrist. *Time to go.*

Ella didn't fight him this time. She looked at her own wrist, where the four rips in her suit stood out like stripes. She'd had enough for one day. A hot shower and a beer or two—or four—at the Jolly Roger sounded like the perfect antidote to this crazy day.

Chapter Eight

At five p.m., with the best seat in the house overlooking the lake, Ella put her feet up on the chair across from her and sipped her beer. All she wanted to do was relax and watch the sun set from the comfort of the Jolly Roger restaurant, if her nerves would allow it. She was starting to enjoy the simple, unadorned atmosphere of the lakeside restaurant, and she regretted not having time to explore the island itself. All she'd really seen of the town was this place and her rented house and the stretch of road connecting the two. Even Mitch's boat was less than fifty yards away, at the dock attached to the pier of the Jolly Roger.

"How's the project coming?" Melissa said. She took a seat next to Ella in the mostly empty restaurant and began twirling one of the many silver rings on her right hand.

"Slowly," Ella said. "But that seems to be the pace around here, doesn't it?"

"You got it. That's why I'm here. Some folks claim it's boring, with nothing to really do—no movie theaters, no dance clubs, none of the amenities of a big city. But that's a plus, for me. My whole family feels that way, even Mitch. He'd rather take *Cassie* out with folks from town than some rich tourons who don't appreciate the island or the ocean. Me, I just dig the quiet. Lets me get more pottery made."

"Even if it's bad for business?"

"Shh," Melissa said with a wink. "Don't let Ben overhear you. He'll freak out if he hears such talk. He's been a bit high-strung lately."

"Order up!" a voice called from the kitchen. "*Tonight,* Mel! Move it!"

"Speak of the devil," Melissa said, rolling her eyes as she moved off toward the kitchen. "I'm coming, boss man."

Ella smiled and thought again about how closely the brother and sister resembled one another. Definitely the eyes. She was impressed at Melissa's ability to find contentment here on Ocracoke, so far from the rest of the world. Ella had trouble finding that sort of peace wherever she went, and she was becoming convinced that it wasn't in Boston anymore.

By the time Melissa had come back with a plate of fries and boiled shrimp, each shrimp the size of Ella's thumb, Ella had finished her first beer. She had forgotten about the events of today's dives and had lost herself in the slowly shifting colors of the early-evening sky. She couldn't remember the last time she'd watched night fall without doing something else.

The sky was turning a beautiful shade of purple when someone set two beers on the table next to her untouched plate of food.

"Thanks, Meliss—" she said, and then stopped. It was Mitch. His face was pale, and he held an envelope in his hands. "Hi, Mitch. You okay?"

The question raised a small smile on his face, reminding Ella of their laugh-fest on his boat after their first dive today. Then his smile disappeared.

"You've got to see this," he said in a breathless voice. He dropped into the chair across from her. "I'm about to lose my mind, I swear."

"What's wrong?"

Ella took the envelope from his hand and shook out a pair of eight-by-ten color photos.

"Look at them. I developed them as soon as I got back," Mitch explained. "I have a darkroom and equipment at my place. Taught myself—it's a lot quicker than sending it on the ferry and waiting a day or two. Just look at them, closely."

Ella held up the first photo of the cavern with the piece of the ship.

"What did you have on your lens, there?" she said, pointing at a pair of discolorations on either edge of the photo.

"Nothing. Today's the first time I used that camera since I cleaned it and put it away for the winter. Look at the next one. It can't be anything on the lens."

Ella stared. In the first photo, floating slightly off-center in the flash-lit cavern, was the barest outline of a small figure, quite possibly a person. The figure was tinged in orange. In the other corner of the cave, near the chunk of ship, was a small bluish-white speck of light.

In the second picture, the first figure had shrunk to an orange dot, losing almost all of its definition. The blue-white light, meanwhile, had grown to ten times its size. It was almost man-sized, with the slightest hint of arms and legs coming from a blurry torso, and it was now floating close to the mouth of the cavern.

Just off to the side of the blue-white figure, Ella could just make out what could have been the frayed end of a rope. The same kind of rope that could have been used, centuries ago, for hangings.

"I don't . . ." Ella began, but her voice wasn't working. *I don't believe this,* she'd wanted to say. Flicking her gaze from one photo to the other, she felt her jaw drop and her mouth go dry. The air felt ten degrees colder.

"I made three other prints, just to be sure," Mitch said.

91

He rubbed his eyes as if he hadn't slept in weeks. "All of them were exactly the same."

With a gentle tug, Mitch carefully pried the photographs out of Ella's grasp. Without realizing it, she'd been slowly crumpling both pictures as she looked from one to the other. At some level, Ella felt a violent urge to destroy these pictures. They simply made no sense. You couldn't take pictures of something that wasn't *there.*

"I was just thinking," Mitch said, "that maybe that tank and hose from your first dive weren't defective after all. I swear I saw something right next to you yesterday, right before the hose came loose. The same . . . thing . . . we saw today. And then, after what happened today—"

"I need some fresh air," Ella said, standing up too fast.

Regaining her balance, she pushed away from the table, taking her beer with her. She nearly ran down the wooden ramp leading back to the road, each step sounding as loud as a blast from a miniature cannon.

In the growing darkness, Ella hurried down the road as if trying to outrun the memory of the strange images in Mitch's photos. She toyed with the idea of simply going back to her house, but that felt too much like giving up. And in any case, she was much too restless to sit in that musty-smelling house and stare out over the lake at the Jolly Roger.

"This was supposed to be the trip that helped me get my act together," she whispered to herself. "Not the trip that made me lose my mind."

She took a long drink of beer, wishing she could bring back the laughter she'd shared with Mitch just a few hours earlier. She pulled up short in mid-stride when she realized she was almost back home already. Off to her left was Owen's produce stand, sitting under a street light that had just flickered to life. The old man was in the process of closing up for the day.

Ella was about to call out to Owen when he reached down into a bucket of cucumbers and plucked one out. He held it up in the fading light and stared at it. He pulled out a knife and carefully cut away part of the green skin.

Spirit fingerprints, Ella thought, remembering their talk from a day ago. *Is* that *what's on Mitch's photos? And is that what caused those scratches on my wetsuit?*

Instead of going across the street to find some answers from the produce man, Ella spun on her heel and turned back to the Jolly Roger. The sight of Owen had calmed her and made her forget the images from the past two days that had haunted her, both awake and asleep.

When she made it back, the restaurant was empty except for Mitch, a fresh plate of shrimp, and another beer waiting for her at the table next to the lake.

"A peace offering," he said. "How many dive masters have you known in the past who buy their bosses dinner?"

"Not many," Ella said, taking a seat. "Sorry. I just needed some fresh air, I guess."

"I'm glad you came back, so it didn't go to waste. I only ate a couple," he added, pointing at the half-dozen shrimp tails on his plate.

Mitch turned over the two photographs on the table and ran a hand through his hair, making most of it stick straight up. Ella noticed that he had circles under his eyes, and she felt a pang of sympathy for him. She could imagine what kind of nightmares he'd been having lately.

"Thanks," she said, peeling a shrimp. Just like that, her hunger was returning.

As she ate, Mitch toyed with the shrimp tails spread out on his plate, flipping them around like bugs.

"You must think I'm one ignorant, superstitious hick, huh?" His voice wasn't angry or bitter, just matter-of-fact. "All I can talk about are ghosts and pirates and old wives' tales."

"Come on," Ella began. "I don't think—"

"I'm not really like that," he interrupted. "Sure, I like a good ghost story and all, but damn, I never *believed* in any of them. Not really. Now I'm convinced there's either something wrong with me, or there's something seriously unnatural about that ship."

Ella didn't know what to say, so she drank her beer and pushed her plate of shrimp closer to Mitch. She felt a bit unnerved, looking at this big guy peeking at the photos on the table next to him like they contained his own death certificate.

"Let me tell you a story, Mitch," Ella said. "I don't know what your dad or anyone else from my university may have told you about that ship down there and what it might be, but I want you to know."

Mitch lifted his gaze from the photos, a half-smile on his face, one eyebrow raised.

"We're pretty sure that the ship down there is a lost ship called *The Revenge*. It used to be one of Blackbeard's ships."

"Of course," Mitch muttered, draining the last of his beer. "Him again."

"But it was more than just Blackbeard's ship. Okay, quick history lesson. You know how the *Queen Anne* was found pretty much empty, right? No gold, no booty, just a ruined ship? Well, it's quite possible that the ship down there is *The Revenge*, Blackbeard's backup ship. You see, Blackbeard knew the *Queen Anne* would be caught eventually, because everyone knew of it, so he moved his treasure.

Guess which ship ol' Blackbeard used to store all his gold and treasure?"

"No way," Mitch said, his eyes widening.

"Yep. Do you see why we can't tell anyone about this? Finding *The Revenge* could be huge, historically. And financially too, of course. But if people hear about it, they're going to go nuts trying to find the lost gold of Blackbeard and company." Ella grimaced for a moment. "I wasn't even supposed to tell you."

"Wow," Mitch said in a soft voice.

His half-smile had turned into a boyish grin, and in that moment, Ella felt something in her chest shift. The look on his face told her that he was feeling the same addictive sense of wonder she felt every time she dove a wreck. She looked down and saw that she'd grabbed his hand at some point, and he was squeezing her hand back as hard as she was squeezing his. They both let go at the same instant. Ella covered her mouth with the same hand, which felt strangely warm, while Mitch fiddled with the pictures once more.

"Hey, I just thought of something," he said at last, breaking the awkward silence. "Maybe the ghosts are guarding their treasure? Maybe that's why they keep bugging us."

Ella made a sudden movement, as if she were getting ready to leave. Tingling hand or not, she didn't want to get started on that train of thought again.

"Wait!" Mitch said. "Don't leave again. I was just joking. Well, sort of."

Ella rolled her eyes at Mitch and gave him a real smile. This time she touched his hand on purpose, just for a second. She could have sworn he jumped from the contact, as if she'd given him a shock. Ella had felt it too, and like a schoolgirl she'd felt her heart skip a beat.

"It's more than just the chance to get rich, you know," she said. "That's not why I'm doing this. That ship is filled with history, and the treasure it may or may *not* have is just a tiny part of that."

"Yeah, but . . ." Mitch's gaze drifted away from her for a moment, toward the lake and his docked boat. He turned his head back to look at her. "I guess you're right."

"Did you know," Ella began, feeling herself slip into lecture mode, but unwilling to stop herself. It felt good. She hadn't given a lecture in a long, long time. "Did you know that on one of the ships, they found a complete Bible, in a leather pouch sealed with wax, perfectly intact? It had an entire family tree written into the front pages, going back to the 1500s. *History*, Mitch. That's what my job is all about."

Mitch was nodding along with her words, his pale eyes intent on everything she was saying. Ella felt herself blushing for no reason.

"Sorry," she said. "I guess I get a bit worked up, talking about this. But that's my field—Maritime History. That's what I do . . . or used to do."

" 'Used to'?" Mitch grabbed a pair of shrimp from her plate. "What do you mean?"

"Oh," Ella began, and then stopped. How badly did she need to go into all this—the terrible semester she'd been having, the untaught classes, the funeral that had started it all off last fall? And how much did Mitch deserve to hear all of this, right now, after the last few turbulent days they'd just shared together?

"It's been a bumpy few months," she said instead. "Let's just leave it at that, okay?"

Mitch nodded and gave her an understanding smile, making the warm feeling in Ella's chest grow. Then his eyes drifted back to his photos on the table next to him. Ella watched him trying, without much luck, to keep from shuddering at the images.

"I'd better get going," he said. He slid the photos back into their envelope. "See you tomorrow around five or six?"

Ella gave him a long look.

What was going on behind those eyes? she wondered.

"Tomorrow," she said at last, and Mitch gathered up his pictures without another word.

Ella watched him leave and realized she'd barely touched her meal. She polished off her beer and tried to eat, but she felt emptier with each shrimp she ate. The warmth in her chest had departed along with Mitch.

To top it off, the sun had set, and she'd missed it. All she had to look forward to on her walk home, alone, were the brilliant stars spread out in the night sky above her.

And that was going to have to be enough, at least for today.

Chapter Nine

An hour after the sun came up the next day, Mitch and Ella dropped into the water, armed with lights and cameras. They were starting a bit later that day, but Ella wasn't complaining. After seeing those images on his pictures, she preferred not to go down there until the sun came up. And after the strange dreams that had kept her tossing and turning all night, she had no problem with sleeping in until six that morning.

The plan was to do more work inside the cavern, getting as much information as she could from the intact piece of the ship. They both agreed that the cave felt like the best place to start. Mitch would stand guard outside the cavern and warn her well in advance if anything strange was coming their way. They would try this for forty-five minutes, then surface, and if everything went well, try it again.

"I'm trusting you," Ella said to Mitch before they dropped overboard. "Don't leave me, Mitch. If something weird shows up, like one of those things from your photo, come in and get me. And I'm not admitting to believing in ghosts or anything like that. I'm just covering my ass, okay?"

Inside the cavern once again, Ella was on her hands and knees, digging in the sand that covered the rectangular piece of the ship. Judging from the curve of the planks she had uncovered so far, along with the way the wood was bound together, she was pretty sure she was looking at a chunk of the external hull of the ship.

She couldn't believe her good fortune at finding this small nugget full of history. Her respect for the ocean and its unpredictable currents had skyrocketed, as it had done so many times before in previous expeditions. Ella guessed that when the ship broke apart on the shoals of the sound, this piece had come loose and came to rest inside this cave. The currents of the ocean may have even nudged it into the cave for all she knew. The end result was that the piece of the pirate ship had been preserved in the sand of the cavern for over two centuries. It was almost like magic, in a way.

Magic? Ella thought to herself. *I'm starting to sound like a certain dive master from Ocracoke.*

Shaking her head at such thoughts, Ella pulled out her dive slate and a tape measure. She took notes about her discovery on the Mylar sheets with a grease pencil. At first she was tempted to bring Mitch in to help with the measuring, but she was enjoying the solitude and the thrill of discovery too much to stop working for the few seconds it would take to bring him inside the cave. They could make more exact measurements later. Right now she had more discoveries to make.

Like what was on the *inside* of this hull wall. Surely something had been preserved under there.

Ella floated over to the jutting section of the wall that she had started to clear of sand. She set down her tape measure and slate. This section, exposed to the elements more than the section that had contained the plate dated 1717, had rotted more, but she could still disperse the sand without ruining the wood.

After five minutes, she had moved enough sand so she could try to raise the wall a fraction and glimpse underneath. She clicked on a handheld flashlight and propped it by her feet so she could see what the underside might hold.

Thankful for the relative weightlessness of objects underwater, Ella fitted her fingers under the wall and lifted.

I could really use Mitch now, she thought as the wall refused to budge. Her arms shook from the effort, and she was about to give up for fear of damaging the wall. With a sudden sucking sensation, the wall loosened, and Ella was able to raise it almost two feet high.

Jackpot! she thought.

Propping the wall up with one hand and her knee, Ella bent low and grabbed the flashlight. She could make out scratches covering most of the wall. Like hash marks, in sets of five—four straight lines, with the fifth line cutting through the four diagonally.

Was this some sort of prison cell? Ella's arm and knee were starting to ache and quiver from the weight of the wall, but she had to get one more look.

Two other marks bigger than the hash marks appeared near the bottom of the wall. They appeared to be numbers—A five and an eight, possibly? Maybe some sort of date?

Or maybe not numbers at all, Ella thought, eyes widening with excitement. *Maybe they were—*

"Dig *deeper,*" an insistent voice said in her ear.

Ella bit down a scream at the sound. She threw her body back while pulling her legs and arms out from underneath the piece of the hull. She *felt* more than heard the impact of the wall hitting the sand.

She hadn't even noticed the water turning cold around her. All of her muscles locked up, and for five seconds she couldn't move. Her eyes were pinched shut.

The wall and its mysterious scratching were forgotten by Ella when she opened her eyes. Her entire attention was focused on the small child floating less than five feet in front of her. The child was giving off an unnatural orangish light.

Oh my God, Ella thought. *You can't be real. This isn't happening.*

"But it *is* happening," the child said, in that same slightly impatient tone of voice. The child had a thick English accent, one that Ella couldn't easily place. "And you're not looking *close* enough."

Ella inched backwards until the rough wall of the cave was at her back. The child hadn't made a move to come closer, but she felt like the boy was only an arm's length away now.

Leave me alone, little boy.

"I'm not a *boy,*" the child said in a suddenly light voice, and the glowing orange color that surrounded the child lightened to a sunny yellow. The child smiled. "I even fooled you! After all these years . . ."

Mitch! Ella wanted to scream his name. *If I could get a hold of him right now, I'd rip him apart for letting this happen. Surely he must have seen this boy—this girl?—slip inside the cave.*

"Is Mitch the gent from outside? He went for a swim, I believe he did! That silly boy! He's long, long gone from here."

Focusing her anger on Mitch helped Ella clear her mind, and she was able to step away from the cave wall.

I'm leaving now, she thought. *Go away, little ghost boy.*

"No!" Orange flames covered the child's face and hands, which were balled into fists. "I need you to dig deeper. And I am not a *boy!*"

Ella felt a sudden pressure on her chest, and she realized that the girl floating in the water in front of her had reached out and touched her. Ella's knees unlocked, and she dropped down onto the sand next to the chunk of the ship.

"That's *better,*" the ghost girl said, her color relaxing to yellow again. "Now you can listen to me. I'm Caroline Amberson, ma'am, and I signed on as a cabin boy, foolin' 'em all, just like I did to you. I had to leave home, you see. Ever since my family came to this new land, life had been nothing but hardship."

Ella nodded, wondering at what point she'd lost her mind and started talking to dead people.

"But I'm not *dead!*" The girl shook her head violently, hard enough to create a flurry of small bubbles around her head. "I'm just a ghost. There's a difference, you know."

Sorry, Ella thought. *Continue, by all means.*

"So I was cabin boy for the *Queen Anne's Revenge,* for almost two years, if you can believe it. Things would've been just right, if we hadn't come across that accursed Stede Bonnet."

Stede Bonnet? Ella asked before she could stop herself. *But wasn't he known as the gentleman pirate? I thought he was a good guy.*

"Oh, no gentleman, this Stede Bonnet," Caroline said. She pointed at the wall below her. "See this? This was a piece of Bonnet's hold, where he kept his prisoners until they died of starvation or . . . worse. No, ma'am. Bonnet was no gentleman. The only thing that kept him from rampagin' all over the seas was the strong arm of Blackbeard. Bonnet even set a ship afire out here in Teach's Channel, and he let Blackbeard take the blame for it."

Ella took a slow, steadying breath, wondering at Caroline's story. *Had all the history books been wrong about these two men?*

"They always get the story wrong, ma'am. All I know is that when Blackbeard took over Bonnet's *Revenge,* he loaded it with all the gold from the *Queen Anne.* And then

Teach made his worst mistake ever. He gave Bonnet his ship back. And guess who was hired on to be Bonnet's cabin boy?"

Ella had a bad feeling where this was leading.

"Bonnet wanted to make burning enemy ships his signature, but he was sick in the head from a bullet wound. After his injury, he was always walkin' about in his nightshirt, moaning for his family and groaning for the arms of his wife. Blackbeard had to lock Bonnet up to keep him out of mischief. About a month later, Bonnet got his wits back and Teach let him free again. And that was when he found me out."

Was that an explosion? Ella wondered, glancing at the mouth of the cave. *And where the hell was Mitch? Surely it was time to go back to the surface.*

But she had no choice but to remain where she was—to leave would mean going through the girl floating directly in front of her, and Ella wasn't about to touch this being, whatever she or it was.

"When Bonnet found out I was a girl," Caroline said, her thin face turning hard and tight, "he claimed he was in love with me. He insisted we be married. He still wasn't right in the head, and never will be."

That was definitely *a cannon blast,* Ella thought, inching away from the girl.

"But I wouldn't let him do it. The thought of him touching me was enough to make me want to jump overboard. Lucky for me, I had friends among the crew, and they helped me get away."

Ella glanced at the gauge attached to her tank and saw it inching into the red. She was running out of air down here, but she couldn't leave, not with this glowing girl in front of her. As another blast of cannon fire filled the air, she couldn't get her body to move. She didn't dare risk touching Caroline. The last time she did, she'd come away with four long gashes in her wetsuit.

"We were passing by these islands at the time," Caroline continued, oblivious to Ella's growing panic, "and the good people in Pilot Town hid me from Bonnet's men. I stayed there for almost a month, and I would've stayed gone, too, if Blackbeard hadn't come back through, with Bonnet's *Revenge* following the *Queen Anne* like a damned puppy. Bonnet wanted to impress Blackbeard, so when he found me in Portsmouth Towne he locked me here in the hold, in the same cell where he'd been locked up by Teach just a few months before."

Caroline pointed at the curved piece of the hull below them. "A week later, the ship ran into a reef, and part of the hull was breached."

No, Ella thought. *I don't want to hear any more.*

The cannon blasts were closer now, and her air tanks were running low. She had to get out of here.

"The lower levels flooded. Including this part of the ship. I had no chance of getting free. I drowned here."

I'm so sorry. Ella knew the words sounded foolish, but she didn't know what to say. *That had to be an awful way to die.*

"But I didn't die! I just . . . *faded.* Something held me here, in the middle lands. In limbo. Nobody mourned me, or gave me a proper burial, for Bonnet wouldn't let them."

Ella stared at the glowing girl floating in front of her. *I don't know what I can do to help, Caroline. But I need to get to the surface, before I run out of—*

"No." Caroline's image was growing fainter, and Ella was able to see the other side of the cavern through the girl's orange-tinted face. "*No.* What you need to do is bring

104

Stede Bonnet to justice, and show that he was responsible for my death. And then I can rest."

Ella reached up a gloved hand to the girl in front of her. Caroline continued fading even as the sound of the cannons grew.

How?

"Search the islands," Caroline whispered. "The clues are there. Find them and show that Bonnet was no gentleman. Don't believe what you may have heard about him from others."

The blasts of the cannons were coming faster now, an almost constant roar. Ella felt her equilibrium knocked for a loop.

"He's coming," Caroline said, winking away completely. All that was left was a tiny orange flash in the water, a speck of light identical to the light captured in Mitch's second picture.

"Don't let him find me," Caroline pleaded. "Dig *deeper*, like I told you earlier. And remember, *he's* caught in limbo just like me. Him and . . ."

Caroline's voice faded before Ella could hear anything further. As deep, unsteady laughter filled the air, Ella kicked off from the rock wall, aiming at the mouth of the cave.

She hated feeling trapped in here, and her only consolation was the thought of the screaming she'd get to do at Mitch when she found him outside the cave and pulled him to the surface.

But all that she encountered outside the cave was more icy water and the thunder of cannons. No Mitch.

Damn it! Ella reached to inflate her BCD once again, but before she could hit the button and rise to the surface, she felt a dead weight on her ankle.

Must have snagged it on something, she told herself, but it took all of her effort to look down to see what was trying to drag her back down.

Instead of a vine, Ella saw a white hand wrapped around her ankle.

"My *lady,*" a wavering voice said, coming from a darkened figure floating a few inches above the ocean floor. "I do wish you wouldn't rush off like this."

Ella kicked and fought, but the man in the black coat never lost his grip.

"Let me tell you something," the man continued. "I don't know what that little whelp said to you, but I was Blackbeard's most trusted captain. I was the gentleman pirate."

Ella looked down to see his yellowed eyes gazing up at her, his wispy black beard unable to hide the thick noose around his neck. The tiniest hint of a sickly blue light covered the man like grease. The thundering cannons suddenly stopped, though the water remained like ice around Ella. Her head ached, and her air was starting to taste stale.

"I thought that bastard would have *approved* of my stern discipline with the girl," he continued, as if they were old friends chatting in a park. A blackened bandage flapped on his forehead like a dead flag. "But damned Teach took my ship away from me *again* after he saw the drowned girl in my hold. And so he imprisoned me, on the *Queen Anne.* I was never happier than when I saw his head removed from his shoulders that day in November."

Ella's left foot was going numb from the grip and icy touch of the creature that may or may not have been the ghost of Stede Bonnet. She did her best not to breathe faster and use up all her air, but she couldn't help but suck in more oxygen as the ghost started to rise up toward her.

Her flipper slipped off her left foot. Ella didn't want to see the man's staring eyes any closer than she already was. She forced her arms to move to her BCD again, even as she willed both legs to prepare to kick harder than they'd ever kicked before.

"Come stay with me down here," Bonnet's ghost said, floating closer. *"Stay—"*

Ella punched the release button on her buoyancy vest as she kicked out. At first the grip tightened on her left leg. She could feel claws cutting through the wetsuit and into her skin.

She kicked and kicked until her right leg connected with Bonnet's head, and he let go of her left leg.

She flew up to the surface, ears popping and lungs burning. She burst through the surface of the inlet just as Mitch swam up next to her.

"Mitch!" Ella screamed at him. "Where the hell were you?"

Mitch didn't answer, but simply stared at Ella, his face white with fear. She was too out of breath to speak, so she pushed past him so she could clamber aboard the boat. A wild sense of panic filled her, and she couldn't stay in the water any longer. It felt like it was filled with cold, reaching hands.

She pulled off her tank and mask and wrapped herself in the blanket again. She couldn't stop shivering. She had felt so alone down there. Alone with those two . . . beings.

Ghosts, Ella told herself. *Admit it. You are seeing ghosts.*

Mitch dropped to the floor of the boat next to her, wrapped in his own blanket and panting for breath.

"I know this looks bad," he said softly. "But I saw this light off in the distance, and . . . I wasn't thinking straight, I know, and I totally ignored your orders, but . . ." Mitch's

107

eyes went from being wide with excitement to being narrow with a focused anger. "Well, I just figured that as long as I had that light in front of me, the ghosts down there couldn't bother you. Damn it, I thought you'd be safe . . ."

"Mitch," Ella said, torn between her fear and her surprise at the intensity of his eyes as he talked about protecting her.

"Next thing I knew, I was way out in the Atlantic, and the light disappeared. I started swimming back as soon as I could. I'm sorry. I should've never left you. I gave you my word."

Ella nodded, no longer angry at him but trying to piece together all that she'd learned down there. She could feel the familiar heaviness in her limbs that went along with the last bit of her adrenaline rush.

"Someone wanted you out of the picture, you think?" she said. "So they could get to me?"

"I think so. I'm sorry, Ella. I keep letting you down."

Ella looked at the scratches on the arm of her suit from yesterday and the claw marks and missing flipper on her left leg from today. She swallowed hard and took a deep, shuddering breath. Her arms and legs were still shaking. She stared up at the sky, unable to remember a time when she'd felt happier to see the sun.

Ghosts, she thought again.

"Now what?" Mitch said at last.

"Mitch," she said, afraid to close her eyes, convinced she'd see Stede Bonnet's senseless yellow gaze looking back at her. She rested her hand for a moment on his leg and felt him stop shaking at her touch. "I think we need to get the hell out of here."

Chapter Ten

"So what now?" Ella asked Mitch over their untouched lunches an hour later.

Mitch set down his plastic cup of iced tea and waved to his sister for a refill. The guy couldn't seem to get enough liquid in him. Ella figured all that swimming he'd done had given him quite a thirst. She was still preoccupied with all that Caroline and Bonnet had said to her—that she had *imagined* them saying to her, she corrected herself. She was so distracted by those stories that she hadn't brought up the fact that Mitch had disappeared on her outside the cavern.

She glared at Mitch and cleared her throat.

"I'm sorry?" Mitch said, as if just now realizing she was staring at him, waiting for a response. Melissa, tired of running over to their table every two minutes to fill Mitch's cup, set a full pitcher of sweet tea in front of him and walked off without a word.

"I need to know what we should do now, Mitch." Ella heard the edge in her voice and tried to calm down.

Don't think about the end of your career just yet, she told herself.

"Well," Mitch said, pouring himself some more tea. "I guess we should eat our lunch. Though I sort of lost my appetite, I guess."

"That's not what I meant," Ella said. "I can't spend the next few weeks here at the Jolly Roger, eating burgers and fries and watching the fishing boats come in. As much as I'd love to do that, my boss at the university is going to want to see some sort of progress from me, and soon."

Ella felt a grimace of unease flicker across her face as she remembered how little air she'd had left in her tanks when she surfaced and taken off her gear. Less than five minutes' worth. She'd come dangerously close to running out down there, thanks to Caroline and Stede Bonnet. Whoever—or *whatever* they were.

She pushed her uneaten lunch away from her and stared out at Silver Lake and the ocean beyond it. She took a deep breath and let it out slowly as she focused her gaze on Mitch.

"Okay, this is the deal. I'm pretty sure I might just be losing my mind, Mitch. But I swear to God, I think I imagined myself actually talking to a young girl down there."

"Really?" Mitch leaned forward. "What was it like?"

"We were able to talk to each other," Ella said, licking her lips nervously. Her voice was barely a squeak. "But the whole conversation was taking place in my *head*."

"Melissa said that they could do that."

Ella stared at Mitch for a long second. *What was that supposed to mean? What kind of ghost stories did people around here tell?*

As if mistaking her shock and disbelief for impatience at being interrupted, Mitch's face flushed. He nodded for her to continue with an apologetic smile.

"She told me she drowned in the ship down there," Ella said. "And the ship—well, the good news is, from the evidence I saw on the piece of the hull in that cavern, I'm pretty sure that this *is* the lost ship of Blackbeard. The bad news is, well, in addition to my friend Caroline, there's another—" Ella couldn't bring herself to call the apparitions *ghosts,* not yet at least "—*being* down there close to the shipwreck as well. He's the one with the cannons, I think.

110

You've heard them, right? And get this—this one tried to *kill* me, Mitch."

Ella looked down at the table, where Mitch had put his hands on her hand. It was like last night's hand-holding, but instigated by him this time. Ella gripped his calloused hands with her fingers. She liked the warmth and weight of his touch.

She took a steadying breath and filled in Mitch with the details to her story: The girl Caroline disguised as a boy until she was found out, the unbalanced Stede Bonnet trying to make her his bride, Bonnet's punishment by Blackbeard and his vow for revenge against the infamous pirate. She even told as much as she could about Bonnet's grip on her leg, still barely able to believe it herself.

When she was done talking, they both sat together in silence, staring out at the blue water of Silver Lake and the boats bobbing up and down on it.

Ghosts, Ella thought for what felt like the hundredth time that day. She slipped her hand out from under Mitch's. Retelling Caroline's story had made her feel foolish and naïve, and her frustration was mounting. She had too much research to do down there to continue getting interrupted like this.

"Ghosts," Mitch said, as if reading Ella's mind. "It always comes back to ghosts, in all our stories 'round here. I always believed the stories, as a kid. Maybe I still believed a little bit of them as an adult. But I have to tell you . . . It's no fun, believing in ghosts."

"Tell me about it."

Before Ella could say anything, someone walked past their table. She was expecting Melissa, so she was surprised to see a white-haired man looking down at her. He tottered slightly, leaning on his cane. It was the same old man that she'd been seeing here and there the past few days. The man from the blue Mercedes.

"Did I hear you young folks correctly?" the man said in a gravelly voice. "Were you telling . . ." He paused for so long that Ella wondered if he'd lost his train of thought. "*Ghost* stories?" the man said at last, puckering his mouth into a tiny circle.

"No," Ella said. "You must have overheard the wrong thing, sir."

Mitch gave Ella a dirty look, as if to say, *Be nice to the touron.*

"No, sir," Mitch said. "But I could tell you a couple if you're interested." He gave Ella a quick glance. "Maybe some other time, though."

"Bah!" the old man said. He spun on his heel and shuffled over to the bathroom, muttering something about kids and being patronized by them.

Ella wanted to call after the man to see how the car's horn was doing after nearly scaring the crap out of her a few days ago, but she bit her tongue.

"Friend of yours?" Mitch said, chewing on his ice.

"Yeah, we go way back."

Ella looked from the closed door of the men's room to the picnic table outside, where the two elderly women sat. Neither women spoke, and when they saw Ella looking their way they suddenly became interested in the ferry pulling into the harbor.

"That's odd," Ella said. "Those three tourists seem to be following me everywhere I go. I wonder . . ."

"It's a small island, Ella," Mitch said. "There's only so many places folks can go this early in the season."

"Yeah, you're probably right. So," she said, turning back to Mitch and more pressing matters than the trio of surly elderly tourists. "What do you suggest we do?"

"I think we have to help her," Mitch said. "I think we need to help this girl, Caroline, before we can return to the ship."

"Help her?" Ella stared at Mitch for a second, and then she picked up her bottle of beer. After swallowing a long pull, she said, "How do you help someone who's been dead for almost three hundred years?"

"Just hear me out. Obviously there's some vital link between her and the other ghost—this Stede Bonnet guy. I mean, that's how ghosts work, you know? They haunt a place until the wrong that was done to them is righted." Mitch stopped and scratched at the stubble on his check. "Wait. I think that's how it works. Crap. Melissa knows all the ghost rules."

"*Ghost* rules?" Ella's bottle of beer was now empty. She could use another one, quickly. "I didn't know there were *rules* for ghosts, Mitch."

"Anyway," Mitch said, ignoring Ella's sarcasm. "I think if we can take care of Caroline's needs, prove what happened to her beyond a shadow of a doubt, maybe they'll both go away. They can both rest. That's what ghosts want. At the very least, this Stede Bonnet won't have another ghost to harass anymore."

Ella gave a hesitant nod.

Mitch sighed in frustration and shook the ice in his empty glass. "That's the best plan I can come up with."

"Mitch," Ella said, her uncertain feelings being replaced by a giddy feeling similar to the one she'd had on the ship with him yesterday, during their laughing fit. It was all too much to handle. "You actually said 'That's what ghosts want.' Did you even realize that?"

"Well . . . I just . . ."

Ella was grinning at him now. She hit his hand lightly with hers, hoping she could at least get a smile out of him.

"Hey," he said with an exasperated shrug, "I guess I *do* believe in ghost rules, okay?"

Ella burst out laughing. At first the sound of it was high, a bit shrill, and then it filled out into honest laughter.

"I'm sorry," she tried to say between chuckles. "I just . . . It's too much . . . I can't help it . . ."

Mitch smiled at her, though the haunted look hadn't fully left his eyes.

"I'm trying to be serious here," he said. He stood up, and his smile was gone, but there was still a glimmer of light in his eyes. "Think about what I said for a minute," he said. "I'll be right back. I need to get a pitcher of beer. This sweet tea isn't strong enough."

Mitch walked off to the bar, and Ella watched as his old buddy Ben poured him a pitcher of Killian's. The old man left the bathroom and gave Ella a huge scowl on his way past her. Ella gave him her sweetest smile, and then she turned that smile on Mitch as he carried the full pitcher back to the table. Mitch almost spilled his beer when he was confronted with the intensity of that smile.

"Mitch," Ella said as he sat down, "I wasn't laughing at you. Just my stupid nervous laughter coming out, that's all."

Mitch set his cup on the table next to Ella's empty one and started pouring. Ella thought about the way she'd stomped off last night at the Jolly Roger, overwhelmed by all that was happening. Just like her, Mitch had come back as well.

"Okay, apology accepted." Mitch said. The guarded look left his eyes, and for that Ella was very glad. "Just don't let it happen again."

"Aye-aye, Mitch."

He picked up his cup, and Ella lifted hers so they could tap them together.

"Cheers," Mitch said.

"Cheers." Ella took a drink, and then she set down her cup. She was tired of all this beating around the bush. She needed some facts. "So tell me, Mitch. What *is* the deal with all the ghosts here?"

Mitch nearly choked on his beer. "You know what? That was the first time you've said the word 'ghost' without making it sound like some kind of swear word. Are you pulling my leg, or do you really want to know?"

"I'm serious. If we're going to help Caroline, which I think we need to, I'm going to need a primer on ghosts and hauntings. Spooks 101."

"Okay," Mitch said, staring back at the lake. "You asked for it."

But before Mitch could launch into one of his ghost stories, a pair of arms wrapped around him and pulled him back in his chair. Ella recognized a sleeper hold from professional wrestling.

"Melissa," Mitch said, wriggling out of her grasp and guiding her unceremoniously into the chair next to him with a thump. "Cut it out, would you? Don't you have a coffee mug or an ashtray to make or something?"

"Oh, shut it, you. I've got to work the dead shift today, from noon to midnight. I probably won't make enough to buy clay for this week and next. Why, you need another ashtray for your nasty cigars?"

"Maybe," Mitch said. "Can you do that for your dear old brother?"

"So why aren't you two out on *Cassie*?" Melissa said, ignoring her brother. "You know, out doing your top-secret diving research stuff?"

"We've already got our research done for the day," Ella said smoothly, and then grinned. "Actually, Mitch here was getting me caught up on the folklore of the island."

"Right. Folklore. Has he told you about the ghosts and the supernatural presences hanging around all over this place?"

"See?" Mitch said. "What'd I tell you? She's *obsessed.*"

"As a matter of fact, we were talking about ghosts. Maybe you'd like to tell us a story or two, Melissa?"

"But of course," Melissa said, scooting closer in her chair. "Would you like to hear about Blackbeard? Red-Eye? The four dead soldiers from World War Two? Or how about the—"

"Let's start with Red-Eye," Mitch interrupted. "We don't have all day. And I think we may have actually seen that crazy pony the other day. But he's not a ghost."

"Right," Melissa said. "Who've you been talking to?"

"No one," Mitch said. "Well, maybe Owen. Why?"

"Because. Seems like every other person who comes in for a burger is talking about seeing a black pony walking around in someone's backyard, or slipping past a sand dune. Owen knows what Red-Eye's really like. Where'd you see him? Red-Eye, I mean, not Owen."

"Slow down, Mel," Mitch said, casting a worried glance at Ella that almost made Ella burst into laughter again. It was obvious Mitch was worried his sister would push Ella over the edge.

"It could've just been a pony from the pens that slipped out," Mitch said. "We clipped it with the car the other day, out on the highway. But when we got out to check on him—"

"He was gone," Ella finished. "What's it mean, Melissa?"

Mitch looked at Ella as if he was hurt that she was listening to his sister when before Ella had simply ignored his stories.

"I think the spirits have been stirred up lately," Melissa said. "It seems to happen every couple of years, around this time of year. Usually the end of March, just when it starts to get nice out again. Plus there was the hurricane last fall. That stirred *everything* up."

"I remember you saying something about how the tourons have been staying away so far this season," Ella said. "Think that has something to do with it? Maybe it's just that they don't want to feel depressed by the hurricane damage. Or maybe there's some low pressure system, El Niño or La Niña say, that's making a trip to the island sound like not so great an idea? Surely there's some logical reason for it."

Melissa rolled her eyes at Mitch, totally unconvinced. "Right. That could be. *Or* it could be something less scientific, something like bad karma, or . . . dark undercurrents we can't see, but we can feel."

"Dark undercurrents," Mitch muttered, but Ella ignored him.

"I was talking to Owen about this just the other day," Melissa said, on a roll now. "He was saying the fruits and veggies he grows were all coming in weird sizes and shapes, and had weird bruises on them. He called them—"

"Spirit fingerprints." Ella had been waiting for that one.

"Owen's a smart guy, and he's in tune with the cosmic order of things."

"Cosmic order," Mitch muttered under his breath and poured himself another beer. "Next thing you know, she'll be talking about the lights of UFOs and all that 'X-Files' crap."

"Shut it, Mitch," Melissa said, and continued telling Ella about Owen.

Ella was only half-listening. Something strange had come over Mitch. He had paused halfway through pouring his beer as if he'd been struck by lightning.

"Mitch?" Ella said, interrupting Melissa. Both women turned to Mitch, who was muttering to himself. Melissa took the pitcher from his hand before he poured beer all over his lap.

"The *lights*," he was saying. "Lights in the water. That's what it was."

Ella's skin began to crawl as she remembered driving over the Oregon Inlet Bridge. Her car had nearly been blown off the road, into the water below. The water had been dark, but flashing with . . .

"Lights!" Mitch said again.

"What is it, Mitch?" Melissa said. "Tell us."

"I'd forgotten about all this. How on the last day of February, I'd been out in that same patch of water where the ship was buried."

"Mitch," Ella said, trying to get him to stop before saying too much about the downed pirate ship. But he wasn't stopping. Melissa stared at her brother with her mouth half-open.

"I was taking *Cassie* out for the first time all year," Mitch continued. "Just cruising around the island, cleaning out the engines, when I saw them. Lights, flashing under the water. Without even thinking about it, I dropped the anchor and put on my diving gear for a quick solo dive. And that's how I found the rusted anchor, and the anchor led me to the rest of the wreck."

"Mitch!" Ella hissed, looking around the nearly empty restaurant. "That's enough."

118

"I probably would have missed the light any other day. So maybe it hadn't been coincidence. Maybe I'd been guided to the ship by a spirit, either Caroline's or Bonnet's, or hell, maybe even Blackbeard himself. Someone had *wanted* me to uncover the remains of the pirate ship."

Mitch looked up, a shocked look on his face as he realized what he'd said, and who he'd said it to.

"Great," Ella said. "Nice one, Mitch."

"I *knew* it," Melissa said. "Mitch, you could *never* keep a secret. This is so awesome. You know, you could've told me. Who am I going to tell, anyway?"

"Oh, just every damn touron who steps foot into the Jolly Roger from now until the end of summer," Mitch said.

Ella thought about getting mad at Mitch, but she felt like she could trust Melissa. And maybe, with Melissa's interest in all things supernatural, she'd actually be able to help.

"Oh, relax," she said. "Melissa, this is just between us, okay? I'm here from Boston University to check out a shipwreck that could be one of Blackbeard's ships. As soon as I can identify it, we'll send down a crew. But for right now, we can't have people out there, diving the site and disrupting everything. So, mum's the word, okay?"

"This is all amazing," Melissa said. "I think those lights were a sign, Mitch. There's spirit fingerprints all over this shipwreck, I'll bet. What do you think, Ella?"

Ella didn't answer. She was staring at Mitch, no trace of a smile on her pale face. A bad thought had struck her while Melissa had been talking—*what* else *had Mitch neglected to share with her?*

"You were probably expecting something bad to happen on our dives, weren't you?" Ella said to him, her eyes narrowing. "I can't believe you didn't tell me about this up front."

119

"Sure," Mitch said. "Like you would have believed me if I said that a ghost light was what helped me find that shipwreck in the first place. You would've laughed harder at me than you did ten minutes ago!"

"Oh boy," Melissa said. She stood up and tied her apron around her waist. "I think I need to go start my shift and let you two sort all this out. See ya!" She walked off, whistling the theme song to *Ghostbusters*.

Alone again, Mitch and Ella sat in silence for nearly a minute. Mitch was looking at something over Ella's shoulder in a distracted manner. She turned and saw he was gazing at *Cassiopeia*, docked fifty feet away.

The guy really loves that boat, she thought. *But that didn't keep him from risking his life and that boat to try to single-handedly uncover what he thought was his own personal buried pirate ship.*

Finally, Ella gave a long sigh and sat up straight across from Mitch, pushing their empty cups and pitcher out of the way.

"All right," she said in a soft voice. "Let's get all our cards on the table, Mitch. If there's anything else related to the shipwreck that you haven't told me, I want to hear it."

Still gazing at his boat, Mitch shook his head.

"Okay, so we've got all these little tidbits of facts going on here. But none of them are fitting together and making sense yet. That girl down there talked about Pilot Town and Portsmouth Towne, and told me to dig deeper. Do you know where those places are?"

"This is Pilot Town," Mitch said. Ella gave him a blank look, not understanding him. "Before Ocracoke became a real place on the map, folks called it Pilot Town. All the ships passed through this area, because of the calm waters. And Portsmouth is just a few miles, thataway," he added,

pointing vaguely out at Silver Lake, toward the Coast Guard station and the dock.

"I think we need to do some exploring," Ella said. "Maybe we can talk to some people and check out some places that Caroline may have visited. We'll see if we can't find some of those so-called spirit fingerprints for Caroline and Stede Bonnet."

"And Blackbeard," Mitch said. "He seems to be a part of this too. Remember, he died around here. And like Melissa said, there have been weird things happening around here lately. We should probably start by chatting with an expert about the ghosts. And I don't mean my sister."

"Oh, man," Ella said, resting her head in her hands. The thought of going over all of this with someone else seemed suddenly unbearable. "I can't believe I'm even considering this."

"Well, we can't do much diving with those two down there harassing us, you know."

"You're right. I know you're right. But damn, Mitch, it just feels *wrong* to me. I'm supposed to be a scientist, and I'm actually considering talking to ghosts."

"Stranger things have happened," Mitch said. "And may happen in the future. There's no promises, you know? You just have to have a little faith."

Ella gazed at Mitch, with his once-sleepy eyes focused on her, a determined look on his face. She was starting to really like this version of Mitch the dive master, so different from the Mitch she'd first met just a few days earlier.

"Okay," she said at last. "When do we get started?"

Chapter Eleven

Mitch had suggested they talk with an expert first. And by an expert, Ella knew he'd meant Owen.

The late afternoon still gave off a warmth that was surprising so early in the year. Ella enjoyed its heat as they walked down Main Street toward Owen's produce stand. The breeze blew her hair back from her face and lightened the weight that had settled on her heart. She'd been feeling that weight ever since she began admitting to herself, thanks to Mitch's influence, that she was starting to believe in ghosts.

Well, maybe she wasn't ready to believe in ghosts themselves just yet, but the *possibility* that ghosts might exist. And for Ella, that was a huge leap.

An occasional car crept up and down the two-lane road next to them as if nobody had anywhere else to be except right there. Ella and Mitch passed a group of three tourists sitting on the front porch of the Creekside Café, nibbling on ice cream cones. She did a double-take when she realized that the tourists were her three elderly friends, out and about once more.

The rest of the people they saw were obviously residents of the island—fishermen in big boots loading up their coolers in front of the convenience store, and darkly tanned men and women driving pickups and old utility vehicles. Kids rolled past on their bikes, digging their tires into the loose sand next to the road as they pedaled home after school.

Ella remembered with a start that today was a Thursday. She'd been so caught up in her diving and her expeditions that she'd completely lost track of time. Dr. Bramlett was going to need an update soon about what she'd found at the shipwreck site. She dreaded having to make that call, and she had no idea what she'd tell him. The truth was definitely out of the question.

As they walked past others on the narrow sidewalk, Mitch would nod or say hello to everyone they passed, greeting most of them by name. Ella could feel the curious gazes of the Ocracoke residents on her, though they also said hello to her.

She could understand the attraction of a place like Ocracoke, where everyone knew who you were. Even if people probably knew most of your business, it also meant that they would be there to help you out and lend a hand, if you ever needed it.

And we may need it, Ella thought, surprising herself.

It wasn't until she and Melissa had started talking that she'd realized how dangerous this entire expedition had become. Even if she and Mitch were simply experiencing some sort of shared delusion while they went diving together, that delusion had almost killed her. Twice.

Ella thought about what would happen if she told Dr. Bramlett about this on the phone, imagining his deep voice pausing for a few long, painful seconds (as he'd been doing a lot more in the past few months when they spoke) before he asked her if she was all right.

She smiled. *What is it with me and men checking on me to make sure I'm okay?*

She decided then and there, in view of Owen's produce stand, with Mitch next to her and a summery breeze ruffling her shirt and hair, that she'd simply keep an open mind to all that was happening and would happen to them in the next few days. They had a mystery to solve, and she didn't want to dismiss any possibility, no matter how far-fetched it seemed to her. At the same time, she knew she had to be the logical one in their group, because Mitch the Superstitious Dive Master wasn't going to be relying on logic and the scientific method.

"Hey," Mitch said, looking over at her for the first time since leaving the Jolly Roger. "Glad to see you smiling again."

"Oh," Ella said. She felt her face grow warm, wondering if Mitch had any idea what she'd been thinking. "I didn't know I was. Guess I'm looking forward to talking to Owen again."

They crossed the street, and she felt her smile widen as Owen looked up and caught her gaze.

"Hi, Owen!" she called out. "How's business?"

"Why, Ella," Owen said. "Good to see you again. Hello, Mitch. How's that new birdhouse, Ella?"

"Looking great on my front porch, though I haven't had much time to enjoy it. Been too busy working, unfortunately."

"Out digging for gold in the inlet, eh?"

Mitch gave Ella a meaningful glance. "What do you mean, Owen?" he asked.

"Don't worry, Mitch," Owen said with a laugh as he stood up to stretch. "Your secret's safe with me. I've just been following the signs and watching you and your *Cassiopeia* leaving the harbor with Ella here, early in the morning. After seventy-five years here on this island and Portsmouth, I know what a research crew looks like."

"Actually," Ella said, leaning on the edge of Owen's cart as she marveled at how perceptive the older man was, "that's sort of why we're here. I guess neither of us are very good at keeping secrets, huh, Mitch?"

"Don't worry 'bout that," Owen said. "Old Owen doesn't tell anyone what old Owen doesn't want anyone to know. And hey, who believes anything this old man has to say, anyway?" He sat back down in his rocker and grinned mischievously at Ella. "So. What would you kids like to know?"

With Mitch sitting in the brown grass next to Owen in his rocker, Ella felt like she was back in front of a classroom of two, getting ready to lead a new discussion. She hadn't known until now how much she'd missed teaching.

"We've found some interesting, ah, artifacts out in the inlet," she began. "Just between the three of us, I think we've stumbled across the last missing ship from the fleet of Blackbeard."

Owen sucked in his breath at the name, but his face wasn't filled with fear. Instead, he looked like someone who'd suddenly realized the answer to a riddle that had been plaguing him for weeks.

"That explains it," Owen said, snapping his fingers. "The pony tracks in the alley next to my house, the finger-prints in the fruit and vegetables, and the missing keys."

Ella glanced at Mitch, who was staring at Owen in utter confusion. She'd expected Owen to mention the spirit fin-gerprints, and she guessed the pony tracks may have be-longed to old Red-Eye, perhaps, but . . .

"Keys?" she blurted out. "Owen, what are you talking about?"

"Don't laugh at an old man and call him forgetful, that's all I ask before I begin." Owen's dark eyes flickered from Ella to Mitch and back again. Ella nodded and inched closer to him. "But I've been studying the spirits on this island since I was a boy, and that's their favorite way of causing mischief. They love to hide keys."

"By *'they'* you mean . . ." Mitch trailed off.

"Ghosts," Owen said, without a second's hesitation.

"Tell us more," Ella said. She reminded herself that she was keeping an open mind, no matter how off-the-wall things got.

"Ever lose a set of keys, Mitch?" Owen began. When Mitch nodded, Owen turned to Ella. "How about you, Ella? I mean recently, just since you've been here on the island. Any other things gone missing that you normally don't lose? Keys? Hairbrushes? Change?"

Ella shrugged. "I guess. Maybe. I didn't really notice."

"Um-hmm." Owen didn't look convinced. "Keep an eye on things like that from now on—you'd be surprised. We've got spooks, and we've got 'em bad. They don't call this stretch of the ocean the Graveyard of the Atlantic for nothing. And hiding your keys is the least of their mischief."

"Okay," Ella said. "Why keys?"

"They hate keys because they don't like the sound of metal on metal. Either that, or, if they're older ghosts, they don't like cars—too new-fangled and noisy. So they hide keys any chance they get."

"But why would they want to cause mischief? According to Mitch, all ghosts want is to find eternal rest so they can quit haunting the real world. Right, Mitch?"

"Basically," Mitch said, giving her a curious look, partially surprise and partially disbelief. Ella winked at him and turned to wait for Owen's answer.

"That's just a *part* of it," Owen said. "Some ghosts want to find rest, but some others enjoy living in between the worlds of the living and the dead. Y'see, they *know* what's waiting for them when they leave our world, and it probably involves lots of heat and flames, if you know what I mean. Some of them want to keep other ghosts in limbo with them, and even bring some of the living into limbo with them. And some of them think they can come *back* to our world. Now," Owen said, setting his hands on his knees as he stopped rocking. "Why don't you tell me what's going on here?"

Owen was looking directly at Ella. She glanced at Mitch, who only shrugged his shoulders, as if to say, "Why not?"

"Okay," she began, surprised at how easily it was getting for her to tell this story, "you remember how we were exploring the remains of what we think was Blackbeard's ship? Well, the ship came with a couple of ghosts, free of charge. The first is a girl who died before her time, and the second is the man she claims is responsible for her death."

"Two ghosts?" Owen said, running a finger across his thin mustache. "That's all?"

"Don't you think two is enough?" Mitch said, his voice full of exasperation.

"Oh, that's not it, Mitch. It's just that usually ghosts are alone or in groups of three. There's power in numbers, and three's an unusually powerful number. Ghosts are 'specially susceptible to such attractions. Anything to make their presence in this world easier for them. Depending on their goals, of course."

"Of course," Mitch mumbled. He dug his hands into the grass next to him, pulling at the brown blades.

"Just hear him out," Ella said before she could stop herself. Again Mitch gave her a look of disbelief. Ella could see his frustration and she could understand why, suddenly— this talk about the nature of ghosts was the kind of thing Mitch had been saying all along, but Ella had ignored him.

She'd done the same thing an hour earlier during their talk with Melissa.

She owed Mitch an apology, if he'd accept it. But first she had more questions for Owen.

And in the back of her mind, she knew she was overlooking something. Something from her first day in Ocracoke. But that would have to wait. First there was the shipwreck and the task she needed to do for Caroline.

"We can't finish our dive with the two of them down there, harassing us," she said. "How can we help them? Or at least get rid of them for a while?"

Owen got out of his rocker and began packing up the contents of his stand. Night had started to fall around them without Ella realizing it.

"My advice to you kids," he said, "is to just ignore those ghosts while you're down there. They can't hurt you unless you let them. If you ignore them, I promise you they'll go away."

"But what about the scratches in my suit? Mitch has some too," Ella said, handing Owen a slightly bruised apple that had fallen from the cart.

Owen paused, apple in hand. "Now *that* I can't rightly explain. Maybe they tricked you into scratching yourself. Or . . . I have heard that the older the ghost, the more powerful they are—their connection to this world is stronger. They can sometimes make themselves solid, for a short time."

"Owen," Mitch said. "Is there anything else we can do to help the girl?"

Owen shrugged. "I'd say find something that may have held some sort of significance for her. Something old, something that would have meaning for the ghosts. Something like . . . well, I'm not sure."

Owen had left his carefully packed cart so he could step

out into the street. He turned to his left and looked up. Ella followed his gaze and saw the white tip of the lighthouse peeking out above the trees and houses to the west. The setting sun was hitting the horizon on the other side of the squat white tower. At that moment the lighthouse caught the fading sun and flashed with an orange light that made Ella think of Caroline.

"I hope that helps," Owen said, returning to his cart. He whistled softly as he wheeled it down the street, leaving Ella and Mitch to stare up at the 200-year-old Ocracoke lighthouse.

Ella and Mitch walked back to her rented house in silence, digesting all of Owen's information. As the few street lights winked on around them, Ella felt the air turning colder, and she wanted to get a sweatshirt before they did anything else.

"So this is my place," Ella said. She pointed at the miniature house on her porch. "My birdhouse, from Owen."

"Nice," Mitch said, glancing at his watch.

"Listen," Ella said, "I'm sorry about all of this."

Mitch gave her a quizzical look. "What do you mean? Why are you apologizing? It's not your fault there's something messed-up going on out there at the wreck site."

"No, it's not that. I'm sorry I didn't listen to you earlier, Mitch. All this ghost stuff—you were on the right track, it looks like now. Hell, even your sister and Owen back you up. I was just being stubborn and not paying attention to you. So, I'm sorry."

"That's okay," Mitch said. He looked over his shoulder at the lake. Ella wondered if one of the lights out there was *Cassie*. From her front porch, Ella had a perfect view of the Jolly Roger.

"Want to come in and plan a strategy?" she said, part of her hoping it didn't sound like she was making a pass at him. The other part of her wasn't sure a pass would be such a bad thing.

"Oh, no," Mitch said, looking at the glowing numbers of his watch again. "I've got to get some rest. Although . . ."

"What?" Ella felt a rush of excitement fill her at the impulsive look on Mitch's handsome face, half-hidden in the darkness. *Look at me, getting all worked up about a possible date with Mitch after all we've been through together in the past few days.*

"Maybe we *could* do something tonight," he said.

Ella gulped. Maybe Mitch had read her mind. "What do you mean?"

"The lighthouse. I'm thinking we could slip in there tonight and look for clues. We'd never be able to get inside during the day. Don't you think that was what Owen was trying to tell us?"

"Oh," Ella said. For a moment, she'd forgotten all about hunting ghosts and solving centuries-old mysteries. "The lighthouse. Right."

"I mean, the lighthouse isn't as old as the island, of course. There would've been fishermen and people called 'pilots' here back in the early seventeen hundreds to help ships through the inlet and sound. But the lighthouse itself didn't come 'round until sixty or seventy years after Caroline would've died. So I don't know if it'll help all that much."

"But you think it's still a good place to start, don't you?"

"Yeah. Ben and I found a way to slip inside it when we were kids. We could wait 'til after midnight and sneak in there. We may be able to see things from up there that we'd never be able to see otherwise. Or maybe Owen meant there could be some clues *inside* the lighthouse. We'll never know unless we give it a try. Like you said, we've got to start somewhere. What do you think?"

Ella was still trying to process all that Mitch had said— this was the most he'd spoken at one time—and in the weak light of the street lights, the passion in his pale blue eyes was threatening to take her breath away.

What the hell is wrong with me? Ella thought. *Am I fifteen years old again?*

"Let's go for it," she said. "But let's go at eleven. Midnight is too melodramatic."

"Sounds good," Mitch said. "I'd better get some rest, I think. I'll meet you back here around eleven. We'll need some flashlights and a camera."

"Got it," Ella said.

"Be back in a few hours," Mitch said. He was already backing away.

"See you then," Ella said, and she walked up to her front door. Her face felt hot, as if she'd been turned down for the prom.

Mitch had nearly run *down the street to get away from me for a while. We could've waited here together until it was time to go adventuring. Or gone inside. Or done something . . .*

Ella had to laugh at herself as she ran her hand along the top of her door frame, where she'd left her key. Acting like Mitch was someone she should even *have* a schoolgirl crush on.

She let her arm drop to her side. Her key was gone.

"Damn," she said. Rubbing her arms until the goose bumps went away, she rested her hand on the white plastic chair on her front porch. She'd have to get the spare key from the rental office in the morning.

"Someone's fooling around with me," she muttered.

"Either that, or I'm getting forgetful in my old age."

Imagining Red-Eye slipping onto her porch and reaching up on his back legs so he could knock down her house key and spirit it away, Ella stared out at the harbor and the stars above. She looked at the window leading into her living room and thought about trying to jimmy the lock to get inside.

I think I could do it, she thought, *but it just seems like too much work right now.* Instead she took a seat in the cold plastic chair, rubbed her bare arms one more time, and waited for eleven o'clock to roll around.

Chapter Twelve

Ella surprised herself by falling asleep on her front deck, in spite of the cold and Owen's tales of wandering, key-stealing ghosts. She was so tired she was dreaming the instant her eyes closed, and it was the same routine—falling planes, runaway ponies, near drownings. Still, in spite of the familiarity of the dreams, the near-impact of the out-of-control plane and the sinking boat and the aching sense of helplessness that filled her out in the middle of the dream-ocean still unnerved her and kept her from getting any sort of quality sleep in her chair.

She nearly screamed when a hand touched her shoulder and gave it a good shake.

Ella tried to cover her surprise by looking at her watch. The time was half past eleven.

"I guess it's time, huh?" she mumbled, rubbing her neck and getting slowly, painfully to her feet. "Time to go break and enter?"

"Yeah," Mitch said. He gave her a curious look with the hint of a smile on his face. "Ella, why were you sleeping outside?"

"You don't want to know," she said. "Ow. My neck's killing me."

Mitch gave her a sheepish look. "I would've been here sooner, but the nightmare I was having made me sleep right through my alarm."

"You too, huh?" Ella rubbed her neck, trying to work the kinks out of it. "I was dreaming about all sorts of wild stuff.

First I was on a plane, then my dad was taking me boating out on the water down here, and we got caught in a storm. And Red-Eye was swimming past with all his pony buddies. And the boat tipped over and I was stranded . . . Well, it was all really weird. What was yours like?"

Mitch shrugged. "I usually forget dreams as soon as I wake up, but this one was pretty intense. What really made it a nightmare was that it had my ex-girlfriend in it."

"That sounds nightmarish." Ella felt her pulse speed up at the mention of Mitch's ex. He had never spoken of her before. "So what happened in your dream?" she said, peering through the darkness at him.

He gave her another curious look at the question, and Ella realized that he'd been pretty disturbed by his dream. He also looked a bit sad. His emotions stirred up an odd mixture of feelings in Ella as well, including a sense of protectiveness for Mitch that was completely new. She remembered what Melissa had said about Mitch's ex, and their turbulent times together.

"I'm just asking because," she added, "both our dreams could have some clues for us. For our search, I mean."

"Sure. I get it." Mitch leaned against the porch railing and took a deep breath. "Well, Julie and I had been arguing in the dream, as usual. It was the same stuff as what we argued about back in the day. She wanted me to move to her place over on the mainland, and I wanted her to live with me here in Ocracoke. The weird thing was that we were locked inside a small wooden room together. We were out on the ocean, and the waves threw us all over the place while we yelled at each other. Then the air was suddenly full of cannon fire, and that's when I realized she and I were trapped together on what could only be a pirate ship."

"Unbelievable," Ella said. "More pirates."

Part of her was fascinated to hear about Mitch's problems with this girl named Julie, while another part of her felt an illogical pang of jealousy. *Why was he dreaming about her, and not me?*

Ella tried to stifle those feelings as soon as possible. She had to focus on the task at hand.

"Yeah," Mitch said, rubbing his arms. "I didn't know which was worse, being a prisoner of the pirates, or being locked up with Julie, the only girl I'd ever gone out with who couldn't stand being on Ocracoke for more than a couple hours."

"That's interesting," Ella said, getting up at last from her chair. "Our dreams have some things in common—the ocean, the sense of danger. I wonder—ow! Ow ow ow!" Ella felt every joint in her body complaining to her all at once. She was all bent out of shape from sleeping sitting up.

Mitch grinned at her in the weak light of the neighbor's porchlight, as if he'd just realized something.

"Say," he said. "Did you lose your keys, just like Owen was talking about? Is that why you were waiting outside?" Mitch hopped up the stairs and rattled the knob to the locked front door. "Did you keep it hidden somewhere?"

"Up," Ella said. Her voice was barely a grunt as she worked the kinks out of her body. "Above the . . ."

"That's not a very good hiding spot," Mitch said. With a flourish, he pulled down the key he'd found at the top of the door frame. "Can you grab a couple flashlights from inside?" he said, holding out the key to Ella. "And a camera with a flash."

"But," Ella began, and then gave up. She grabbed the key from his hand.

"You've had a visitor, I guess," Mitch said.

"Stupid ghosts," she muttered on her way inside her

135

house. She grabbed the flashlights, a camera, and her Boston sweatshirt. When she came back outside she made sure Mitch saw her put the key in her jeans pocket. Before she left the porch, she looked down and could have sworn she saw a circular impression in the dust of the porch boards.

Could be a hoofprint, she thought, but she decided not to bring that up with Mitch at that moment.

"Ready to go?" she said instead, and Mitch nodded.

Finally warming up with the help of her thick sweatshirt, Ella felt the kinks in her neck and shoulders and legs untangle themselves as they walked to the lighthouse. She realized that she hadn't seen any light coming from the lighthouse since she'd been in town, and she asked Mitch about that.

"They've been working on the lamp inside the lighthouse today," he said. He began whispering as they walked through the tall grass next to the road. "When we were kids, Ben and I snuck into the lighthouse. We climbed to the top and both of us were almost blinded by that lamp when we got up there. We were lucky neither of us slipped and fell." Mitch gave a dry laugh. "Me and Ben were true hellions, back in the day."

"You're lucky you survived childhood," Ella said with a soft chuckle of her own. "So are we just going to walk up to the lighthouse and break in?"

"Sort of," Mitch said. "But we're going in the back way."

They passed by the spot where Owen usually set up his cart and turned right onto the shadowy Lighthouse Road. The big gray bulk of Albert Styron's general store was on their right, its wooden façade reaching high above them, followed by a row of one-story houses.

Two houses down from Styron's store, Mitch turned off the road and plunged into a clump of trees and bushes. Ella paused for the briefest second, wondering if he'd lost his mind, and then she followed him. With branches slapping her in the face, she pressed through the undergrowth after him until she could see the back of a garage with peeling white paint covering it. Mitch slipped out of the trees without a sound.

"Shortcut," he said when Ella was able to pull herself free of the overgrown greenery.

"I see. Thanks for the warning."

They were standing fifteen feet from the lighthouse, which rose up into the night sky like a fat white finger. The rough walls of the tower were unbroken except for a pair of windows, one five feet off the ground, the second directly above it, twenty feet away. Off to their left was the long white picket fence leading to the tower from the road. He and Ella were on the side of the fence that nobody was supposed to use, unless they worked for the Coast Guard or the Park Service.

Mitch grabbed Ella's hand and pulled her toward the squat white generator building next to the lighthouse.

"Careful," he whispered. He plucked a pair of leaves from her hair. "Don't let anyone in the lightkeeper's house see you. Usually it's empty, but you never know. This is where it gets a little tricky."

"Why do I not like the sound of this?" Ella whispered.

"Don't worry." Mitch pointed up at the lower window, which was barely visible in the weak moonlight. "I'm just going to need you to squeeze in through that lower window."

"You've got to be kidding," Ella said. She shook her head. "I'm going back home."

"Come on. I'll boost you up. I'd do it, but I'm a bit bigger than I was the last time I broke in here. You just have to jimmy the window a bit, a couple times to the left, then push up and to the right, and it'll pop right open."

Ella made a face, and then set down the flashlight and camera she'd been carrying.

Keep an open mind, she reminded herself. *They've probably fixed the window since Mitch was a kid.*

"For this," she said, stepping into the cup formed by Mitch's interlaced fingers, "for this I got my PhD?"

Mitch held her up for almost half a minute as she worked on opening the window. She pushed the window to the left a few times, and then to the right, but nothing happened. She tried it again to no avail. Mitch's arms were starting to shake when Ella slid the window to the right one more time, and it opened. She pulled herself up and squeezed the top half of her body into the lighthouse. For a few bad seconds she thought she would drop right to the bottom of the lighthouse, but instead her hands made contact with the cold metal of the spiral stairs that led to the top. She was in.

"Damn," she could hear Mitch say outside. "Not bad for a city girl."

Ella hurried down the steps on legs that were quivering the slightest bit and unlocked the lighthouse door. Armed with the camera and flashlights, Mitch slipped inside. He closed the door behind them and locked it again.

"I heard that 'city girl' crack," Ella whispered, elbowing him lightly in the side. "But I'll let it pass if you let me turn on a flashlight. I've *got* to take a look at this place."

"Okay, but be careful where you shine it. We don't want to attract any unwanted attention."

"Come on, Mitch, cut me some slack," Ella said in a

voice tinged with excitement and awe. She clicked on the smaller flashlight. "Oh man, this is *awesome.*"

Looking like the bottom of a merry-go-round, a series of over a hundred metal steps circled up and up to the top of the lighthouse. Ella felt her balance shift for a second as she gazed straight up—for a second she felt like she was falling upwards. She'd forgotten about that wonderful feeling of vertigo she'd experienced at the last lighthouse she'd been to almost a decade ago.

Anxious to see the rest of the tower, she was already climbing the rusty brown stairs, not caring if Mitch followed her or not. After only a couple steps she felt the staircase sway.

"Crap!" Mitch hissed from behind. "I forgot these steps weren't attached to the wall. Be careful, Ella."

For the first time all night Ella felt a twinge of unease as she thought about how old this structure really was.

All in the name of science, she told herself. *These steps will hold us.*

A hundred steps later, Mitch caught up to her at the top.

"About time," she said, and climbed up a ladder leading to a trapdoor in the low ceiling. She saw Mitch cringe, and she hoped he'd be able to fit through the small opening.

"Follow me," she said with a grin that felt as wide as her entire face. She worked the trapdoor open and went through it. "That's a fourth-order Fresnel lens," Ella said, talking softly, afraid to breathe. "It's probably a hundred and fifty years old. They don't *make* these anymore, Mitch."

Mitch was noisily pulling himself up through the tight fit of the trapdoor. The moonlight glistened in through the wall of windows around them.

She turned to Mitch. He was hunched over in the

cramped room, and in the darkness she could see that his face was red from getting through the trapdoor. At least she thought that was why he was so red. He was giving her one of his looks that she couldn't quite comprehend, as if he was seeing her with a new set of eyes.

Ella knew she was still probably smiling like a kid on her birthday, right before the cake and ice cream.

"Thanks," she whispered, pulling her gaze away from the lens. "Even if we don't find any clues, seeing all this was worth risking a breaking and entering charge. I'm so glad you brought me here."

"Just wait." Mitch stepped carefully around the ancient lens and pushed past her with a gentle touch that made Ella shiver for an instant. Then he opened a tiny door in the windows that was barely two feet wide. "There's *more.*"

Mitch squeezed through the door first, and Ella followed him in a heartbeat. They were standing on the catwalk outside the lighthouse. Ella held onto Mitch's arm, taking comfort in his solid bulk close to her.

"Wow." Her head moved slowly, taking in as much of the star-filled sky as she could. She gripped the balcony railing with her right hand, still keeping a sturdy grip on Mitch with her left. The balcony slanted a little, and she wasn't taking any chances.

Mitch led her slowly around the entire catwalk so she could take in the entire island, the sound, and, far off to the south, the Atlantic. The black stretches of water, reflecting the stars, made the island look like it was surrounded by outer space, above and below. Ocracoke didn't look just like an island in this star-lit emptiness—it looked like its own *planet,* floating alone in serenity.

"Wow, Mitch," Ella said again. The night breeze blew onto her skin, cooling the light layer of sweat she'd raised climbing the steps, and she moved closer to him without re-alizing it.

The island itself was a patchwork of lights throwing out circles of glowing whites and yellows, surrounded by a blackness so thick Ella wanted to reach out and touch it. She tried to get her bearings, doing her best to pick out landmarks. She thought she could see the Jolly Roger just off to the north, on the other side of Silver Lake.

"I see *Cassie*," Mitch said. "See her? Doesn't she look lonely?"

"Where? Wait, I think I see her. And there's the ferry landing, and . . . What is that?" Ella let go of Mitch so she could point at a pale, flickering light farther to the north, past the Jolly Roger and *Cassie*. The light flickered orange for a split second, and then faded out of existence.

"Isn't that where the cemetery is?" she said in a soft voice. She was getting colder by the second.

"I think so. That's weird. Must be someone burning gar-bage or something."

"At two in the morning?"

Ella inched away, looking at the rest of the island off to the right of the cemetery. She stopped on the other side of the lighthouse balcony and squinted at a flash of orange.

"Mitch? There's another one of those lights."

"Where?" The catwalk creaked as Mitch crept around to where she was standing.

"I could have sworn I saw another orange light out that way." Ella was pointing off to the south, as best as she could tell in the darkness. "But there's nothing out there, is there?"

"Just an old island. Nobody lives there anymore. It's called Portsmouth."

Ella grabbed Mitch with her free hand, keeping the other

one glued to the railing. "Portsmouth! That's the place Caroline was telling me about. Can you see anything out that way? Any lights?"

"Nah," Mitch said, eliciting a frustrated sigh from Ella.

She moved off to the right and glared out at the darkness in search of clues. Something wasn't quite connecting in her mind, and all these lights popping up felt too convenient, like someone was playing with them. And then she saw a third flickering light out in the blackness of the water. This light, unlike the first two, flickered bluish-white at first, and then turned bright white.

"Okay," she said. "Now I *know* I'm not going crazy. Mitch. Come look. What the hell is going on here?"

When Mitch moved closer to Ella and looked at where she was pointing, he let out a gasp.

"What's wrong?" Ella hissed.

"I've seen this light before," he said. "On the day I found the shipwreck. But that light's coming from Teach's Hole, not the shipwreck. And Teach's Hole is . . ."

Ella finished the sentence for him. "Where Blackbeard is reported to have died."

No sooner did she finish her sentence than a loud slam came from the ground below them.

"I thought you shut the door behind you," Ella whispered.

"I did. And bolted it from the inside," he said in a breathless voice.

"Mitch, quit playing around. I mean it."

"I wish I was."

"Mitch—"

"Shh . . ." Mitch grabbed Ella's hand in his.

Standing on the catwalk at the top of the lighthouse, Ella tried to stay calm. If someone was coming up to them, they'd surely hear them creeping up on the unattached metal stairs. She was already putting together a cover story for the local authorities, something about how she'd needed to see the island at night, from the lighthouse. For her research. Mitch reached his arm around her, and she resisted at first, and then leaned into him.

"Someone's messing with us," he said. "We'll just wait them out and then get the hell out of here."

Ella hoped he was right. She listened hard for the creak of stairs, but there was nothing. Instead of being able to relax, though, she felt even more panicked. Her eyes kept returning to the strangely pulsing lights of Teach's Hole Channel. She thought of Mitch's stories about finding the shipwreck, as if the lights had led him to it, and his nightmare about the hand reaching up from the water and pulling him in, dragging him under the depths.

She looked away, trying to reassure herself that she was imagining all of this, when she saw the channel called Teach's Hole. The flickering white lights had spread and transformed into a blood-red fire.

"*Look,*" she said. "Blackbeard's channel is burning."

When she squinted to try and see more clearly, she saw what may have been the outline of a burning ship. The ship was headed south, toward the inlet. The lights began to shift back to white.

"Blackbeard?" Mitch whispered.

And then the night went black as something blocked her vision. A cannon exploded in her ears as Mitch and Ella both pressed themselves back against the lighthouse, away from the shadow in front of them.

Ella tried to aim her flashlight onto the shadow, but all she could see was blackness. But it was blackness in the shape of a man. And the man was headless.

Oh no, she thought. *Not again.*

"Aye," the shadow growled, the sound coming from somewhere inside the space where the man's chest would have been. " 'Tis me again. An' the two of ya been makin' enough noise to wake the dead."

Ella's fingers went numb at the sound of that impossible voice. She dropped her flashlight, and it clattered down the side of the lighthouse and smashed onto the pumping house next to the tower.

"So tell me," the shadow said, floating five feet next to the balcony where Ella and Mitch were cowering. "What do ye be needin', on this night blacker'n my soul, from ol' Teach?"

Chapter Thirteen

"Ella," Mitch hissed. "Get back from the edge."

Ella heard him, but she couldn't be bothered to acknowledge him. Not right now. She had pushed away from the lighthouse wall as soon as the headless figure began talking, and she now stood directly in front of the talking shadow, within grabbing distance. Frigid air flowed out of the figure, and she was convinced it was coming from the man's headless neck. She could smell burnt matches and a hint of rot.

This was the missing piece, right in front of her. He'd been there on her very first day, dancing in the flooded sound next to the highway. Blackbeard.

"We need your help," she heard herself say, raising her voice to be heard above a sudden burst of wind that pushed her back against the windows of the lighthouse. "If you are who you say you are."

"*Always* ye livin' ones be needin' the help of the dead," the black figure rumbled back, but with a hint of humor in its deep voice. "Never lettin' us rest in peace."

"It's not for us, but for a girl. A girl who died too young. Surely you've seen her in your . . . hauntings?" Ella didn't dare look at Mitch, but she could feel his hand on her shoulder, holding her. Thanks to his steadying presence, she was able to inch closer, even as the chill air coming from the headless figure covered her. She could see a faint light outlining the being in front of her, just like Bonnet and Caroline, but this time it was white instead of light blue or orange.

"Aye," the figure said, appearing to relax somewhat, as much as a headless body floating almost seventy feet in the air could relax. "Ye've met Miss Caroline, I see."

"Yes! She's the one. And I'm sure you know the other one, Ste—"

"*Don't,*" the figure warned. His face—or at least the empty space that would have been his face—was suddenly inches in front of Ella. The cold flowing out of him numbed her skin, and she could barely breathe for the smell of fire and death he left in her nose.

"*Don't* be sayin' his traitorous damned name around me."

"Okay," she squeaked, feeling her first pangs of true fear. She'd been able to hold it back by simply acting on instinct and not thinking, but that voice, coming from nowhere, and the cold and the smells were all starting to unnerve her. She pried her left hand off the railing and reached back for Mitch. She didn't have to stretch her arm far to find him—he was right there behind her. Their hands met and locked together.

"Okay," she continued. "We're trying to help Miss Caroline find peace. Right now she's caught in limbo, and she can't get free until her killer is brought to justice. Even if they are both dead." She realized who she was talking to and winced. "Uh, didn't mean to remind you about that. Being dead and all."

The headless figure's hands began to take shape inside the shadows, and thick fingers reached up to stroke a beard that was no longer there. The fingers curled up into a fist of frustration, becoming even more solid. Ella leaned back, away from those hands.

"Aye," he said. "I hope to find that same peace, myself.

But I cannot, not 'til I am whole."

"We'll keep an eye out," Mitch said from behind Ella on the narrow catwalk. He moved even closer to her, until his chest touched her back. "If we see your head, sir, we'll grab it for you. Now how about you leave us alone now, so the lady can step back from the railing?"

The shadow figure—the *ghost*, Ella thought, and immediately dismissed the term—paused for a long moment, long enough for her to shiver from the cold air whistling out of his chest and up from his neck. Finally, he burst into hearty laughter. The sound echoed in his chest like the pounding of drums. Mitch's right arm went around her stomach, gripping her tightly. Any other time, Ella would've relaxed into that strong, comforting embrace. But not now, not with that unearthly laughter filling her ears.

"Ye've got a good man there, lass," the ghost laughed. "Best hang onto him the way he's hangin' onto *ye*."

Ella wanted to correct the man's mistake about her and Mitch, but the renewed laughter pouring out of his chest was too loud to interrupt. When she moved her gaze away from the shadowy figure in front of her, she froze. Out of the corner of her eye, he came into sudden focus. She could just make out a bloodied and torn blue jacket, and the glint of a broken cutlass in the figure's black-gloved hand.

"Now then," the headless pirate said, "if ye do indeed find me ugly old head, I'll be keepin' the two of ye safe the rest of yer lives t'gether. Ye have my word on it."

Ella caught her breath as she suddenly realized she was standing at the very edge of the narrow balcony. Her toes were hanging off the edge. She let go of Mitch's hand and gripped the cold metal of the handrail with both hands again. She had to force herself not to look down.

"And jus' because I like ye, I'll be keepin' the 'Gentleman Pirate' off yer tails, for a short time. He and I been needin' to talk for decades now. I been thinkin' about how easy that damned Royal Navy man from Virginia caught me unawares like that, back on that terrible November day. I been thinkin' my ol' friend *Stede* mighta had somethin' to do with that surprise attack."

With Mitch still holding onto her, Ella eased her way back from the railing as the pirate talked. He seemed to be speaking as much to himself as the two living humans in front of him. She could barely feel her fingers for the cold in the air.

"We'd better go," Mitch whispered. "I think we've pressed our luck far enough tonight."

"Wait," Ella said. "There's one more thing I need to know."

"I'm thinkin' he wanted all the gold we'd been storin' on his ship," Blackbeard continued from almost ten feet away now, his black shadow bobbing and swaying farther out into the night sky, blocking out the stars. "Yeah, that's what I'm thinkin', and he double-crossed me to get it. Can't believe he called his own damned ship the *Revenge*, too. As if there could be more than one *Revenge* on the seas. As if he—"

"Excuse me," Ella said, even as Mitch groaned next to her. "Ah, Mr. Teach, sir?"

After a low rumbling sound of annoyance at being interrupted, the dead pirate floated closer. Icy air covered Ella again, cold as the water of Ocracoke Inlet on their ill-fated dives. With a sudden flash of vertigo, she felt the lighthouse sway underneath her.

"Ye're still *here,* lass?"

"Ah, yes, sir," Ella said, hoping her voice sounded steadier than it felt to her. "I was hoping you could give us a hint as to where we should start looking, sir. To help Miss

Caroline. She spoke most highly of you, sir, by the way."

"Aye, flattery will get ye everywhere with Blackbeard," the ghost said, more laughter bubbling out of his chest. "I do believe I like talking with ye two. Everyone else I've visited here jus' runs off screamin' when I come 'round. All I get to do is hide their keys and move their lawn ornaments around for my leisure."

"What about the lights in the channel?" Ella said. Blackbeard's ghost was drifting away now, as if he'd lost interest. "Out in Teach's Hole? Or the lights near the cemetery? And the island next door, Portsmouth?"

"All devilry. Though sometimes a bit of mischief is a good thing, lass. And—speak of the devil and he shall appear!"

From far below came the slow clopping sound of hooves. Ella shivered, guessing the source of the sounds below them, but she was afraid to look down and have Blackbeard slip away.

Mitch gave a hissing sound. "Red-Eye," he said. "He's in on this too, I'll bet."

"Curse that damnable pony," Blackbeard muttered, starting to drop to the ground. Ella could barely see him anymore. "Always on my tail, chasin' me off like I was some curse-spittin' spook, on my own island. I'll show him some *curses*," he said, his gravelly voice coming from below them now.

"Blackbeard!" Ella called out as loudly as she dared. "Mr. Teach! Where should we start?"

For nearly ten seconds the air was filled with the sound of Blackbeard swearing and the angry squeals of Red-Eye. Ella looked down, but could only see a faint red glow in the blackness. She heard a sharp grunt, and Ella imagined the pony's back hooves connecting with Blackbeard's headless body. The pony gave a final bray of triumph and then ran off with a pounding of hooves.

For a long moment, the night was silent again. Ella stood trembling at the railing, savoring the feel of Mitch's arms around her and trying not to think too much about the impossible visitor they'd just had. At some point Mitch had put both arms around her in a big, protective bear hug.

The guy probably thought I was going over the side, she thought, *trying to make my point in my little chat with the old pirate.*

Her moment of peace ended when she heard Blackbeard's voice again.

"The lights are as good a place for ye to start as any," he said, his voice fading with each word. "Though I'd tell ye to start at Teach's Hole. And follow yer instincts. Dig *deeper.*" His voice was nearly lost in a sudden gust of wind coming off the water. "Now . . . I must rest . . ."

"That's it," Mitch said, whispering in her ear so closely she could feel his breath in her hair. Together they inched away from the edge. "Inside."

At the entrance, Mitch let go of Ella, and she felt suddenly vulnerable again. He waited for her to enter the tiny room containing the lighthouse lamp, and then he squeezed in after her. He shut the door and threw the bolt. When he turned to her, Ella gave him a hug of victory. She squeezed him so tight she could feel his heart pounding against her own chest. After a second or two, Mitch hugged her back. She inhaled his clean, slightly salty smell, and rested her forehead against his whiskery cheek.

We found our clues, she'd wanted to say to him, but the reality of all that they'd just done hit her like a punch to the gut.

She let go of Mitch and dropped to the dusty floor. Out

of breath, she rested her back against the glass walls of the lighthouse.

"Mitch," she said, gasping for air and shivering even though the cold breeze had disappeared. "What the hell just *happened?*"

Mitch's only answer was to look at her for a long moment. The darkness inside the lighthouse was too complete for Ella to see what sort of expression he wore, though she could feel his disbelief and shock.

"I wish I knew," he said at last, slipping through the trapdoor leading to the spiral stairs below. "I wish I knew."

Morning came much too soon for Ella, but despite the surreal discussion that had taken place last night at the lighthouse, she woke completely rested. Not a single nightmare haunted her, not even a dreaming visit from old Red-Eye, the Pony that May or May Not Be a Ghost.

I should talk to ghosts more often, she thought, and began laughing. Her laughter filled her small bedroom along with the bright glow of the early-morning sun, and getting out of bed wasn't a problem at all. She had a lot to do today, and no time to waste.

On her way to her closet, Ella paused to look at her grinning face in the mirror on the wall. She hadn't felt so good—so *alive*—in ages. Winter in Boston had never seemed so far away, like a bad memory that had happened to someone else, really.

She stretched and began pulling on her clothes, thinking about the short walk back to her house last night. She had chattered nonstop with Mitch the whole way, her words tripping over each other as she did her best to analyze the clues the pirate had given them. The whole time she'd been trembling with excitement mixed with fear, not to mention a crazy sense of euphoria at what she'd just seen and done. And the memory of Mitch's arms around her was still wonderfully fresh in her mind.

"So what do you think is out there, in the channel?" she'd asked Mitch. He hadn't said a word since they slipped out the front door of the lighthouse. "Do we dare try to dive there, do you think? Think anyone will bother us out there? Mitch? What do you think?"

Instead of answering, Mitch had plopped himself down onto the front steps of Ella's house.

"Ella," he said at last, his pale eyes catching the street light next to her driveway. "I am *completely* freaked out."

"Come on," Ella said. "It wasn't that big of a deal."

"You were talking to a ghost! I mean, I know that's become sort of a hobby with you, but this was Blackbeard! Damn, but this is crazy, Ella! I thought you didn't believe in stuff like this, and there you were, chatting away with ol' Teach like you guys were old buddies."

"Mitch," Ella said. "It's okay, really."

Sitting next to Mitch, Ella remembered the secure feeling she'd gotten at the top of the lighthouse, when he'd held her close on the catwalk. The fact that his arms were shaking with fear didn't bother her. She'd felt like she could do anything with him at her side. Including talking to ghosts.

Standing next to him outside her house, she'd wanted to do the same to him them, put her arms around him and calm him, give him that same confidence he'd given her when she'd needed it.

But when she reached out to touch his shoulder, Mitch stood up suddenly, as if desperate to get away from her. He'd taken almost a dozen steps before he stopped and turned back to her.

"Sorry," he said. He shrugged sheepishly. "Like I said, I'm just a bit freaked out. Blackbeard's *ghost*. It's like all my childhood horror stories, coming back to life. Even Red-Eye made an appearance."

Ella had tried to get Mitch to sit and talk, but he'd been too worked up. He refused to say anything further about it, not while it was still nighttime. He left after promising to meet her at eight-thirty at the coffee shop, far from the water and the lighthouse. She was sad to see him go.

On her way out of her house that morning, Ella grinned at the thought. She was looking forward to a nice strong latte at the coffee shop just up the road. For a change, she felt like one of the many tourists who would be coming soon to this sleepy island town, getting up late and spending the morning sipping expensive coffee drinks with her—

Her *what?* What *was* Mitch to her?

He's more than just a colleague, Ella thought. *More than just the dive master on our botched series of underwater excursions.* She'd felt his arms around her and held his hands tight in her own far too many times in the past few days for him to be just a guy she was working with.

She'd seen a look on his face, every now and then. This sort of surprised look, when he thought she wasn't paying attention to him, as they were talking or working on something together. As if he'd expected her to be different, somehow, and she kept pulling the rug out from underneath him. Sort of like the look on his face when they first met, but with the disappointment replaced by surprise and something else. Something deeper.

"Oh boy," she said, pulling her unruly brown hair into a ponytail. "I am really losing it."

Ella had left the house early, so she took her time getting

to the coffee shop. She checked out her birdhouse on the front porch, but nobody had taken up residence there yet. Instead of walking past Owen's stand, she looped around Creek Road, keeping her eyes on the lighthouse off to her right. The wind was cool, but nowhere near as frigid as the air coming from Blackbeard's headless, floating body last night.

Ella shivered. Her bright good mood from the morning was starting to fade, and on the breeze she thought she could smell a hint of burnt matches and something worse underneath. She picked up her pace and hurried down Lighthouse Road, away from the source of their misadventures the night before.

On her way down Main Street, she thought she heard the sound of hooves pounding up the pavement to meet her, but it was just an old truck with a bad muffler. Laughing at her overactive imagination, she crossed the road and ran her hand across the dozens of faded pink conch shells sitting in an oversized canoe outside the Pirate's Chest store. "Only a Dollar a Shell," the sign read. She passed by Blackbeard's Lodge and Teach's Hole gift shop before the coffee shop came into view on her right.

Pirates were everywhere in this town, she realized. *But these pirates were just safe, sanitized versions, completely unlike the real thing. Tourist-pleasers. If these people knew the real history of pirates, they'd probably change the name of their store or hotel.*

Mitch was already at the Ocracoke Coffee Shop, sitting outside under a gigantic cedar tree with twisting branches stretching out above him. Ella had half-expected to see him sitting in a corner inside, safe from the crisp morning air and the sudden bursts of wind, but instead he had commandeered a picnic table. Maps, notebooks, and diagrams covered every available inch of the table, weighted down by coffee mugs and dusty hardcover books.

He sat as far as possible from the three elderly tourists huddled together over their mugs on the front deck of the coffee shop. The three of them looked to be deep in discussion. Ella looked away from the now-familiar tourists before they could bother her again about ghost stories, like the old man had done at the Jolly Roger.

Mitch scribbled something into a notebook and grabbed a thick reference book from his pile, completely oblivious to her approach. He was now bent over an old map of the coast, making tiny marks on it with a pencil. Ella bit her bottom lip to keep from smiling at his expression—he looked like a young boy cramming at the last minute for a big test.

"Good morning," she said in a soft voice.

He looked up with a sudden start and almost knocked over a giant mug of black coffee with his free hand.

"Oh, hey," he said. He set down his pencil and took a sip of coffee. "Just doing some research."

"Oh really?" Ella said. She watched with more than a hint of jealousy as Mitch took a big gulp of coffee.

When he set down the mug, she could see Mitch's hand shaking slightly. She could see that it wasn't trembling with fear or excitement, but caffeine. Lots of it, apparently.

"How long have you been here?" she said. "And how many mugs of coffee have you had?"

"Since about seven," Mitch said, running his hands through his hair, mussing it even further. "And this is mug number three of their blackest stuff." He gave her a bloodshot look, eyebrows raised sarcastically. "Why do you ask?"

"No reason," she answered. "I'll be right back with a

drink. I see I have some catching up to do. Can I get you anything to eat?"

"Nah, not hungry," Mitch mumbled and turned back to his papers. "And I just got a fresh refill."

Ella crept past the still-whispering trio of tourists on the front porch and went inside. She was greeted by the smell of fresh coffee and warm pastries.

Surely there were more tourists visiting the island than just those three folks, she thought. A quick look around the L-shaped sitting area inside the coffee shop didn't convince her, however. Other than the young guy behind the counter, the coffee shop was empty.

She nodded at the barista and wandered to the back, her steps creaking on the smooth wooden floor. A small bookstore, Java Books, was attached to the back of the coffee shop.

A great idea, Ella thought, wishing she could camp out on the beach with a fat book and a latte. But the bookstore had a "Closed for the Season" sign on the door.

She walked back to the front of the coffee shop, passing shelves stuffed full of bags of coffee, pottery mugs, and T-shirts. Ella winced in sympathy for the owner—the place was full of souvenirs that weren't being bought by tourists who weren't coming to the island. At least not yet this year.

"Slow day?" she asked the twenty-something guy behind the counter.

"Slow *month,*" he said, rubbing his sandy blonde goatee and shaking his head. "My boss is really getting stressed out, y'know? People haven't been coming to the island much lately. But it's early in the season, I keep telling him. Wait until April, man, we'll be so busy he won't know what to do."

"I hope so," Ella said. "How about one of those blue-berry scones? And a triple latte, please, skinny, hold the foam, with a shot of mint."

"You got it," the guy said. "You've ordered that before, I can tell."

"Just a few times," Ella said, remembering many frigid Boston mornings when sipping her latte on her way to the university was the high point of her day.

As the barista worked the cappuccino machine and steamed a small metal cup of milk, Ella wandered off again. She gazed at the big glass jugs of black coffee beans stacked in rows against the wall and inhaled the rich scent of the small shop. For some reason she thought of Melissa, serving beers and platters of fried food at the Jolly Roger, and how she'd like all the pottery scattered throughout the small café area of the shop. And the bookstore area would make a great pottery shop.

On a whim, Ella picked the mug that most reminded her of Melissa, and sure enough, she found the initials "MT" on the bottom of it, next to an elegant sketch of a dragonfly. It had to be the handiwork of Mitch's sister.

"Here you go," the man behind the counter called out. He passed her a gigantic, steaming mug. "So what brings you to the island?" he asked. "Early vacation?"

"I wish," Ella said. "I'm doing some research for a university up north."

"Oh yeah? You know any paranormal psychology re-searchers up there?"

Ella was about to sip on her latte when his question brought her up short. "No. Why do you ask?"

"Oh, people 'round here've been talking about spirits, that's all," he said, rolling his eyes as he attempted to act nonchalant. Ella could tell there was something more to his

comments than just idle chatter. He seemed serious, underneath his slacker demeanor. "Rumor has it people don't
want to come here because of the ghost stories they hear
about the island from other tourists. We're sort of getting a
reputation as a haunted island. And not in a good way, like
New Orleans or other cool places with lots of history to
'em. Haunted in a stay-the-heck-away-from-there way."

"Really?" Ella said. "So what do you make of that?"

"Hey, whether ghosts are real or not, people get all
weirded out by 'em. Even if they're just in their imaginations. So maybe everyone just decides to take their spring
vacation somewhere else? It kills the economy here, and
makes for slow days for me. What can you do, y'know?"

"Good point," Ella said. "Glad to hear you're not
freaked out by all those rumors."

"Yeah," he said. "Well, I wish I could tell you I wasn't.
But I could've sworn I've seen some weird lights at night
lately. I don't sleep much—all this caffeine, y'know?"

"I'm sure there's a logical explanation for it," Ella said,
and gave the guy a genuine smile. She knew exactly how he
felt. "Where did you see these lights?"

The coffee guy was suddenly busy polishing the cappuccino maker. "Oh, here and there," he mumbled, obviously
embarrassed now. "Um, out on Silver Lake once. Out by
the cemetery once. But I'm pretty sure it was just my eyes
fooling me."

"Well," Ella said, "you never know." She picked up her
mug and scone. "Tell you what, I'll keep my eyes open for
any weird stuff, and you do the same. And I'll let my buddy
Mitch know about it, too."

"Ah," the guy said, giving her a relieved smile, as if all
this talk about ghosts and weird lights at night had been
cramping his relaxed style. "You know Mitch, huh? Guy's

been here all morning. Tell him he owes me a trip on his boat for all the coffee refills I've given him, will you?"

"Sure. Well, I'd better get going." Balancing her drink and her scone in one hand, Ella grabbed the door. She was tempted to stay and quiz the obviously lonesome coffee guy some more about what he may or may not have seen at night, but she doubted he was going to say much more about it and risk ruining his slacker image. And she had work to do.

"Thanks for stopping by," the guy called as she left the store.

Flashing a quick smile at the three elderly tourists, not caring that they didn't return her kindness, she walked back to the picnic table. Mitch was finishing off a list he'd made on a piece of notebook paper.

"The natives are restless," Ella said, sitting across from him. She nodded in the direction of the shop. "The coffee guy is convinced the island is haunted, and that's what's keeping people away. I think the island could be in trouble if we don't do something soon."

"You may be right," Mitch said, setting down his pencil and pushing away from the table. He stretched and cracked his knuckles. "I mean, after last night, can you argue with what the guy in there said?"

"Yeah, yeah," Ella said. "Drink your coffee."

As Mitch did just that, finishing off the last of his mug, Ella looked at the stubble on his cheeks and the weatherworn, rugged look of his hand holding the mug. She caught herself thinking again about the touch of his hand on hers, from when he grabbed her hand at the Jolly Roger a few nights ago, to when he'd wrapped his arms around her last night at the top of the lighthouse.

"What's wrong?" Mitch said, setting down his mug. Ella

saw the dark circles under his eyes and realized he probably hadn't slept much last night. "Do I have something hanging out of my nose?"

As Mitch rubbed the stubbly mustache growing under his nose, Ella laughed. The sense of urgency she'd been feeling all morning began to recede to a manageable level.

"No," she said. "You're fine. I was just spacing out."

"Hey. That's *my* job, isn't it? You're the logical professor, remember."

Ella almost snapped back at him when she realized he was teasing her. She hadn't expected that from Mitch. She sort of liked it.

"You got me there," she said, laughing again. "So. What have you figured out this morning? Are we going treasure-hunting? And if so, where?"

"Maybe we are," Mitch said, shifting back into serious mode in a blink of an eye. Still hyped up on coffee, he began running through their options at a rapid-fire pace. "We've got three major areas to cover in the next day or two. The faster we take care of our friends' problems, the faster we can get back to diving the wreck."

"Sounds good," Ella said.

Mitch rattled his fingers on the top of the picnic table, as if annoyed at being interrupted. Ella remembered the feeling well from her teaching days, and she gestured at him to continue.

"So," Mitch said, "today I want to hit the first two—the cemetery and then Teach's Hole Channel. You'll forgive me if we visit the graveyard here on the island first, during broad daylight. I'm recovered from last night, mostly, but I don't want to push my luck." Mitch took a breath and then plunged onward. "Since we saw lights at those two spots, I figured that would be where we'd start."

"Okay, that's the first two," Ella said, talking fast to interrupt Mitch. She was afraid he'd jabber on and on all day long in his over-caffeinated state if she let him. "What's the third place? Portsmouth?"

"Yep. You don't mind, do you?" he said, breaking off a chunk of her scone. He took a bite and tried to talk around his mouthful of scone. That intense look was back in his eyes again, and Ella felt her pulse quicken. "Now, if I remember my island history from school, plus what I read in these books and found on these maps, Portsmouth was pretty active back in the old days. Our Caroline may have spent a good amount of time there, hiding out from Bonnet. Plus," he said, slowing down for breath and swallowing his scone at last, "they have a couple cemeteries there as well. We'll go there tomorrow, as soon as it's light."

Ella nodded. "What do you think we'll find out there, Mitch? I mean, really. Are we just chasing our tails and wasting our time?"

Mitch reached for his mug and lifted it to his mouth before realizing it was empty. He sighed.

"This feels right to me, doing this. Don't you think? I mean, there's some reason all of this is happening right now. How I just happened to find the ship that day, and how all the ghosts are sort of waking up right now, spooking people. Keeping tourists away and hurting the businesses here. I think that if we don't help Caroline soon, and get rid of Bonnet, the island is going to be in big trouble."

"I thought it was just early in the season."

"Ella," Mitch said in a soft voice. "I've lived here all my life. The only time the shops and restaurants have been this empty this late in March was when we had a freak snowstorm when I was a kid. People come here to get away and relax. We even have crowds of folks in the middle of winter.

This is serious. Whatever it is, bad karma or evil spirits or something else, it's keeping people away, and lots of folks are going to go broke or move away. As much as I hate to admit it, we need the tourons."

Ella nodded. With the leaves of the trees rustling above her, the only sound other than the occasional passing car, she realized that the sort of serenity and escape that this island provided was something worth preserving.

Mitch, she realized, *could be quite convincing. Especially when he locked those eyes on you when he was talking.*

"What do you say," she said, passing Mitch the rest of her scone and brushing her hand against his in the process, "we gather up all your paperwork here and do some *real* detective work?"

Chapter Fourteen

Still wound up from their caffeine, Ella and Mitch walked through the side streets of town at a speedy clip. Mitch's house was on the way to the Howard-Wahab Cemetery, and he wanted to drop off his armload of books and papers, so they took a quick detour to his place. Still thinking about the flashes of orange and white they'd seen last night from high above the island, Ella waited outside Mitch's when he went inside. She caught herself pacing back and forth in front of his front porch, and she forced herself to stop.

She stepped back and took a good look at Mitch's house. He lived in a modest two-story almost hidden by a ring of tall oaks whose shadows fell on the screened-in front porch. The lawn was surprisingly neat and green, not an easy feat at the end of winter, though Ella thought the crooked blinds inside the upstairs windows and the trio of faded pink flamingoes in the front yard made it obvious that a bachelor lived there.

Ella waited for Mitch for what felt like an eternity, but was probably closer to half a minute. Now that they had a plan, she was having trouble waiting to get started, and she felt the need to keep in motion. If she stayed in the same place for too long, she knew she'd start to analyze her situation too closely.

She left Mitch's house and walked alone to Cemetery Road. The cemetery was less than two blocks away, and it was a somewhat jumbled collection of graves fenced off by three different rectangles of unpainted pickets. The largest section contained a dozen weathered, whitish-gray head-stones, most of them choked with weeds and creeping vines. Uneven brown grass poked out at the bottom of the fences, ready to be trimmed for the first time that year.

Ella bent down in front of one of the graves in the front-most section and peeked through the fence at it. Mitch had mentioned that this graveyard belonged to the two oldest families of the island, the Howards and the Wahabs. She didn't want to go inside the fence unless she had to. Even though she knew better, she still remembered all too well her father's theories about walking on top of the graves of the dead and waking them.

"Sometimes people come back," he'd say whenever they passed by a cemetery. "And when they do, they come looking for whoever woke them. Is *that* what you want them to *do?*"

Ella shook her head, turning back to the graves on the other side of the fence. The last cemetery she'd visited had been where her father had been buried.

Just as she was remembering the cold fall day of Dad's burial, a hand gripped her arm. She nearly jumped over the picket fence in surprise.

She turned to see Mitch next to her, carrying a small notebook in his left hand.

"Find anything yet?" he said, wearing an exasperated grin. He moved closer, still holding onto her upper arm with his right.

Ella didn't try to wriggle free. She looked for that burning light in his pale blue eyes again, and was glad to see it was still there, along with something else. *Irritation at being left behind, maybe? Or was it something more?*

"Not yet," she said when she found her voice again and remembered his question.

"Thanks for waiting for me, by the way," he said. His hand slid down her upper arm, cupping her elbow for a moment before moving to her hand.

"Sorry." Ella shuffled her feet closer to Mitch's, until they were toe-to-toe next to the cemetery fence.

"You're not excited about this scavenger hunt, are you?" Mitch's voice was soft as a whisper, and he still wore that curious grin.

Ella wondered if he was talking about their mystery that needed solving, or something else.

"I just wanted to . . . get started."

"I hear you." Mitch squeezed her hand and moved his head a fraction of an inch closer to her face.

The sound of an old car with a bad muffler filled the air as a car passed on the street ten yards away from them, and Mitch pulled back from her as if realizing where they were. Ella took a step after him, but he had moved off. He was now looking over at the three interconnected cemeteries.

"Yeah," he glanced back at her, his face flushed, "I just needed to get a fresh notebook—spilled coffee all over the other one."

"That's . . . too bad." It was all Ella could think to say. And she wasn't just talking about his notebook.

"Anyway," Mitch said as he cleared his throat. "I've got to show you something over here."

He hurried off toward the third and smallest graveyard, and Ella stood there for a long moment after he'd walked away, heart still pounding away, arms suddenly empty. She wasn't sure what had just happened.

After she caught her breath and composed herself, she followed Mitch over to the third graveyard. The tiny cemetery contained a careful arrangement of concrete crosses adorned with bronze plaques, all of them surrounded by a white picket fence. Two of the crosses bore only the word "Unknown" on their faces.

"They were British sailors," Mitch said. He sounded relieved to have something to take his mind off their too-intimate moment. "Their ship was sunk by a German sub in World War Two. The locals found their bodies and the sailors were buried here. Hard to believe that the war came this close to our country."

Ella stood in front of the enclosure of graves, reading the metal marker dedicated to the memory of the sailors and England.

"I've read about this," she said. "But I'd forgotten they were here. Amazing to think that there's a little piece of England right here in your town, holding these four soldiers."

"Yeah," Mitch said. "You probably won't want to hear about the stories Melissa made up about the ghosts of those four soldiers to scare my buddies and me. I just hope . . ."

"What?" Ella said, looking over at Mitch. He was staring at the four crosses with his arms crossed tightly in front of his chest, chewing his lip. She remembered how close he'd been to her, how she'd wanted to touch those lips with her own. Just once, just for a second or two.

"Oh nothing, just . . . Well, I just hope Caroline, Bonnet, and Blackbeard don't wake up *all* the spirits around here. There've been a *lot* of ships that have gone down all over the Outer Banks."

Ella felt a chill, as if someone had run a hand directly down the line of her backbone. She didn't even want to consider the number of lost souls that could be haunting this section of the ocean, up and down the coast.

The Graveyard of the Atlantic, indeed, she thought. *Good thing I don't believe in ghosts. Right?*

166

"Anyway," Mitch said, shaking his head as he pointed at the section of the graveyard farthest from the road. "Check this out over here. This is the oldest section of the grave-yard, the Howard section. We're talking old-*old* stuff here, professor."

"What should we be looking for, do you think?" Ella was a few steps behind him now, having pulled herself away from the graves of the soldiers.

"Clues," he said. He rested his hands on the rough wood of the four-foot-high fence.

"Smart guy," Ella muttered, but caught herself smiling just the same.

A second later she heard a car pull to a stop behind them. When she turned, she saw her old friends, the three older tourists, getting out of their idling blue Mercedes. The muffler was coughing like it was about to fall off at any minute, and then one of the old ladies clicked off the engine. The other two were pointing at the memorial for the four soldiers, consulting a handful of pamphlets and papers. All of them were dressed in matching dark blue sweaters and khaki pants, like some sort of uniform.

Surely they had to be hot in those outfits, Ella thought, as the temperature today was probably already in the seventies. The trio left their car in the narrow parking section in front of the graveyard and hobbled up onto the wooden sidewalk.

"Shh," Ella hissed at Mitch. She wanted to see what the trio was up to, and she was starting to get suspicious at the number of run-ins they'd been having with these three tourists.

She and Mitch were both partially hidden by the big oak tree between them and the tourists, and she didn't think the three elderly folks would bother risking a walk over the uneven ground near this section of the cemetery. Most of the markers around her were unreadable anyway, and people weren't allowed inside the fenced-off area.

Ella watched them approach the small British cemetery and listened to them murmuring to one another as if comparing notes. One of the ladies carried a thick, leatherbound book that she would hold up to her face for a moment, then look back at the four graves, and back again.

After another minute, they walked back to their Mercedes without looking back.

"Our tourons get around," Mitch whispered. "Good thing they didn't see us. They'd probably think we were grave-robbing or something."

Ella let go of the breath she'd been holding after the Mercedes drove off. She was about to say something about them when she heard Mitch rattle the latch to the gate behind her. She watched, shocked, as he walked into the Howard graveyard.

"Mitch. What are you *doing?*" Ella whispered. "That's private property. Don't tell me you *are* going to do some grave-robbing."

"It's private only to family," he said. "Come on in, Ella."

He bent close to a tall, narrow slab of white rock containing the faintest outline of words. The wind and rain had worn the rock smooth.

" 'Fallen from our hearts, beloved Johnathan's soul did leap,' " he said softly, " 'And into heaven he flew, leaving us behind to weep.' "

"Who was he?" Ella crept closer, right to the edge of the old cemetery. She was fascinated by the line of ancient poetry and Mitch's obvious familiarity with it. She squinted at the gravestone but couldn't make out any words. "A great-

great-great-great grandfather?"

"Sort of. He only lived for a year before he died of tuberculosis. His father, Donald Thompson, married Eloise Howard. Back in their time, they would have called the town Pilot Island, not Ocracoke."

"Where's the oldest grave in here?"

"Probably Donald or Eloise, or . . ." Mitch looked at the other mismatched markers filling this section of the graveyard. "There. That's Eloise's oldest brother. Come on."

Ella rested her hand on the gate. She knew she'd have to help Mitch look through the thick undergrowth around the gravestones if they were going to make any progress today. But the heavy weight of history, combined with all the strange events of the past few days, made her hesitate before entering the graveyard. She could almost hear her father's teasing voice, asking her, "Is *that* what you want them to *do?*"

"Ella?" Mitch said. "You're not getting freaked out already, are you? It's just a graveyard."

Ella made a face at that and pushed open the gate. *Mitch was supposed to be the superstitious one,* she thought, *not me.*

"I know," she said and forced a smile onto her lips. "I just didn't want to start trespassing again so soon after last night in the lighthouse."

"Ah, you'll be fine so long as you're with me," Mitch said, examining another faded stone marker. "I'm family, and that's—"

"What's *that?*" Ella said, pointing at the ground next to Mitch. As soon as she'd walked three steps inside the fence, she'd seen a flash of light coming off something on the ground.

"Where?"

"Here," Ella said, tiptoeing through the cemetery. She

nudged Mitch out of the way and went down on one knee, pushing aside random blades of grass. She saw another flash of light as something metal caught the sun peeking through the two trees next to the fence. Ella plucked something metal from the ground. It felt hot to the touch.

"What the hell?" Mitch said. "How did you manage to find that?"

"It's part of a locket, I think." Ella held the tiny piece of blackened, curved metal up so Mitch could see it. The initial heat she'd felt coming through it had disappeared already. Just as Mitch was reaching out to take the locket, she heard the sound of hooves, pounding through sand.

"Did you hear that?" she said, pulling her hand back with the piece of metal still in her grip. Some of the silver from the bottom shown through, but for the most part the piece was black with age.

"Hear what?" Mitch was still staring at the piece of the locket. Ella looked around, trying to catch a glimpse of the source of the noise, though she had a good idea who it was—a pony with reddish eyes, most likely. But the sound had stopped as suddenly as it had started.

"Never mind," she said. She passed the piece of the locket to Mitch, feeling a sense of sudden sadness when it left her hand. Sadness and loss, along with something else. Something darker than those other emotions.

"I think this is one of our clues, Mitch. Maybe there's something else around here." Ella thought about asking for the locket back, but she wasn't sure she wanted to feel those intense emotions again.

"Can you hang onto that for me?" she asked Mitch.

Mitch nodded and slipped the piece of metal into his jeans pocket. Together they combed through the grass around the graves and checked out all the remaining tombstones. Ella wasn't surprised that, after fifteen minutes of searching, they didn't find anything else.

When she saw the locket, something had clicked inside her mind. She didn't dare tell Mitch this, but she knew that the piece of the locket was what they'd come to the cemetery to find.

And they had one more place to search today.

"I think we need to move on," she said.

"Sounds good," Mitch said without hesitating. He must have been thinking the same things that she was. He pulled out the locket again and squinted at it. "Do you think this is something important, Ella?"

She shrugged, not wanting to get either of their hopes up just yet. "I don't know. Maybe."

"Oh, come on." Mitch stepped closer, holding out the locket. It had been cut neatly in half, leaving a rounded shape that looked like half a heart. "You *know* that this means something, Ella. Maybe it belonged to Caroline."

"I don't know." She tried to remember all of Caroline's story. "Wasn't she pretending to be a boy all the time she was on Ocracoke—Pilot Island?"

Mitch stared at the locket as well, rubbing his chin as he considered her theory. "Well, she would have been here *after* she escaped from Bonnet, so she wouldn't be hiding the fact that she was a young woman." Mitch put the locket away again and led Ella out of the fenced-in cemetery, closing the gate behind them. "Maybe she met someone here on the island, and her new guy gave it to her?"

"Maybe," she said, even as the breeze carried what sounded like the echo of distant hooves. "Do you think Caroline didn't tell me her whole story?"

They had left the cemetery behind them, walking on the sandy shoulder of the road. As if on cue, the dusty blue

Mercedes puttered past them, and Ella nodded at the three elderly tourists giving them the eye from inside their car. She was glad Mitch had hidden the locket away, feeling suddenly very protective of it with the tourons around.

"Good question," Mitch said, staring after the Mercedes with a troubled look on his face.

"You were talking about ghost rules," Ella said. *I can't believe I'm saying this,* she thought. "Can they lie to living people? Is that within their, um, guidelines?"

"Your guess is as good as mine. Maybe you just didn't get the whole story from Miss Caroline. I don't think she lied—not sure that's allowed in the ghost rules—but she may not have given you *all* the facts in her story."

Ella had a sudden urge to look at the locket again. "That's true. She didn't have a lot of time before Bonnet interrupted her," she said. "But I do think she wasn't telling the whole story. Can I see our clue again?"

Mitch pulled out the locket and handed it to Ella. She stared at the blackened piece of metal, with its jagged edge. As she ran her finger across the back of the locket, feeling a tiny indentation that may have been some sort of letter or design, she felt all the excitement she'd been trying to hold in slip free.

"I think we're onto something here, Mitch," she said, her voice quivering the tiniest bit. "Something that may re-write history books. At least the ones dealing with a certain two pirates."

Mitch blinked in surprise at her response, as if that was the last thing he'd expected her to say. After a moment, he said, "Meet me at my boat in half an hour? Teach's Hole is the next stop on our whirlwind tour of the great Ocracoke metropolitan area. Bring your diving gear."

"*That,* my partner in crime, is an excellent idea." Ella

looked at Mitch's smile and his sparkling eyes. She could tell he was feeling the same wild surge of excitement that she was. "I'll see you there."

Still looking at the piece of the locket in her hand, Ella walked away. They were probably both crazy to even consider another dive, but she wasn't one to give up easily when it came to something that mattered to her. And with the appearance of this locket, the mystery of Caroline Amberson was starting to matter quite a bit.

Chapter Fifteen

Less than an hour later, Ella was about to let go of the side of Mitch's boat and drop into the water of Teach's Hole Channel when she saw the stampeding ponies.

Removing her mask so she could see better, she saw over two dozen white, brown, and spotted ponies thundering down the narrow sliver of sand on the western edge of Ocracoke Island. Some kicked up plumes of water from Pamlico Sound, while others threw sand into the air with each pounding step. As she dangled, half in and half out of the boat, Ella could see the wide whites of their eyes and the gray foam around their mouths.

"Mitch," she whispered, but he'd already seen them.

"How'd they get out?" he said, reaching for his cell phone next to the wheel. "Let me call Sheriff Austin and tell him."

Ella pulled herself back into the boat and grabbed his arm before he could key in the number. "Recognize that last one?" she said, pointing at a squat black pony bringing up the rear. Ella could almost imagine the redness of the creature's eyes.

"I think I see who made the ponies start running," Mitch said, squinting. "See him?"

"*What?* That can't be right," she whispered.

Fading in and out of her vision, a man in a black overcoat stood on the sand behind the ponies. Ella could just barely make out the loose rope from the hangman's noose around his neck trailing behind him like a tail. Ella thought she could hear the explosions of cannons with each dull thud of pony hooves in the sand.

The man was looking right at Mitch's boat.

And then Red-Eye turned and charged back toward the man, dodging his fellow ponies, and leaped onto the man in black, who promptly disappeared.

"Whoa," Mitch said. "I'm not sure how I feel about seeing him moving around out of the water like that. He should be underwater."

Now that Red-Eye had chased off Bonnet's ghost—or whoever that was—the ponies began to slow, cantering onto the scrabbly grass next to the narrow beach, blowing hard. Within seconds they were grazing on the grass, within sight of the old lighthouse a few blocks away.

"What do you mean?" Ella looked up at Mitch, her arms shaking. She tried to keep her voice light, but it wasn't working. "Think he's not following the ghost rules?"

Mitch didn't answer. Instead, he pressed some more numbers on his cell phone and let the sheriff know the ponies were out. Apparently, Ella was guessing, this sort of thing happened more than once.

"Still feel up to this dive?" Mitch said after he put his phone away. He rested his hand on Ella's shoulder.

Still staring at the runaway ponies, Ella placed her hand on top of his. Her fingers felt numb, while his hand was warm. She saw the scratches on the sleeve of her wetsuit, the same scratches that Mitch had on his own hand, and she felt a surge of defiance fill her.

This is my project, damn it, she thought. *No ghost is going to muck it up for me. At least not without a fight.*

"Yep, I feel up to it," she said, grudgingly removing her hand from Mitch's. "Got the tether ready?"

Mitch pulled on the ten yards of sturdy rope between

them, coiled on the floor of the ship. He snapped one end to his belt and the other end to Ella's belt.

"You still okay with the plan?" Mitch said. "We hang tight down there together, no matter who shows up?"

Ella nodded. "But if either of us gives three tugs, we're surfacing."

"Got it." Mitch's smile was a mix of reassurance, excitement, and a trace of fear.

"Let's see what's down there," Ella said, giving one last glance at the now-deserted beach. The ponies had already moved on. The coast was as clear as it was going to get.

On the count of three, Ella and Mitch dropped together into the water of Teach's Hole Channel. The water was murkier here than their usual diving area south of the island, out in the Atlantic. Ella let herself sink, eyes peering at the glowing bits of silt and sand floating in front of her face. She could barely see Mitch just a few feet away from her.

Mitch had brought them to the deepest section of the channel that was still within sight of the lighthouse, using what Ella thought of as a mix of technology and instincts. She thought about the flashing light she'd seen in this area last night from the lighthouse, and how the light had grown, illuminating what looked like an ancient ship that had caught fire. The ship had burned bright for an instant before disappearing into the sound. Mitch's choice of location felt to Ella like the right place to start looking.

She soon felt the sandy bottom of the channel under her flippered feet. She shone her light on the sand, hoping to find something down here as easily as she'd found the piece of the locket. If she did, they'd have this mystery solved in the next day or so, and she and Mitch could get back to work.

With Mitch tethered to her and almost within arm's reach of her, Ella was able to block out her worries about getting separated from him again and focus on searching for clues. Half an hour slipped past as they covered a wide swatch of the channel floor. They found nothing more than sand, silt, and shadows.

As she looked, Ella wondered about Caroline's story. She didn't think Caroline was lying about the way history had distorted the reality of Blackbeard and Stede Bonnet—as a history expert, she knew that what really happened in the past and what was in textbooks or shared in legend were often very different creatures. Even the most truthful and unbiased historian often had an axe to grind against certain events and people from the past; everyone had some sort of agenda.

What Ella couldn't understand was how Bonnet could have allowed Caroline to die in such a heartless manner—locked in a cell as water poured into it from the damaged hull. Even if the man was touched in the head, surely his men wouldn't allow such a thing to happen to her. If she had worked beside these men for years, as she said, even disguised as a boy, there would have been some sense of loyalty and camaraderie. Someone would have kept Caroline from drowning in her cell.

Thinking about Caroline made her touch the locket tucked into a pocket of her wetsuit. Once she was sure it was safe, Ella thought about what had been engraved into the locket. All she'd been able to make out were two hard-to-read impressions, probably initials, or part of a word. She guessed the first was a C, but she'd have to clean the silver tonight to be sure.

The other half of the locket was out here somewhere, she knew. As impossible as she knew it was going to be to find it, Ella had a feeling they would come across it. Her time with Mitch and the wild events of the past few days were giving her the belief that there were stronger forces at work all around them.

Ella gave a start when she felt Mitch pulling gently on the tether. He was trying to get her attention, and she'd been so lost in her thoughts that another ten minutes had slid past. All she'd discovered down here so far were layers of shifting sand and the occasional hermit crab. And she'd managed to wander a good eight or nine yards away from Mitch.

On her way back to Mitch, Ella felt the trace of a chill enter the water. She stopped in mid-kick, holding her breath for a second, as if waiting for a cold hand to grab her or pull at her hose.

Get a grip, she told herself and kicked her way to Mitch. The water returned to its normal temperature. *It's just water currents.*

He was hunched over a long piece of blackened wood that he gently pulled free of the sand and silt. Two metal pellets were embedded in the burnt timber.

Ancient bullets, Ella realized. This may have been the site of Blackbeard's final stand, after all. Their clue had to be here.

Giving Mitch a quick thumbs-up, Ella began digging in the sand where he'd found the board. Every time she displaced a handful of sand, two more would rush in and undo her work. So she simply thrust her hands into the channel floor, searching for something, anything.

Her arms were buried almost to the elbow when the water turned to ice around her. A now-familiar exploding sound filled the air, and Mitch was pulling at her arm, ready to surface. Ella shook her head at him.

178

Just a little bit longer, she wanted to tell him. She gave one last push into the sand, and her probing fingers were rewarded with the touch of something metal.

Accompanied by a cannon blast that changed into a resounding laugh coming from directly above her, Ella pulled her treasure out of the sand. She didn't even get a chance to look at it before a black figure swam between her and Mitch and cut through their tether. Mitch went one direction, and Ella went the other.

How can Bonnet do that? Ella wondered, forgetting about the metal object still cradled in her hands. Then she remembered how Bonnet had become solid long enough to grab her leg and Caroline had been able to scratch her arm.

Stay calm, she told herself, even as Stede Bonnet turned his back on Mitch and dropped down through the water toward her. Still booming out laughter that came from all around her, filling Ella's ears, Bonnet pulled something from inside his overcoat.

For a long, blank moment in which her breath became lodged in her throat, Ella couldn't comprehend what it was the floating man was holding out to her like a trophy. She felt a sudden heat from the pocket of her wetsuit, right in the spot where she'd placed the broken locket earlier.

"You see," he said in a voice as echoing and deep as his laughter, "what happens to those who cross Stede Bonnet."

In her left hand, Ella lifted the object she'd found in the sand just as she understood the impossible item dangling from Bonnet's hand. She was holding an ancient pistol, while Bonnet was holding the dismembered head of Edward Teach, better known in these parts as Blackbeard.

"This is where he died," Bonnet continued. "This is where he got what he *deserved*."

Back off, she thought, taking aim at the ghost with the

rusted pistol. The locket felt white-hot inside her wetsuit. *Back off, and drop the head.*

Bonnet laughed at her. The sound burbled out of his bony chest and turned the water in front of him into half-frozen slush. The locket went cold inside her wetsuit, and she forgot about it immediately. He floated closer to her, becoming more solid with each passing second.

Before Bonnet could get any closer, Ella saw movement from behind him. Mitch had taken it upon himself to test just how solid the ghost had become. He dove at Bonnet, trying to take him out at the knees.

Mitch's desperate move succeeded. The ghost pitched forward, launching Blackbeard's head into the water above them even as ghostly gold coins flew from Bonnet's pockets. Bonnet's mouth went wide with shock. As he fell through the water, a delicate silver chain flew out from his neck as if it had a mind of its own, and it had decided it no longer wanted to be attached to this wicked old pirate.

Ella caught the chain in her right hand. Just like the piece of the locket had been for a few painful seconds, the chain was hot the instant it touched her, melting part of her wetsuit before it cooled off a second later.

That's it, Ella thought. *That's enough of this diving business, for now.*

When she waved at Mitch and pointed upwards, he didn't even hesitate. He grabbed her under one arm, and together they kicked up to the surface. Clutching her two treasures to her chest, Ella surfaced along with Mitch a few seconds later. They were back in the boat in no time.

Ella hoped Bonnet would think twice before coming after them again, but she knew Bonnet had little to fear from her and Mitch. And in any case, the pirate was already dead; he had nothing left to lose.

★ ★ ★ ★ ★

As Mitch aimed *Cassie* toward Silver Lake, Ella didn't think they'd ever get out of Teach's Hole. She felt like Mitch had taken forever to start the boat's engines and get them turned around. Now they were creeping back to the harbor. Worried about the shallow bottom, Mitch claimed he'd had to take it slow through the ditch leading to Silver Lake.

"We'll be there in a minute," Mitch said.

Now that they were moving at last, getting away from the deep, haunted channel outside the island, Ella barely heard him. She was gazing at the antique weapon she'd dug out of the ocean bottom, holding it in her still-shaking hands.

"I wonder where we can get this gun analyzed," she said. "And this chain, too. It was almost too easy . . ."

"You call that *easy?* He was on us as soon as we hit the water."

"You may be right." Ella set the gun into the salt-water container she'd set aside for her artifacts.

We should have filled this container five times over by this point in the dive, she thought. She was going to have to call Dr. Bramlett soon and give him an update. She dreaded it.

"My dad's been studying guns all his life," Mitch said as they glided up to the dock next to the Jolly Roger. "I'm sure he could tell you how old it was, and he probably knows a good bit about that chain and locket we found, too."

Ella nodded and looked up at Mitch once they had drifted to a stop. "Sounds good. We'll have to talk to him about it. I've got some research to do online, and I want to clean up that locket and this chain and see what I can find. Do you still want to try visiting Portsmouth tomorrow?"

"Yeah, that'd be good." Mitch killed the engine and

began tying up his boat.

Ella glanced at Mitch, hoping her next question would come out sounding innocent. After all that had happened, she wasn't crazy about being alone for the rest of the day, even though she had some research to do on the gun and Portsmouth Island. She took a quick breath and asked Mitch her question.

"Maybe we can meet up for dinner tonight?"

"Sounds good," Mitch said in a distracted voice. He was busy putting away his equipment and their wetsuits and straightening everything about *Cassie*. He paused and looked at Ella with a half-smile. "Stop by my house around seven?"

Ella nodded. She gathered up her equipment and was about to leave *Cassie* when Mitch called her name.

"Don't forget to bring your gun for dinner," he said.

In response to his question, Ella's look must have been completely unreadable to Mitch, because he burst out into the same contagious laughter Ella had heard on his boat a few days earlier. Then Ella remembered the old pistol she'd found in the sand of the channel, and she laughed along with him.

"Sorry," he said with a big smile. "I've always wanted to say that to a pretty lady."

"Right," Ella answered, trying to match his light tone. "You Ocracoke guys have all the lines us ladies love to hear. See you at seven."

In spite of her fatigue after yet another burst of adrenaline had drained away, Ella's walk back to her rented house took no time at all. She'd forgotten about Bonnet and the icy water and cannons he brought with him. She'd even managed to put Caroline's plight and her upcoming phone call to her boss into the back of her mind.

She kept thinking about the way Mitch had smiled at her when he called her a pretty lady. That smile said more than his words.

Dinner tonight could be an interesting endeavor, she thought. *I just hope the guy knows how to cook.*

Chapter Sixteen

When Ella knocked on Mitch's front door at ten past seven, fashionably late, she was almost knocked off her feet by the smell of something spicy and mouthwateringly good from inside the house. The screen door leading into Mitch's house was open, and she had to knock again to be heard over the sounds of Louie Armstrong's trumpet and the sizzling coming from the kitchen.

Ella looked down at her faded jeans and mostly wrinkle-free white blouse and wondered if she should have gotten more dressed up. She didn't know it was going to be that kind of meal. She'd been *hoping*, but . . .

"You must be Ella," a deep voice said from behind her. Soft footsteps approached, following by the mad patter of dog paws on the sidewalk. Ella set down the bag that held the ancient pistol and a six-pack of Killian's and turned to meet a tall, gray-haired man with pale blue eyes, his hand on the collar of the fattest chocolate-brown Chesapeake Bay retriever she'd ever seen.

"I'm Bill Thompson," the man said. "Mitch's dad. And this is Barny, short for Barnacle—the resemblance is striking, isn't it?"

"Nice to meet you," Ella said. She shook the man's free hand and took Barny's leash from his other. "And it's so nice to meet you, pup!"

Barny's response was to put his paws on Ella's midsection and almost push her off the porch. She laughed and wrestled the dog off her, escaping with only a wet face.

She should have known, judging by the dog's belly, that Barny was a licker.

"Looks like we got here just in time, huh?" Bill said. He opened the door and pushed Barny inside. "Come on in. When the kid's cooking, he goes into his own world. He must really like working with you to go through all this effort."

With a wink, Bill picked up her bag of goodies and motioned for her to go inside. They passed through a cluttered living room and entered the kitchen, where it looked like three dozen crabs and their accompanying side dishes had exploded. Three pots sat atop the stove, steaming and giving off a zesty odor of spices.

Two plates of hush puppies sat next to a cooling pan of oil, and Ella felt her stomach growl. She'd been so busy all day that she'd forgotten to eat anything since breakfast.

Mitch was at the sink, arms and hands almost a blur as he worked on tossing a huge salad.

"Beer's in the fridge," he called out, wiping flour from his cheek with his shoulder while holding Barny back with one foot. "Food should be ready in a minute." He looked over at Ella and gave her a sheepish smile. "Glad you could make it. You met Dad already?"

Ella nodded. "Sure you don't need help? I'm not the world's greatest cook, but you look a little bit over your head."

"Nah," Mitch said. "This is how I usually work. Grab a beer and have a seat. I told Dad about the gun you found."

"Mind if I take a look?" Bill asked from where he was sitting at the kitchen table, scratching Barny's belly. The bag sat on the table in front of him.

"Sure," Ella said, feeling a bit disappointed that Mitch wasn't preparing this massive crab boil just for the two of them.

But then again, she reminded herself, *I'm not here for romance. I have work to do.*

"It's a pistol," she said. Taking a seat at the table next to Mitch's dad, she carefully opened the bag and removed the chain first. She then took out the pistol and began unwrapping it, peeling off the rags soaked in salt water one by one.

Bill whistled lowly when Ella finally uncovered the rusty old gun. "That's a beauty, Ella. A real find. Mind if I touch it? I've got some experience working with antiques—your Dr. Bramlett and I go way back—and I promise not to muss it up."

Ella nodded, surprised she didn't feel more protective of the gun. It had helped save her from Bonnet, distracting the pirate long enough for Mitch to attack the ghost. But she could tell that Bill knew what he was doing. She pulled out the piece of locket from her jeans and set it on the table as well.

"Have you found a date on it anywhere?" he asked her, holding up the gun and squinting at it.

"Not yet," Ella said. She gestured at the other two items on the table, the chain and the piece of the locket, both of them gleaming silver now instead of black. "I actually haven't looked at it much. I've been busy examining some other finds we've come across today."

"This gun looks to be from that era—it's got the standard firing mechanism and would shoot the round metal shots that the pirates liked to use. And right here . . ." he said, turning the pistol on its side, "looks like a possible date: one seven one five."

Ella squinted at the rusty gun with a smile forming on her face.

"Bingo," Mitch's dad said. "Looks like we have a winner."

"Tell me, Bill," Ella said, leaning down so she could scratch Barny's fat belly. "Can you tell me anything about these?" She pointed at the chain and the locket.

"Hmm," he said. He rubbed his chin in a manner that reminded Ella of Mitch. "Where did you find these?"

"It's a long story, trust me."

"Well," Bill said. He gave a meaningful look over at Mitch. "Looks like we have a little bit of time before we eat. So . . ."

"Okay," Ella said, and she launched into a recounting of where and how they'd found both items. Bill became more and more excited with each sentence, even though she carefully avoided mentioning the three "visitors" they'd encountered on their dives and at the top of the lighthouse. She didn't want the man to think she'd gone completely nuts.

"Sounds like you've got ghosts following you," Bill said once she'd finished. "Maybe they *needed* you to find this locket and chain."

Ella nearly choked on the beer she'd been drinking. *Was everyone in this family obsessed with the supernatural?*

"Amazing," Bill continued. "I know Mitch and especially Melissa have always loved a good ghost story, and I never thought I'd live to see the day when they'd actually start believing in them. No wonder Mitch has been so distracted lately. Poor guy's been haunted."

"Dad," Mitch said. He'd been listening along the whole time, and at some point he'd turned down the music. "Give me a break. You make me and Melissa sound like a couple of flakes."

"And?" Bill said, then he whistled lowly. "I hope one of those is my plate."

When Ella looked up from the table, away from Bill and

Barnacle, the kitchen had been transformed, as if by a miracle. All of the disarray of the crabs and the food and pots and pans had been cleared away, leaving just three plates piled high with crab legs, ramekins of butter, hush puppies, boiled potatoes, slaw, and salad. Another platter of crab legs sat waiting on the counter.

"Who's hungry?" Mitch said.

For the next fifteen minutes, all ghosts, shipwrecks, antique guns, and newfound jewelry were forgotten as the three tore into the crab legs and devoured the hush puppies and all the other trimmings. Ella was amazed at the flavor of the meat, which most likely had been caught that day, and she tried to figure out what spices Mitch had put into the boil. Ordinarily, spicy food made her eyes tear up and feel like steam was coming from her ears, but Mitch had managed to add a certain spiciness and kick to the meat that made Ella sit up straight, but without setting her mouth on fire at the same time.

"That's what we call a 'therapeutic amount' of cayenne pepper," was all Mitch would say when Ella asked about the spices. "Family secret—can't tell you any more. Sorry."

Thanks to her mother's failures in the kitchen, Ella had never been a big fan of cooking, so Ella was always impressed when she met someone who could do such magical things with food. Especially when the cook was a guy like Mitch.

"This is fantastic," she said, cracking open another crab leg with the pliers Mitch had provided.

"Sorry there's no corn on the cob," Mitch said. "Out of season."

"Yeah," his father laughed. "The whole meal is just ruined, all because of the lack of corn on the cob, right, Ella?"

Ella answered by stealing more hush puppies from the

rapidly dwindling bowl in the middle of the table. Barny was whimpering for a treat, but nobody was about to share any of the feast just yet.

"You should see it when he and his little sister get together to throw a party. They have to come over to my place to take advantage of the big stove and extra space we—I—have." Bill's smile faltered for a second, but he continued after a playful nudge in the side from Mitch. "They can sure tear up a kitchen and clean out a fridge and pantry, but the Thompson kids really know how to throw a party. Nobody who's at one of their shindigs needs to eat for days afterwards."

"What can I say? I like to cook every once in a while." Mitch was grinning from ear to ear. "Like every once a year. Good thing the old man here enjoys eating as much as he does, otherwise all our food would go to waste."

Ella liked that smile on Mitch's face, and she liked watching him and his dad laugh and tease each other. There was a kind of sadness that lingered in Bill's eyes, and that sadness had come to the forefront when the older man was talking about his house and he'd corrected himself from "we" to "I." Ella remembered Melissa's story about the death of their mother last year.

As she remembered that fact, she felt something move in her heart. She wanted to get up and give both Thompson men a big hug. She knew what it was like to lose someone.

For the next hour, ignoring the wreckage of crab legs and mostly empty bowls of food in front of them on the kitchen table, Ella listened to Mitch and Bill Thompson tell stories about Mitch, Melissa, and the other kids on the island as they grew up. First Bill told a story about Mitch and Ben going into business, at the ripe age of ten, herding the feral cats around the island and trying to tame them and sell them. Both boys were saved from a painful round of rabies shots when Melissa told on them before their business got off the ground. Then Mitch told about his father's tired old boat losing a race with the ferry one night after Bill and his buddies had been spending the day drinking. Ella laughed until tears spilled from her eyes.

As Mitch kept the beers and stories flowing, Ella felt that same growing warmth in her heart for both men, but especially for Mitch, as she started to learn what he was really like.

All this time, she'd been wrong about him. His silence wasn't caused by a lack of intelligence, as she'd suspected since the first day she'd met him. Watching him and his father together, sharing stories about Mitch's misadventures with Ben and his high school buddies, Ella could see that he was actually a careful, methodical person, choosing his battles carefully even as a teen. Mitch had rarely gotten caught in any of his harmless pranks, including his trip inside the lighthouse, or setting the ponies free late one summer night, only to admit to doing it the next morning and being the first to help corral the ponies again.

Ella tried not to look at the new Mitch across the table from her and gape in amazement just the way he did with her. But the three and a half beers she'd had were making that more difficult.

"I'd better get Barny home," Bill said at the end of yet another story, this one about Melissa and what he called her tree-hugging days. "It's late, and us old pirates need our sleep, you know."

"Thanks for your help with these artifacts," Ella said, feeling a shudder creep up her back when Mitch's father mentioned pirates. "You've helped us a lot."

"Let me know how it all works out, okay, Ella?" He held

out his hand for her and she shook it. "You're nowhere near the mean old Yankee woman that Mitch made you out to be," he added with a wink that almost came too late.

"*Bye*, Dad," Mitch said, leading Bill toward the back door. "Don't fall into the ditch on the way home. I know it's a long four-block walk for an old pirate like you."

"Good luck to you on the expedition, Ella," Bill called. "Ignore my son's rudeness, please."

"Good night," Ella called, just as the door slammed behind Bill and Barnacle the chocolate retriever.

When Mitch returned to the kitchen, Ella was sitting at the table, staring at the kitchen table's wreckage, a sharp contrast to the rest of the clean kitchen. She finished off her bottle of beer and gave Mitch a look when he walked up to her.

"A 'mean old Yankee woman'?" she said. She wasn't sure if she should be laughing at the comment, or if she should be mad about it.

"Dad was a bit drunk," Mitch began.

"I'm surprised he didn't take Barny and go running back home the second he saw me on your front porch."

"Ella, I'm sorry. He was exaggerating what I really said. I think I may have said something about you being pushy—"

" 'Pushy'?"

"Um, I mean, a little impatient?"

"You're digging yourself in deeper, Mitch."

With a long sigh, Mitch threw out his arms. "I surrender. I'm sorry. I was just mad after that first dive, mostly at myself. So I said some things about you to Dad that I didn't mean. And I'm going to kick my old man's butt for bringing it up tonight."

Ella laughed, shaking her head. "Let's just say that neither of us made a good first or second impression on each other, and leave it at that."

Mitch took the empty beer bottle from her hand and held out a hand to help her up from her chair.

"Let me make it up to you by buying you a drink." He nodded at the sliding glass door next to the kitchen that led out onto his back deck. "If you'd like to take a seat on the back deck, I'll bring you a beer."

"Okay," Ella said. She pushed the door open and walked outside to the sound of Mitch's fridge opening, followed by the hiss of two bottles being opened.

Ella barely heard the sounds. She was looking up at the night sky, and the view combined with all her beers and her huge meal made her nearly fall over. She made her way to one of the cold lounge chairs sitting on the deck, and eased her way down onto it. Mitch flicked off the kitchen light, and the stars turned up their wattage even more.

"Mitch," Ella said as he fumbled around looking for her in the darkness of the back deck. "Down here. This is *amazing*."

With the blinds to the windows closed behind them and the big oaks on his lawn blocking all light from the neighbors and the street, Ella had found the perfect spot to gaze at the stars.

"Keep an eye out for shooting stars." Mitch handed Ella her beer and sat in the other deck chair. "Cheers," he said.

"Cheers," she said, clinking her bottle against his on the third attempt to find it. "Thanks for dinner."

"You're welcome. And hey, I hope you didn't mind, me inviting my dad over like that. He was dying to see that pistol."

"It was no problem," Ella said. "I enjoyed meeting him. He's a great guy."

Now that her eyes had adjusted to the darkness, she

could just make out Mitch's face. He was staring up at the night sky, smiling.

"Yeah," he said. "He's had a pretty rough year. But I think he's coming to terms with being a widower. My mom died last year. Cancer."

"I know. Melissa told me. I'm sorry. My dad passed away recently too. Late last year, actually."

"Really? God. I'm sorry, Ella."

"It's okay. Just one of life's little reminders to chase your dreams, I guess. To not waste any more time, because you don't know when your time may come."

"Yeah," Mitch said in a thoughtful voice. "Got to chase those dreams."

Ella leaned back in her chair and watched the night sky. There were too many stars to take in all at once, and talking about her dad had made the stars double, then triple as unexpected tears filled her eyes.

"Tell me about *your* dreams, Mitch." She didn't dare say any more, for fear that he would be able to hear her getting choked up, and she didn't want that.

"Ah, you don't want to hear all that," he said. Ella could hear him squirming in his chair.

"Shooting star!" Ella called out. She nudged Mitch in the side. "Did you see it? That was awesome! I guess I get to make a wish, huh?"

"Sure."

Ella wished for a happy outcome to this diving expedition, figuring that was a general enough wish to cover all sorts of possibilities and outcomes.

"You know, you're really lucky," Ella said, "growing up and living here. It's so peaceful here, so far from the noise and filth of the big cities. And you even get to sit and watch the stars." Ella turned toward him slightly, not wanting to take her eyes off the sky, but needing to see the outlines of Mitch's face at the same time. "I'm still waiting, you know. Tell this mean old Yankee woman about what a guy like you from Ocracoke dreams about. Seriously, I want to know."

After a long pause, as if Mitch was trying to determine if she was pulling his leg or being serious, he gave in.

"Okay," he said. "I told you a little bit about this earlier, on the day we met, about how I've always wanted to own my own diving boat, one twice the size of the *Cassiopeia*. *Cassie*'s a good boat, but she's limited in what she can do and where she can go. With a big boat, I can take more people out onto the water, and go deep-sea fishing or touring or wherever they want to go."

"Wow. But doesn't that mean you'll be dealing with us tourons all the time?"

"That's the other part of my dream. I don't need to overcharge folks to make a living, and I can get by on just a little bit of cash. I want to show people the beauty of the ocean. People who would otherwise never know about it. Regular people, not tourons. I think that would be the perfect job in the world."

Ella was silent next to him, taking it all in.

"Shooting star," Mitch whispered. Ella looked up in time to see it pass overhead, leaving an almost green streak of light in its wake.

"Your turn to make a wish," Ella said. She inched closer to him.

"I don't know what to wish for," he began. "I've got pretty much everything I need . . ."

Ella realized Mitch was looking back at her in the darkness. She jumped and took a quick swallow of beer. She imagined him looking at her with that curious, intense gaze of his.

"Anyway," she said. "I think that's an awesome dream, Mitch. Thanks for sharing it with me. Makes my dream of uncovering Blackbeard's lost ship sound . . . selfish."

"Come on, cut yourself some slack. You're bringing history back to life, discovering these shipwrecks and sharing them with the world. That's about as noble as it gets. I bet your family and friends are totally proud of you."

Ella leaned back in her chair, shrugging her shoulders before she realized Mitch couldn't see that gesture. "I don't have too many friends in Boston anymore," she said. "And I don't have too much to do with my family anymore, not after my dad . . . My mom and I were never close."

"Well, I think what you do is great work, and I'm not just saying that. I remember you talking about the ship at the Jolly Roger the other night, and I could see how much you loved what you were doing. You were . . . you were *on fire* when you were talking about history and discovering lost ships. That's what life's all about, doing what you love to do."

"Thanks, Mitch."

They were both silent for a while, watching the stars and sipping their beers.

"You know," Ella said in a small voice, "being here makes me really miss him. My dad. He's the one who taught me to love the ocean and its history. How you can lose track of time out there on the water, just you and your boat and the waves."

"Smart guy," Mitch said. "Reminds me of my dad."

"They *are* a lot alike," Ella said, reaching a hand over to rest on Mitch's hand. "Good sense of humor, but serious underneath. The way your dad looked at that pistol—that's something my dad would've done. He was suddenly all business, and then a minute later he was bubbling over with excitement over the new find."

"Yeah," Mitch whispered. His hand squeezed Ella's a tiny bit tighter.

Before she knew what she was doing, the words were spilling out of her in a rush.

"Dad went fast, once he was diagnosed. Almost faster than we could get his affairs together. I'd never wanted to have a brother or a sister more than those last months with Dad. And my mom wasn't much help. We went sailing almost every day, toward the end. That was the best part, just my dad and me."

Ella used her free hand to wipe her eyes.

"Yeah," Mitch said. "My mom was tired all the time, but the woman refused to rest, and she was working part-time at Styron's store and cooking meals for all four of us right up until the day before she had to go to the hospital on the mainland. Even though he knew it had been coming for over a year, Dad was devastated."

Ella sniffled next to him, but she didn't let go of Mitch or wipe her eyes.

"I'm sorry, Mitch, to bring up all this—"

"Shh," he said, and she could hear the tears in his voice. "Just look at the stars. It's okay, Ella."

"Thanks." Ella sank back in her chair and tried to open her eyes as wide as she could so she could take in all the stars. Soon her tears had dried up.

"You know, I haven't talked to anyone about all that before."

"You're welcome, Ella. Now, just look up."

For almost half an hour they sat like that on his back deck, hand in hand, watching the sky move slowly past. The silence of the night was interrupted only by the occasional rumbling motor of a car passing Mitch's house, a car that sounded suspiciously like an old Mercedes. Ella imagined the white-haired tourons passing by in their Mercedes, looking for trouble, and smiled. Then her attention went back to the stars above the two of them, and she forgot about everything else.

Chapter Seventeen

Somewhere in the course of their late night together, Mitch had gotten up and started mixing drinks and then sharing them with Ella. By the time she left at half past one—Mitch insisted he walk her home—they were both leaning on each other to keep from falling onto the dew-heavy grass of the lawns around them.

As they staggered down the road in the dark, Ella couldn't stop talking and talking. She didn't even know what she was saying anymore, something about teaching one minute, something about sailing with her father the next minute. It felt so good, she had realized, to just *talk* with someone else again. Especially someone like Mitch, someone she'd misjudged so badly.

Mitch just laughed at her constant chattering and aimed her up her front sidewalk.

And then they were standing in her doorway. Ella had to adjust to standing still again, and her balance felt off, just like it sometimes did after a long day of diving.

"Hope Red-Eye left my key alone," she said, and burst into a fit of giggles.

"Got to be careful of those ghosts," Mitch said, stepping close to her just as she lost her balance. He kept her from falling by putting his hands on her waist.

"Thanks," Ella said. She didn't know where to put her arms, caught inside Mitch's grasp, so she rested the palms of her hands on his chest. His heart was thumping like a tiny engine barely contained by the muscles of his chest.

She looked up at him. "Did I thank you for supper already?"

"About ten times on the walk over here," he said, sliding his hands up a few inches higher.

Ella took a shallow breath. "Right. It really was a good meal. And the drinks, too."

"You're welcome," he whispered. His head angled down to her, just as it had outside the cemetery that afternoon.

Ella felt the world begin to spin a tiny bit faster as she angled her face up to his, and their lips met.

As they kissed, her mouth opened the slightest bit so her tongue could touch his lips. He tasted like bourbon and cayenne pepper. She put her arms around him and pulled him up against her. In return, his arms swallowed her up.

She reached up to touch his cheek and continued on to touch his hair, something she'd wanted to do ever since the day they'd met. She'd wondered how it would feel, if it was soft or thick or tangled. But before she could find out, Mitch pulled away.

Ella stepped back, swaying slightly in the doorway and trying to catch her breath.

"Ella—" he began.

"Mitch—" she said at the same time. She'd been alone for so long, even when she'd been with others, that she couldn't stop the words from her mouth now.

"Will you come in?" she said.

"Oh, Ella," Mitch began. "I just . . . I don't . . ."

Ella barely heard the rest of his answer, something about not mixing business with pleasure. But she'd seen the glitter of desire in his eyes, she was certain of it.

"Mitch, it's okay. Just stay here."

Mitch was already stepping down onto the first of her three front steps. "Maybe at the end of the dive," he whispered. "It's late . . . We need to get up early tomorrow to get to Portsmouth . . . I should just . . ."

Mitch gave up trying to explain and stepped down to the sidewalk. At that moment, Ella remembered why she never opened herself up to anyone else like that anymore. Not since her dad was alive, and probably never since.

"Damn it, Mitch," she said, but she didn't think he'd heard her. He was on the sidewalk, backing away from her.

She turned to reach for her house key and accidentally elbowed the birdhouse Owen had given her. It rocked back and forth as she leaned against the closed door. Feeling like she was being thrown around on the ocean during a storm, she slowly slid down to the floor of the porch.

There had been a look in his eyes, hadn't there? She needed to get up, to run after him and look once more to confirm what she'd seen in those pale blue eyes.

But he was gone now, his footsteps fading into the night, leaving Ella alone with her swinging birdhouse and whirling head and churning emotions. After half a minute of fumbling around for it, she found her house key, which had been in her jeans pocket the whole time, safe from passing ghosts.

In her bed that night, as she slept with the room slowly turning in circles and her lips still tasting the spices of Mitch's lips, Ella dreamed of Caroline, her ghost girl.

In the dream, Ella was back underwater. She wasn't wearing her mask or her mouthpiece, and she couldn't feel the reassuring weight of the air tanks on her back. But she felt completely at ease under the water. The water was warm as bath water, caressing her skin. She blinked her eyes in her dream and found herself inside the small cave again, where she'd first met Caroline.

But this time the chunk of the ship hull was no longer half-buried in the sand. Someone had lifted it up and leaned it against the dark rock of the cave wall. The twelve feet of exposed wood from the underside of the hull had remained untouched by time. Ella felt a dream-thrill run through her. The wall was covered in scratches and words—evidence and history.

In the dream, she looked down and saw she was still wearing the faded jeans and blouse from her dinner with Mitch and his father. Something felt off about her clothing, as if she were missing some important article of clothing or wearing something that didn't belong to her. Had Red-Eye stopped by her place to hide one of her necklaces?

But Ella didn't care about that now. She needed to read what was on that wall.

She remembered the chicken scratches and hash marks from earlier, the signs that somebody had been keeping track of how many days he—or she—had been imprisoned. But that was only on the lower section, which had been the section she'd been able to raise from the sandy bottom during her last visit. This time she saw more initials and numbers. The "58" she'd thought she'd seen before was actually an "S" and a "B." Those letters made sense now; they were the initials of the pirate who once commanded this ship. He probably made those marks during his imprisonment by Blackbeard on his own ship.

When Ella reached up to touch the scratches in the piece of the hull, she felt the water go icy. A tiny, scared voice whispered in her ear.

"Dig *deeper*," Caroline said. "Save me, Ella."

The familiar orange glow grew on Ella's right, and when she looked away from the wall, she saw Caroline again. This time the girl was dressed in a simple white dress that reached to the ocean floor, though the girl floated a good two feet above the ground.

"I'm digging as best I can," Ella said, speaking out loud instead of simply thinking her thoughts. "But I'm missing something. You haven't told me everything, Caroline."

"What more do you need to know? Prove that Bonnet killed me out of spite, leaving me trapped in his prison to drown like a rat. Prove it." Caroline's eyes opened wide with fear and something else, something that Ella couldn't see clearly. "You found the locket he gave me, and his chain? Have you been *talking* to him?"

"We've met a few times," Ella said, gazing at the almost-transparent girl's dress. "And I'm none the worse for it. Tell me, Caroline, why are you wearing that lovely dress? It looks like a wedding dress."

Caroline reached down to touch the lace of her bodice. Her face seemed to flush, if such a thing could happen to ghosts.

"You didn't tell me you were married, Caroline."

"I didn't think," Caroline began, "that is, I didn't want . . . I mean, I'm not . . ."

"Caroline," Ella said, feeling the water growing colder around her as a distant thumping sound tickled at her ears. She had suddenly made the connection she'd been missing for the past few days. "Why didn't you tell me you married Stede Bonnet?"

"You're just dreaming," Caroline said, floating away from Ella. She was starting to shrink, somehow, and her orange-tinted light was fading. "If you bury the locket and the chain, I think that will be enough. I can rest then, I think."

"Don't leave yet," Ella hissed. The pirate Bonnet was coming, she could feel it. "I *do* want to help you. Where's

202

the rest of your locket? And you're only telling me half of your story. What happened to you, Caroline?"

Caroline's ghostly lips quivered, and her eyes suddenly went dark with anger. Ella stepped back against the scratched-up hull of the ship and felt it teeter, as if it was about to topple over on her. She looked down and saw that her skin and body, just like Caroline's, were becoming more and more transparent with each blast of the approaching cannons.

Bonnet will be here soon.

"No!" Caroline shrieked, her voice harsh as a banshee. "You don't need to *know* any more about me! Just show the world that Stede Bonnet was no gentleman, especially to his new wife Caroline!"

Caroline's tiny hands went to her mouth even as she faded farther from Ella's sight, as if Bonnet's presence made the girl shrink inside herself.

Shivering now with the cold, Ella inched away from the wall of the cave. She was afraid she'd pass right through it if she kept fading like this. The thunder of the cannons was making the wall quiver. Her hands had grown suddenly, painfully cold.

"Caroline," she whispered, and the air—water?—burned in her lungs. *All of this was impossible,* she thought, but she couldn't convince herself this was just a dream. "He's *coming.* Stay with me and talk to him. He can't hurt you if you don't let him."

"You don't know that!" Caroline was tearing at her dress, shredding the long white sleeves. "If he can let his own Caroline drown, he's capable of anything."

"Stay," Ella said, but Caroline had already shrunk to a small dot of weak orange light. The glowing light hovered for a moment in the spot where Caroline's heart would have been a moment earlier. When the final explosion of the approaching cannon merged into Bonnet's mad laughter, all traces of Caroline disappeared completely. Ella was freezing cold, her hands almost invisible even though she held them in front of her face.

"And here you are again, my little meddler."

Turning her body toward the entrance took so much effort that Ella felt like she'd been encased in ice. At the entrance to the cave hovered the sickly looking presence of Stede Bonnet, glowing with an unhealthy blue light. The pirate had changed, and for the worst. Most of Bonnet's beard had fallen out, leaving just strands of graying hair on his chin. His dark coat was covered with barnacles and snails, and his silky shirt was pockmarked and filled with worms.

"You don't look so hot, Mr. Bonnet," Ella said, fumbling at her words with her numb lips.

This is my dream, she decided suddenly. Her hands thawed the tiniest bit as she thought, *I refuse to let him scare me anymore.*

"You know nothing about heat," Bonnet said, inching closer. The skin of his face looked perilously thin, the bones too close to the surface. "I've seen the very fires of hell, and let me assure you, I prefer the icy touch of water."

With each word, the cold increased all around her, covering her and overwhelming her dream self, until Ella felt herself going numb again.

Her response—surprising even herself—was a smile. She knew Bonnet's secret now, and she wasn't afraid to use it against him. The man deserved it.

"Your wife was none too pleased with you, Bonnet. What did you do to her? Why did you let her drown?"

"Stay out of business that's not yours, lass," Bonnet

said. Ella thought she saw a flicker of pain cross his gaunt face. "She was only supposed to stay locked up for a day, as punishment for running away, but then we came under attack."

Bonnet stopped, his face darkening in much the same way that Caroline's had earlier.

Apparently, Ella thought, *ghosts weren't that good at keeping their own secrets. At least not in dreams.*

"Damn it all to hell. This is not your concern, lass! Meddling people like you often get hurt, and you can end up hurting those around you as well. Begone!"

Accompanied by a sudden fusillade of cannon fire, Ella felt herself being pulled up out of the cave. Ears popping and frozen legs and arms kicking, she fought against Bonnet's pulling, but the ghost's will was too strong.

She burst out of the water to more cannon fire. For one moment she was out in Ocracoke Inlet, above the shipwreck, and the next moment the dream had shifted her to Teach's Hole. Close enough to touch, Mitch's boat passed by her, aiming for Silver Lake Harbor. *Cassie* was under attack by an ancient ship, and she already had a pair of round holes in her hull. The cannons of the fiery ghost ship were remarkably accurate and lethal. It was the same ship she'd seen from the lighthouse.

Ella saw Mitch at last, picking himself up from the floor of his Sea Cat, struggling to get to the wheel. In his hand he held the ancient pistol.

"Mitch!" she screamed. "Get out of there! Get—"

Before she could say more, Ella was launched into the air. With another ear-popping sensation, she looked around and saw she was inside the cockpit of a tiny six-seat plane, flying a thousand feet above the ocean.

Don't panic, she tried to tell herself, but her dream body wouldn't cooperate. She was screaming as the plane bounced up and down through turbulence.

She heard one last cannon blast from far below her as the plane flew higher. She was pushed back into her seat, knowing what would happen next. Pinching herself to try to wake, she saw nothing but clear blue sky in front of her.

We're too high, she thought. *We shouldn't be this high. Not in this little puddle-jumper.*

And then the twin engines of the plane died. Their forward momentum in the air stopped, and the plane began to freefall back toward the water, nose-first. Ella stopped screaming, and the sudden silence was deafening. She could feel the brute force of gravity pulling the plane down to the ocean like a greedy, hungry monster. Their freefall was picking up speed.

"Wake up, wake up, wake up," Ella muttered until she was shushed by the pilot.

"It's okay," the pilot said, and Ella wasn't even surprised when she saw it was Mitch sitting at the controls of the plane. "We just hit a bad patch of air. Hold tight. We'll be okay."

Her stomach in her throat, Ella couldn't even inhale as the ocean approached. The last thing she saw before the impact was the sight of *Cassiopeia* sinking slowly into the blue waters of Silver Lake Harbor.

The image was so wrong and out of place that Ella had no choice but to end her dream and wake up.

When she opened her eyes, gasping for breath and gripping the sheets around her, she half-imagined that Mitch was sleeping next to her. She even went so far as to touch the emptiness of the bed next to her. Nothing.

He should be here, she thought, more disappointed than

she cared to admit, even to herself. *But no, the only occupant of this bed,* she thought, *is one hungover professor who had way too many beers and who knew how many mixed drinks last night, watching for shooting stars.*

And then she felt the sinking feeling of having done something incredibly stupid last night while she was drunk. As the images of the ghosts from her dreams and the sensation of falling out of control began to fade from her mind, she thought hard, trying to remember just what had happened when Mitch escorted her back to her place late last night.

The events were coming back to her, slowly. The walk back, her constant chattering, the kiss in her doorway. The *long* kiss, which should've been longer. The invitation—*her* invitation—for Mitch to come inside.

She put a hand to her aching head. She didn't want to think about how she'd wanted so badly to keep him close while they were kissing, needing to ease the pain of both their losses and push away the fear that had followed them for the past few days.

"I invited him in," she said with a groan. "I must've *really* been drunk."

She also remembered, right before she'd dropped off into her dream-filled sleep, experiencing a flurry of emotions—feeling both aroused and frustrated, happy and angry with Mitch all at the same time.

"I am such an idiot," Ella said, falling back onto her bed. She was afraid to close her eyes for fear that she'd find herself back on the plane, heading straight down. Or back in Mitch's arms, trying to pull him closer.

The sudden trilling of her phone knocked her out of her guilt-induced reverie and growing disbelief at what she'd done and said last night. *How am I supposed to work with him after all that happened last night?*

She had no answer to that question, so she picked up the phone instead.

"Hello?"

"So tell me," a deep, familiar voice said, with a trace of impatience, "what's the news for your expedition? I'm assuming because you haven't been e-mailing or calling me with updates that you've been incredibly busy taking notes and getting all the facts straight about Blackbeard's ship. Am I correct?"

"Well," Ella said, trying to talk despite the cotton-mouth she was feeling, "of course. It's been an interesting week, Dr. Bramlett. Let me, um, tell you *all* about it . . ."

Chapter Eighteen

Ella made her way down to the Jolly Roger, where Mitch had docked *Cassie*. She was glad that her headache had finally gone away. Talking to Dr. Bramlett hadn't been nearly as bad as she'd feared it would be, and he was actually under the impression that the dive was going pretty much as planned. He would be sending a crew down in a week to start the intensive detail work on the wreck, and Ella just needed to get everything in order by then.

"Plenty of time," Dr. Bramlett had said, "for you to explore every nook and cranny on your own."

"No problem," she'd answered, looking at the piece of the locket, gleaming silver now that she'd polished it along with its accompanying chain. "Everything will be taken care of by then."

With the sun warming her face and the breeze wiping away almost all traces of her hangover, she hoped that she and Mitch were up to the challenge. Time was running short, for all of them.

She hadn't taken more than two steps on the walkway next to the Jolly Roger before she realized something bad had happened. Something from a nightmare.

"Oh my God," she said, looking out into the harbor and dropping her bag of equipment.

Half-sunk into the shallow water of the harbor, the *Cassiopeia* listed at an unnatural forty-five-degree angle. Water filled the lower compartments, and the raised console containing the wheel and navigation equipment now rested against the pier. As Ella stared, mouth hanging open, the ship sank even farther into the lake.

A gray lump sat on the dock in front of the flooded ship. The lump moved, and Ella realized it was Mitch, sitting slumped forward with his arms wrapped around his knees.

"God damn it," he was whispering in a dead voice as Ella approached him.

Tell me I'm dreaming, Ella thought, *and I need to wake up.*

"Mitch?" she whispered. "Mitch, are you okay?"

Mitch didn't move to acknowledge Ella's presence. Ella took careful steps toward the ruined boat, holding her breath, afraid to jar the pier and cause *Cassie* to sink any farther. She wanted to go to Mitch, but she was afraid of what might be going through his head. Instead, she peered over the almost-horizontal console at the starboard hull.

She gasped at what she saw. Two ragged holes had been blasted into the side of the hull, and it looked as if the holes had gone straight through the boat, through the port side.

Just like my dream last night, she thought, her headache coming back full force.

"Mitch." Her voice was barely audible above the blood rushing through her ears. "Mitch, what *happened?*"

Mitch lifted his head and looked up at Ella for the first time. His bloodshot eyes were wide and full of shock. His hands balled up into fists.

"What *happened?*" He got to his feet, shaking visibly. "Your damn expedition happened! How do I explain this to the insurance guys? Do I tell them that Stede Bonnet, a pirate who's been dead for, oh, about three hundred years, dropped by Silver Lake in the dead of night in his resurrected ship and blasted two holes into my ship? Think that'll fly?"

"Mitch," Ella said. "I'm so sorry. I . . . I don't know how

this could have happened."

Mitch turned back to his boat again. Ella followed his gaze. Seeing *Cassie* like this made her heart hurt along with her head. The boat was most likely damaged beyond repair. *But how?*

"What can I do to help?" she whispered. "Anything, Mitch."

"No," Mitch said, getting to his feet in a flurry of motion. He turned his back on *Cassie* and stormed up to Ella. He looked her straight in the eye.

"This is too much, Ella. This project has been cursed from the start. I've had enough." Mitch swallowed hard. "I quit."

As if determined to get away from her and the wrecked ship before she could stop him, he hurried past her, his feet pounding on the wooden walkway. He trudged into the main section of the Jolly Roger and disappeared behind a table at the far side of the building.

Ella stared at the swamped Sea Cat in front of her, still feeling her heart hammering inside her chest at Mitch's words.

I've had enough. Cursed from the start. I quit.

Most of their diving equipment was still aboard *Cassie*, she noticed. Mitch always secured their gear in the lock boxes below the front section of the boat, and they'd need to get that equipment out and salvage what they could from the rest of the boat.

All was not lost, she decided, in spite of what Mitch had said.

She tried not to think about the dreams about the future he'd shared with her late last night as they were stargazing. He wouldn't be able to chase those dreams without a boat. But she knew if she stopped to think about all that he'd lost

211

with the sinking of his boat, she would surely give up hope just like he had.

Instead, she found help with Melissa and Ben. Sneaking up to the side entrance of the Jolly Roger, which would open for the day in half an hour, she managed to pull Ben and Melissa away from the restaurant without getting Mitch's attention. She glanced inside the restaurant for a moment; Mitch sat in the corner, head down on the table with his back to *Cassie* and the harbor. He looked like a broken old man there.

Ella was determined to keep him from losing hope. She felt responsible for his loss, as if simply dreaming about the destruction of *Cassie* had made it a reality.

"What do you think happened?" Melissa said. Ben had been silently fuming ever since Ella and Melissa had led him from his restaurant. He'd taken the vandalism of Mitch's ship personally.

"I wish I knew." Ella pointed at the locked boxes strapped to the uneven deck of the boat. "Think we can get some of that stuff off there without killing ourselves?"

By eleven, Melissa and Ben had helped her clear out all the diving equipment from *Cassie*. She could tell the boat had stopped sinking at last, and it was now resting awkwardly on the lake floor. After they'd hauled the equipment back to her place in four trips of her Escort, Melissa and Ben told her they had to get back to the Jolly Roger to work.

"I owe you guys, big time," Ella said before they left.

"Just find out who did this," Ben said, "and that'll be payment enough for me."

"Mitch is going to have a hard time getting over this," Melissa said. "What are you guys going to do now?"

Ella shrugged at Melissa and looked at the two holes

blasted into *Cassie*'s hull. It had been a long time since she'd studied the effects of cannonballs on ship hulls, and the effect was somewhat distorted by the fact that Mitch's ship was made of mostly fiberglass and metal instead of the wooden ship of pirate times. But there was no doubt in Ella's mind of what had caused the damage.

Somehow Stede Bonnet had managed to resurrect his sunken ship and hold it together long enough to blast two holes into the Sea Cat. That was the only explanation. To hell with logic and physics at this point.

Bonnet was getting stronger and stronger, making more of a physical presence on the island, and he had to be stopped. As painful as it might be to Mitch right now, they had no choice but to continue on and solve this mystery. Caroline needed them to get to Portsmouth, and even more importantly, the island of Ocracoke needed them to put to rest the ghosts of Stede Bonnet and Caroline Amberson.

With that thought in mind, Ella set off toward the Jolly Roger to do some serious convincing with Mitch Thompson, captain of the submerged *Cassiopeia*.

From the start, Mitch refused to listen to any of what Ella was saying.

His head in his hands and his elbows on the table, he barely moved as Ella spoke, even when Melissa put a plate of fries and onion rings in front of him and touched his shoulder.

"One more week," Ella said. "Even one more day, Mitch. Stick it out with me, please. I know you're hurting. I know what *Cassie* meant to you—"

"Don't talk about her in the past tense," Mitch said without raising his head.

"*Means* to you. What *Cassie* means to you, Mitch. But

what's happening here is bigger than all of us—you, me, *Cassie*, your friends and family here in Ocracoke. Something got jump-started on the day you found the shipwreck, and now we've got to stop it before it runs out of control."

"So it's all my fault," Mitch said in a muffled voice. "Since I found the shipwreck, it's my fault. Great. Thanks, Ella. You're doing a *great* job of cheering me up."

Ella took a deep breath. He seemed so beaten, so different from the way he was last night.

Can you blame him? she asked herself. *He just saw the love of his life sink almost completely into the harbor.*

She picked up an onion ring and nibbled on it. There was something that Mitch hadn't told her at first, something that had slipped out the other night. She squinted at his lowered head and tried to remember. She ate the onion ring and was reaching for another when a gleam of sunlight flashed on the lake next to the restaurant. The light reminded her of the story Mitch had told about how he'd found the shipwreck.

"Mitch," she said. "Do you think that this could all be Blackbeard's doing?"

He lifted his head and looked at Ella for the first time. She flinched at the black look in his eyes.

"What are you talking about? This was someone sabotaging my ship. Maybe Bonnet's ghost, or maybe just some crazy bastard with a cannon who's out to get me. Blackbeard had nothing to do with all this."

"You're right—about your ship. But I think Blackbeard started it all." Ella put her hands on the table to keep them from shaking wildly. She was starting to see the patterns, now that she had all the various threads of the story. "You said so yourself, the other day. How you saw that strange light that led you to the shipwreck. What color was that light, Mitch?"

"*Color?* I don't remember any color. What does it matter now?"

"It matters, believe me. Let's just suppose each ghost"— she winced when she used the word, but reminded herself to keep her mind open—"suppose each one has a signature glow or hue that it carries with them. I've seen it. Caroline's is usually orange. Bonnet is usually a sickly blue color. And Blackbeard, I think, is more of a—"

"Bright white," Mitch finished for her. He was looking at her, a hint of the old Mitch intensity in his eyes. Just a hint. Yet his voice was still dead and emotionless. "Almost a pure white, but flickering sometimes, like a strobe light."

He picked up a pair of fries and started munching on them. Ella smiled, glad to see signs of life in him at last. Something tight in her chest suddenly loosened.

"So let's just theorize wildly for a minute here," she said. "Let's say that Blackbeard is instigating all this. Not Bonnet, not Caroline. And it's been a long time coming— almost three centuries. Maybe he's tired of haunting the island, too. But for him to rest, I imagine he'll want to get his head back. He told us that much at the top of the light-house."

Ella smacked the table, surprising herself. Mitch simply stared at her. "And Bonnet has his head! See? It's all coming together!"

Ella thought she saw the flicker of enthusiasm in Mitch's eyes, and then the flame dwindled and died. She spoke quickly, needing to finish with her crazy hypothesis.

"And Bonnet doesn't want to let Caroline rest in peace, because he's up to . . . something. More mischief, maybe some unfinished business with his sunken ship? So maybe

Blackbeard wanted us to help with Caroline first, and then . . ."

Mitch was shaking his head.

"Ella," he said. "Listen to what you're saying. And you thought I was crazy with all my ghost rules." He sighed and dropped the half-eaten fry from his hand. "I'm sorry. I just can't do this anymore. I'm done."

Mitch gave Ella one last look before lowering his gaze to stare at the cooling plate of fried food in front of them. In that look, Ella had seen a kind of desperate sadness that was so unlike the Mitch she'd gotten to know in the past week that she was half-convinced she'd imagined it. His pale blue eyes had looked empty instead of thoughtful and filled with the dreams of the future.

Without wanting to, she remembered the spicy taste of his lips, and how she wanted to taste them again. But she was afraid if she ever kissed him again, all she'd taste would be ashes. With the sinking of *Cassie*, Mitch had given up.

Ella rubbed her face, massaging her sore temples. She couldn't let Mitch's sense of despair continue. She gazed out at the glistening lake and cloudless sky outside. As if on cue, a line of over a dozen pelicans flew overhead, all long gray wings and rounded beaks.

"Mitch," she said, touching his chin and moving his head so he could see outside. "Just look up."

The pelicans formed a ragged V, moving fast as they headed toward Pamlico Sound. Without speaking, she watched the birds until they disappeared into the horizon. Ella left her hand on Mitch's chin, feeling the stubble there that she remembered from their kiss last night. Then he suddenly pulled away.

She looked at Mitch, expecting another angry outburst.

"That's *it*," he whispered, his eyes wide not with shock

or rage, but pure, unadulterated excitement. "I know how we can get to Portsmouth. We can go right now. We've *got* to go right now, while it's still light."

Mitch was already on his feet, stuffing a five-dollar bill under their plate. "Can you drive us there?"

"Where are we going?"

"The Ocracoke Airport. It's been a while since I did any flying."

"What do you mean?"

Mitch gave her a determined look. "I can fly us to Portsmouth."

Oh no, Ella thought, following him out of the restaurant, almost overwhelmed at the familiar sense of dread she felt whenever she thought about flying. *Looks like all our nightmares are coming true this week, for Mitch and me both.*

Chapter Nineteen

A half hour later, Ella was sitting in Mitch's plane, her hands shaking so badly she couldn't get her seat belt closed. She hoped Mitch, busy with the instruments on the small plane's control panel, hadn't noticed. In spite of all she and Mitch had been through, she still had her pride, and she was afraid he'd just scoff at her fear of flying, or act like her worries were groundless, just like Steven had done.

"So," she said in as calm a voice as she could muster once she'd managed to get her seat belt locked, "how long have you been flying, Mitch?"

"Got my pilot's license a year and a half ago," he said. His voice was distant as he worked the engine and tapped on dials and pressed buttons.

Ella jumped when the plane began to move forward to the end of the runway. She forced herself to stop holding her breath.

"I used to take my parents and Melissa for a ride over Ocracoke and Portsmouth every now and then. My mom always said the trip between the two islands felt like the longest flight she'd ever been on."

Mitch paused for a moment in his preparations, as if suddenly reminded of all he'd lost. Ella pushed back most of her fear of flying as best she could so she could touch his hand.

He took a quick breath and looked over at her. "Sorry," he said. "Just thinking about . . . Never mind. Let's get up in the air, what do you say?"

"Sure," she said. She was already dreading the sensation of weightlessness that was coming, but she didn't dare say a word about it to Mitch. Not after this morning. He had enough to worry about. She took her hand away from his and held onto her armrests instead.

"It's okay," Mitch said as the plane began to roll forward and pick up speed. "I know what I'm doing. Just relax and enjoy the sights."

"Just get us there," Ella whispered, and then they were up in the air. She held her breath until her ears popped, and she stared out the window only at the sky, refusing to look down. Her hands began to ache from squeezing her armrests so tightly. She wished she would have sat in the back of the plane, with a blanket over her head.

When her vertigo reached the point where she wasn't sure if she could stand it any longer, the plane began to drop. Convinced he was about to crash them into the ocean, Ella almost reached over to grab Mitch. Then she saw the green island in front of and below them, growing larger by the second. Her stomach leaped into her throat. The island was nearly lost in the deep blue vastness of the Atlantic and Pamlico Sound. The island was way too small, and it was approaching much too fast.

"Portsmouth Island," Mitch announced, oblivious to Ella's torment. "Man, that place brings back the memories. Me and Ben and all our friends from Ocracoke have spent a ton of summer days here. We'd boat over with our parents—or we'd borrow one from our parents—and then we'd spend a couple nights here, camping out and getting eaten alive by the mosquitoes."

Ella forced her gaze back up at the sky, away from the upcoming ground. She tried to focus on their mission to distract herself from gravity.

According to what Mitch had told her over lunch, the island had been deserted for the past thirty years. The last people on the island were descendents of the so-called "pilots" who helped guide ships through Ocracoke Inlet and Pamlico Sound, and they had all moved away in the early seventies. All that was left were two dozen buildings, a couple cemeteries, and swamp land. And the departing islanders had also left the narrow grass airstrip that the plane's wheels had come to rest upon.

They had landed. Ella opened her eyes, not knowing when she'd closed them.

"We're here," Mitch said, turning to her for the first time since entering the plane. "Ella. You can breathe now."

She had no trouble with the seat belt this time. She was out of her chair and pushing her way out of the little twin-propeller plane before Mitch could turn off everything. By the time he got outside she was already a hundred feet away from the plane, tempted to kiss the ground. She was already dreading the flight back to Ocracoke.

Slapping at a fat mosquito, Ella turned in a slow circle to see what the island had to offer. Off to the north was a long sloping roof of what had to be the old Coast Guard station. Mitch had told her that it was one of the few buildings on the island still open to the public. He'd also told her how he and Ben had spent summer afternoons inside that big gray barn, pretending to be heroes and trying to spot pirate ships from the cupola.

As she stared at the main building and the empty stable next to it, Ella heard a distant tromping sound. It sounded like the beating of horses' hooves on the dirt path next to the airstrip, but it was gone before she could tell for sure. Ella brushed away more of the aggressive mosquitoes from around her ears. She shivered and squinted at the beach to the east, but she couldn't see any horses or wild ponies anywhere. She half-expected a ghostly team of white Coast Guard horses to come thundering up the path toward them, chasing after a fire or shipwreck close to the island.

"So," Mitch said, tossing her an industrial-sized can of bug repellant. "Why are you so afraid of flying? It's just as safe as driving, or . . . going out in a boat . . ." Mitch grimaced at the mention of boating.

"It's a long story," Ella began. She coated her bare skin with the bug repellant and handed it back to Mitch.

"Well, we've got some walking to do," Mitch said, nodding at the dirt road leading east and west, away from the airstrip. "The first cemetery is up by Henry's Creek, off to the west there. So why don't you tell me that story on our way there?"

"Okay," Ella said with a sigh. Her pulse was finally returning to normal. "It was my second plane flight as a kid, and my parents and I were going to a cousin's wedding in Florida. Hurricane Hugo was tearing up the coast at the same time, and we got caught in the windstorm. We dropped over a thousand feet before the pilots regained control."

"Oh, man."

"Well," she continued. "I freaked out. I was about ten years old, and I just started screaming. I didn't stop until we landed. Needless to say, my dad rented a car, and we drove back to Boston from Florida. And I've done my best not to have to get into a plane since. I'd rather drive—at least I have some sense of control over what's happening."

"Ah, damn, Ella, I didn't know." Mitch stopped and gave her an apologetic look. "We could've chartered a boat, you know. I'm sorry. You could've told me."

"No," she said. "Flying here was quicker. I think things

are coming to a head here, and we need to move fast." They started walking again, and Ella looked back over her shoulder at the plane off in the distance. "And sometimes you just have to face your fears and plunge into the great unknown. Don't get me started on the bad dreams I've had lately, almost all of them about flying." She took a deep breath and added, "And, anyway, Mitch, I trust you. I knew you wouldn't crash."

"Thanks," he said with just the slightest touch of sarcasm and, even better, the hint of a smile. Ella hoped he was finally recovering from this morning's shock.

As they walked, the silence of the island was heavy as a blanket wrapped around them. Even the oversized mosquitoes had left them alone. Ella wanted to tiptoe to keep from disturbing the peace. They passed a clutch of trees, and an old church came into view.

"Look at that," Ella whispered. "It's beautiful."

The bright white church stood proudly by itself, its black and white steeple rising above the sparse trees surrounding it. The brown grass around it was struggling against the creeping approach of the sand, leaving it a bit patchy, but it was all a uniform length. Someone had been here recently to cut the grass for the first time this year.

"The old Methodist church," Mitch said. "The preservation society people have been working on restoring the old buildings here. The church was one of the first places they fixed up."

Next to the church was a slow-moving creek that drained into the sound. It was surrounded by prickly green marsh grass. Mitch led Ella to an almost-hidden path running parallel to it.

"And here we are," Mitch said. "Cemetery number one."

Overgrown and nearly hidden in the tidal flatland next to the sound, they would have missed the graveyard altogether if Mitch hadn't known it was there. In front of them sat half a dozen battered markers, and all of them looked blank and washed-out from where she was standing. Ella began to take a step closer when Mitch grabbed her hand.

"Do you smell that?" he said, his face scrunched together. He slapped at a mosquito as big as a bee that was trying to take a bite out of his neck. "Like something burning, maybe?"

"But you said nobody lived here anymore, right?" Ella slipped out of his grip and waded through the weeds to the first marker.

A cold breeze blew onto her from the northeast, carrying with it the smell of burning wood and oil. Ella paused, sniffing the air. The wind and the smell were both coming from the inlet, in the approximate direction where Bonnet's shipwreck was. But the shipwreck was at least ten miles away.

"I smell it now, too," Ella said, and then stopped. Just as quickly as it had arrived, the wind changed direction, and the odor disappeared.

"Maybe it was just our imaginations," Mitch said after a few more seconds of sniffing the air. "All these poltergeists are getting to us, I guess."

Ella gave him a lingering look. "I hope not," she said. "Tell you what," she said, "I'll cover your back if you cover mine. Deal? Now let's do some weeding."

But after half an hour of searching the grass around the crooked, forgotten gravestones of the cemetery, with the sky clouding up and the wind blowing even harder now, Mitch and Ella came up with nothing. Not even the headstones, when they were able to make out what was engraved upon them, gave any clues. Just a name—either a Dixon or a Babb—and if they were lucky, a date of birth and a date of death. Nothing more. The Dixons and the Babbs, like the other former residents of Portsmouth, had been hardworking, straightforward people. Nothing fancy for their cemetery.

At least, not this one.

"Let's check out the other graveyard," Ella said. She almost had to shout so Mitch could hear her above the rising wind.

"Wait," he said. "Do you hear that?"

At first all Ella could hear was the wind, and then she caught the rustling sound coming from the other end of the cemetery. The weeds were moving back and forth, as if something was digging into the dirt back there, behind two faded headstones.

Or, she thought, a thrill of fear flashing through her so fast she lost her breath, maybe it was something digging its way *out* of the dirt.

"Let's leave it be, whatever it is," Ella began to say, but Mitch was already creeping up to the pair of gray headstones.

The rustling sound increased and spread, until what seemed to Ella like the entire field north of the old graveyard was alive with it.

"Mitch," she whispered, but he wasn't listening, and the wind was growing stronger, bringing back the smell of smoke.

Mitch took another step closer to the edge of the field just as the grass in front of him exploded. A harsh blatting sound filled the air, along with the mad fluttering of gray and black wings.

"Geese!" Ella said, ducking as one of the black-necked

birds tried to take a bite out of her head. Dozens of them came spilling out of the weeds and bursting into the air above them. "Run for your life, Mitch!"

Mitch picked himself up off the ground from where he'd hit the deck to avoid the first flight of angry birds. Ella grabbed him on her way past, with the geese still taking to the air around them. They ran parallel to the creek, away from the cemetery.

By the time they'd made it to the church, the geese had given up on them and flown away. Ella sat with her back against the church, breathing heavily and pulling her long brown hair back into a ponytail. A couple of the geese had almost scalped her.

She was laughing so hard her face was red.

Mitch gave her a wide-eyed look for a long moment, as if wondering if the goose attack had been the final straw in their crazy week together.

"Mitch," she said. "Come here."

He took a knee next to her and the church as she wiped her eyes.

"Wild geese," Mitch said, shaking his head. Ella chuckled for a few more seconds at that comment, and then she touched his hand.

"Mitch, I'm so sorry about all of this." Ella wiped at her eyes again. "This expedition has been a disaster from day one."

"It's not your fault, Ella. I forgot to tell you about the crazy geese here. They used to hassle us as kids all the time."

Ella laughed at that. "I'm not just talking about the geese, you know."

"I know," Mitch said. He reached up to wipe the last of the tears from her cheek. "You don't have to say any more, okay? I don't think I'm ready to talk about . . . this morning in the harbor yet."

"Or last night?" Ella did her best to meet his gaze, but they both ended up looking away.

"That was just one of those things that happen, Ella," he said. "I overreacted, I think, before I left. But don't let that get in the way of our friendship, and the job we've got to do."

Friendship, Ella thought. She didn't like the sound of *that* word. She got to her feet, not sure why she was feeling angry all of a sudden.

"You're right," she said. "Let's try the next cemetery, then. I don't think there's anything in that one back there, except for goose droppings."

Mitch gave her one last look, and she met his gaze for only a moment before they left the comforting presence of the church. As they followed the waterway known as Henry's Creek south and returned to the dirt road, Ella touched the silver chain in her jeans pocket. It rested there next to the broken piece of the locket, and for a moment both pieces were filled with a wild heat, as if to say "Getting warmer, getting warmer."

Touching the ghostly chain, Ella felt a moment of paranoia. Less than a day ago, this chain had been around the neck of someone who appeared to be, for all intents and purposes, not only dead, but a ghost.

She exhaled slowly and told herself to get a grip.

You're letting the ghosts—and your imagination—get to you. What had Owen's advice been? "They can't hurt you unless you let them. If you ignore them, I promise you they'll go away."

Ella hoped the old guy was right.

On their left was the old post office, nothing more than a barn, really, though it had recently been repainted. Ella wondered how many spirits now hung out there, waiting for letters to arrive on an ancient skiff coming from the mainland. Energized by such thoughts, she picked up the pace until she and Mitch were almost jogging to the entrance of the other cemetery on the island.

Closer to the main port of entry to the island, which Mitch had called Allover Landing, this cemetery was also the larger of the two. Ella counted almost three dozen graves, and most of them had been well-tended.

Just as Ella walked through the faded white gate of the picket fence enclosing the graves, another harsh burst of wind blew down from the north. She took a step back to keep from falling over, and Mitch had to grab the gate to keep it from swinging shut on her. The smell of smoke and fire was back. And the sky had turned almost completely black.

Mitch closed the gate behind them and grabbed Ella before she was bowled over by the wind. They were chest-to-chest again. Still thinking about his "friendship" comment, she tried to pull out of his grip at first, but then she relaxed and wrapped her arms around him. Against her own chest, she could feel the fierce beating of his heart. She took a strange sense of comfort in the fact that he was as scared as she was. Then she learned what was frightening him so badly.

"Over there," he said. "On the other side of the graves."

"What are you—" Ella gave up trying to talk in the howling wind. She fought back a sudden fit of coughing from the smoke in the air being flung at her on the wind. The sky was as dark as twilight, and all the shadows were elongated and distorted.

When Ella was able to see who Mitch had been talking about, the wild wind suddenly died. She tried to find her voice, to no avail. She and Mitch could do nothing but stare in shocked silence at the new arrival, dressed all in white.

Chapter Twenty

Floating two feet off the ground, wearing an ornate white dress, was the girl who was once a cabin boy on a pirate ship, Caroline Amberson. The bottom of her oversized dress almost touched the headstone beneath her, and the lace and fancy beadwork brought a moment of perfect understanding to Ella. The girl was wearing her wedding dress, and it had probably been stolen for her by Bonnet, which would explain the poor fit.

Ella opened her mouth to speak to the girl, and then she saw Caroline's eyes. They were glowing like orange coals. A slowly gathering storm seemed to be emanating from those eyes, as if she were on fire and the clouds in the sky behind her were the smoke she was giving off. The smell of burning wood had returned, along with the hint of lilacs.

"Why are you *here?*" Caroline said, her voice filled with both anger and a childish whine. Her small mouth didn't move. "This isn't where you should be digging deeper."

Thunder rippled across the sky, followed by a fork of lightning. The echoes of the thunder sounded too much like the cannons of Stede Bonnet for Ella's taste.

"We're close to figuring everything out for you," Ella said. Her voice was much calmer than she'd expected it to be. "But something keeps stopping us, Caroline. Something, or some*one*. Why didn't you tell us the whole story?"

"Nothing more to tell," Caroline said, her semi-transparent lip twitching. Ella could see storm clouds building through the girl's body. "Bonnet drowned me, and left me unburied and unmourned. That bit of locket and the chain he took from me surely proves it. Now that you have your evidence, you must tell the world of all his cruel deeds he committed aboard *The Revenge* out there in the ocean. And then I will have *my* revenge."

"Where is it?" Ella said.

Before she realized what she was doing, she was slipping away from Mitch and walking forward, taking one steady step at a time without taking her eyes off Caroline. She felt a rush of excitement at finally figuring out the connection between Caroline and Bonnet, combined with a frustrated anger at Caroline's attempts to manipulate her. Ella hated being tricked and lied to.

"Where is *what*?" Caroline looked down at her dress as if noticing for the first time she was dressed like a young woman and not a boy. She started running her thin, orange-tinted hands over her dress, as if trying to turn it back into the vest and pants of her cabin-boy outfit, but she couldn't make it change. The orange coals of her eyes were growing brighter.

"You know what I'm talking about," Ella said, less than a foot away from the floating girl.

"I really must be going now," Caroline said in a bitter voice.

"Where's the rest of the locket, Caroline?"

She looked up at the girl, arms out and open as if approaching a wild animal.

"Show us where it is, and we can help you. It's in this cemetery, isn't it? That's why you showed up here. That was all the memorial Bonnet left for you—half a locket here, and half in Ocracoke. Isn't it, Caroline?"

Behind her, Ella heard a scuffling sound as Mitch moved through the weeds surrounding the gravestones. Ella didn't dare look behind her and take her eyes off of Caroline, even as the scuffling sounds stopped, and she heard Mitch take a sudden breath.

"*No!*" Caroline's scream was loud as thunder.

Ella couldn't help but recoil from that tortured scream. She spun and saw Mitch bent over, picking something up from the ground. The thunder continued even after Caroline's scream ended, transforming itself into the now-familiar thud of cannon fire.

Damn it, Ella thought. *Company was on the way.*

Even though she could see that his hands were shaking, Mitch calmly brushed dirt off the tiny, blackened piece of silver in his hand. She knew exactly what it was. The other half of the locket.

"We needed this," Ella whispered to Caroline. The ghost girl in her too-big wedding dress drifted backwards, passing directly through the pickets of the cemetery fence. The instant she left the cemetery boundary she began to fade.

"This completes your story, doesn't it?" Ella called into the wind, trying to keep her eyes on the girl's dying orange light as it moved away from her, faster now. "Why did you try to keep us from finding it?"

"No," Caroline whispered, fading even further. "Not complete . . ."

In a few seconds she was just an orange glow that was quickly eaten by the dark clouds and the sickly blue light coming from the northeast, from the direction of the shipwreck.

"Mitch," Ella called. She winced as another cannon blast rolled across the stormy sky. "Quick. What do you see on the back of that piece of metal?"

"Um," Mitch said. "Couldn't we examine this later? I need to get you out of here."

"No," Ella said, hurrying across the cemetery to stand next to him. She was digging in her pocket for the other half of the locket. "Remember what I said about everything coming to a head before? We've got to finish this, right here, I think."

Mitch held up the locket so they could both look at it. In the fading light of the stormy afternoon, Ella could just make out a letter on the back of the locket, with two numbers underneath it.

"It looks like a *B* and a *seventeen*," she said. The cannon blasts were closer now, accompanied by more wind and the first spatters of rain. Ella put the two pieces together. They were a perfect match.

"Oh shit," Mitch whispered as soon as the locket was complete. "I get it now."

"I knew it," Ella whispered to Mitch. "Caroline!" she called out to the purple and black sky. "Caroline Amberson *Bonnet!* Come back! We can help you!"

The stink of something burning filled Ella's nose again, a much harsher scent than she'd smelled with Caroline. She wanted to grab Mitch and run like mad from the cemetery, but she understood now that this was the place they had to be for this showdown.

Where else to deal with ghosts than a graveyard?

She pulled out the silver chain and wrapped it twice around the same hand that was holding the two pieces of the locket. With all three pieces in her grip, she could feel their shared weight of history and something deeper, something that Ella had felt on rare occasions with her previous boyfriends. She was feeling the emotions—the *love*—that had been placed into this locket and this chain, centuries earlier. It was almost too much for her to bear.

Because along with the love was an almost blinding

sense of pain and loss. And betrayal.

All the emotions tied into the locket and the chain filled her hand with a sudden blast of searing heat. Ella would have dropped the pieces of the locket and the chain if Mitch hadn't taken her hands in his, cupping the artifacts together. Almost instantly, the powerful emotions subsided to a dull roar, as if they were being shared with Mitch. With the cold wind blowing her hair into Mitch's face, she leaned close to him.

"Hold on," she said, kissing Mitch so hard on the lips that she saw stars and forgot about the burning sensation coming from the locket. "I have a feeling that this is when things get a bit crazy."

When Ella pulled away from Mitch, her lips still tingling from his and her heart pounding in triple time, the sky exploded with one final cannon blast. Floating ten feet above them, arms outstretched and black jacket flung wide, was Stede Bonnet. His eyes glowed angrily with his signature weak blue light, and his bruised neck was livid with purplish-black flesh on either side of his rotted noose.

"You *fools*," he hissed. "You couldn't let sleeping dogs lie, could you?"

Still holding the locket and chain, Ella looked at Mitch. He didn't look like he was ever going to let go of her hands, even as he glared at the ghost that had been dogging them for days.

"Fools!" Bonnet shrieked again, his voice louder than the howling wind.

"It's okay," she said to Mitch, ignoring Bonnet and pulling her hands free of his. "I'll keep hold of it."

The wave of emotions from the locket and chain hit her again—pain, loss, betrayal—but she was ready for it. And she had her own emotions to fight them off. More than anything, Ella was mad. She'd had enough of Bonnet's meddling and posturing, and she'd definitely had enough of his damn dramatic cannons.

With one last look at Mitch, Ella turned her back on the ghost.

With a knowing, calm wink, Mitch turned away from the ghost a moment later.

"Don't you *dare* ignore me!" Bonnet shouted. "You know what I am capable of!"

Ella could feel the cold coming off of Bonnet as he floated closer, but she didn't turn to look up at him. Instead she took a deep breath and focused on the locket, which had again started giving off more heat in her hands.

"Caroline Amberson Bonnet!" she called out again. "Come back here, now. We hold your destiny in our hands, and we want to help you! But we can't help you if you don't help yourself."

"I *can't*," a tiny voice answered: Caroline's. "Not by myself. Not with him there."

"Caroline!" Mitch called. "We won't hurt you!"

"Yes, you will! You're a man," she said. "That's what you do."

"Oh Caroline," Ella said, almost whispering. *You're so wrong*, she wanted to say. *You just got caught up with the wrong man.*

But her voice failed her when she felt the hairs on the back of her neck stand up. If she turned around now, she knew Bonnet would be staring down at her from inches away.

"Ready?" she said, hoping Mitch remembered Owen's words about what to do with ghosts you didn't want to see anymore. "On the count of three?"

"One," Mitch said, reaching out to take Ella's free hand. Ella could feel the heat from the locket intensify even more, then it spread from her hand into Mitch. From somewhere off to her left, she could hear the sound of distant hooves. She focused on the hooves to keep from thinking about the burning pain in her hand.

"The girl is right," Bonnet shouted from behind them. "I *will* hurt you, if you don't turn around and face me. I expect this behavior of a woman, but not of someone who would call himself a man."

"Two," she said, looking Mitch in the eye. The heat of the locket was making Ella's hand turn red. "Ignore him," she hissed.

Wind blasted onto them from the south, pushing them back toward Bonnet's ghost. Ella leaned into the swirling currents of the air, which had changed direction and now blew at them from the right. From the left, the pounding of the hooves grew louder.

"Coward!" Bonnet shouted. "Face me like a man! Don't you dare turn away!"

Out of the corner of her eyes, Ella saw a black streak emerge from the path leading from the old white church.

"Three," Ella and Mitch said together, and they walked out of the graveyard together. The taunting insults of Stede Bonnet were suddenly cut short by a gurgling sound of pure fear. Ella turned to see the black pony from Ocracoke leap the cemetery fence and slam into the ghost. Bonnet's challenge had been answered by Red-Eye, who had apparently become the resident ghost-chaser of both Ocracoke and Portsmouth islands.

"Come back!" Bonnet's fading voice cried after them as he struggled with the pony. "Hand over your treasure . . ." he added, as if from a growing distance, "or I'll return . . . with friends of my own . . ."

Ella and Mitch ignored the shouts of Bonnet as well as

the angry neighing of Red-Eye. Ella didn't want to see any more of what was happening back there in the graveyard, though from the sounds she was hearing she could imagine the unearthly altercation all too clearly in her mind. She held onto Mitch's hand and walked as fast as she could back to the plane.

By the time they made it back to the landing strip, most of the clouds had blown away. The sun was fighting to show itself through the remaining gray clouds. Ella dropped to the ground, for the first time in her life glad to see a plane.

"Is your hand okay?" Mitch said.

She opened up the hand that had held the burning locket, expecting her flesh to be charred or at least blistering from the locket's sudden heat. But her hand was only bright red, just a bit warmer than usual from the strange heat of the locket.

"I think it's okay," Ella said. "It hardly even hurts any more."

She realized with a start that she had to squint at the locket and chain in her injured hand, due to the sudden darkness creeping up on them. Somehow they had lost a couple of hours in the cemetery, facing off with Caroline and then Bonnet.

She looked over at Mitch. "When should we take off?"

"Not today," Mitch said from above her. He must have been watching her the whole time, ever since she sat down. He cleared his throat and leaned against the main cabin of the plane. "It's too dark for me to fly. I'm not even going to risk it."

Ella stared at those faded blue eyes, a flurry of emotions running through her: fear, excitement, hope, and the steadily increasing tingle of desire she'd felt ever since meeting Mitch, less than a week ago. Their too-few kisses only intensified that tingling sensation.

"Can you call someone to come get us, in a boat preferably?" Ella realized that she was hoping Mitch's answer would be no.

"I could," he said, leaning closer to her the tiniest bit. "I *could* probably find someone on Ocracoke to come get us. If . . ."

"If what?"

Mitch shrugged, a gesture that was almost lost in the gloom. "If that's what you really want to do," he said.

She met his gaze, hoping her emotions weren't showing on her face. And if they were, she hoped that the darkness that was now almost entirely surrounding them would hide those telltale emotions.

"We always carry a couple sleeping bags in the back of the plane," Mitch said. "You can sleep inside the plane if you want."

Ella could just make out his hand waving at the sky above them. The stars had come out, brighter than last night, a wash of white stars marred only by the sliver of moon, almost enough to see by.

"Since the skies have cleared up again," he continued, "I think I'll sleep out under the stars, just like the old pilots of Portsmouth probably did. I've had a hell of a day, and I'd like to get some perspective. We could also use someone to stand guard." He touched Ella's shoulder, and she jumped the tiniest bit. "If you'd like to join me," he whispered in her ear, "that would be great."

And then he left her side, going to the plane to pull the sleeping bags out of the compartment at the back of the craft.

"So," Mitch said softly. "Want me to leave your sleeping bag in the plane?"

Ella got to her feet and touched Mitch's hands. They were still warm, just as she'd remembered them.

"I don't think so," she said. "And here I thought you were incapable of being subtle."

"Shh," Mitch said. "You'll wake the ghosts."

Moving far enough away from the plane so that its wings wouldn't block their view of the sky above—but not so far that they couldn't run back to it if necessary—Mitch and Ella unrolled their sleeping bags and dropped onto them. Ella hadn't realized until that moment how tired she was.

Mitch balled up a blanket for a pillow and rested his head on it. Ella sat down next to him on her sleeping bag. She felt suddenly exposed on the grassy airstrip in the middle of the deserted island. She put her hand on his chest, letting it rise and fall as he breathed, and she smiled when he covered her hand with his own.

"Why did you have to mention ghosts?" she muttered at last, needing to say something to fill the void of silence between them.

"Sorry," Mitch said, his voice distracted. Ella turned and saw that he was busy staring up off into space, much like he'd done on their drive into town on the day they met. That day felt like years ago, now.

She exhaled slowly, trying to let her frazzled nerves unwind. Lying here on her side, with Mitch so close, helped her relax, though her brain kept going over the events of the day. With her eyes focused on the sky, watching for another shooting star, she thought about Caroline's story.

"I hate to admit it," she said, "but our girl fooled me with her innocent act. Who knows if Bonnet is even responsible for her death? I don't know what to believe now. All I know for sure is they seem to be tied up together, and they can't find peace until they find some sort of peace together."

Ella shivered in the cool night air. The storm that had been building all afternoon had dissipated almost as soon as they'd walked away from Bonnet in the cemetery, and the air had warmed at least twenty degrees since then. Yet she still felt a chill pass through her. Without realizing it, she had inched closer to Mitch. He squeezed her hand in response, and Ella could tell he was smiling.

"I'll bet you never thought," Mitch said, still gazing up at the sky, "that you'd be sitting next to the world's biggest redneck from Ocracoke on a mostly empty island off the coast, talking about the motivations of a couple of ghosts."

Ella elbowed him in the side as she lifted her hand from his chest and rested at last on her back next to Mitch. Once again, her hand found his.

The tension in her neck and back began to slowly unravel as she smiled.

"Oh come on," she said. "You're not a redneck. At least not the world's biggest one."

Mitch slid some of his blanket over for her so she could rest her head on it. After all the excitement from that day, her pulse had finally begun to settle down. And then Mitch's head touched hers, which set her heart to galloping again.

Ella wondered how much this piece of the sky had changed since 1718. She was about to say something about it to Mitch, but when she looked over at him, she was surprised to see that his eyes were closed.

"Mitch? You okay? Don't tell me you're sleeping."

"Shh," he said, keeping his eyes closed. "Just stop for a second, would you? Isn't it enough to just listen to the wind and the surf?"

"What?" Ella said, putting a hand on his cheek and turning Mitch's face to her. A strange sense of déjà vu passed through her, but she couldn't figure out why she felt it. Being this close to Mitch was making everything fuzzy in her mind. "What did you say?"

"Just listen," he said. "Don't talk, don't worry, don't analyze. Just relax and be alive."

Ella left her hand on Mitch's cheek, reveling in the touch of his stubbly beard. His jaw was relaxed and soft, and his lips brushed against her hand as he spoke.

"Shh . . ." he whispered.

Ella turned her head on the makeshift pillow until her forehead rested against Mitch's, and she inhaled his salty-sweet smell of soap and sea. She could feel his chest rise and fall slowly, and she moved closer, so she could feel every move he made.

At last, she closed her eyes. She let her sense of hearing come to the forefront, listening to Mitch's slow breathing next to her, air hissing almost silently in and out of his nose. From the field of marsh grass around the landing strip, frogs had gathered to sing their repetitive, cheeping songs, while farther away to the east was the low roar of the Atlantic.

Creating a counterpoint to all of this was the wind, ricocheting off the wings of the plane and picking up speed over the flat tidewater marshes surrounding them.

Ella was so intent on the sounds around her, noises she'd never heard all at the same time before, especially in Boston, that she never knew if she or Mitch had started with the kissing.

All she knew was that one moment she was alone with the sounds of the uncivilized world surrounding her, and the next she was sharing it with Mitch. Their lips pressing together, tongues touching tentatively at first, and then with more confidence. Soon they were exploring each other's bodies with their hands and torsos and feet as well as their lips. Each new touch was like a tiny explosion of bliss in Ella's heart.

So long, she thought. *It's been so long since I'd felt this kind of fire take hold of me.*

She refused to open her eyes, just in case this was a dream.

Mitch's arms were around her now, an almost familiar sensation after the events of the past few days. He was holding her tight, comforting yet nicely overpowering at the same time. So she gripped him tighter in her arms, squeezing him around the shoulders as tightly as she kept her own eyes squeezed shut.

Ella moved on top of Mitch, feeling all of her fears slip away as he rolled with her, off the sleeping bags and onto the brittle grass of the landing strip. Ella reached behind her and opened up Mitch's sleeping bag with one deft flip of her hand. With the other hand she pulled off his shirt, which was over halfway off already. Mitch returned the favor as they rolled on top of his sleeping bag, still kissing without saying a single word.

Then he was on top of her, careful not to crush her, but still maintaining a steady pressure as they kissed and touched one another, reveling in the fact that they were alive here in this dark land, surrounded by so much history and the pair of long-suffering spirits.

The feel of his skin against hers was heavenly, almost more than she could handle, but she wasn't about to stop. Ella had never felt so right, so sure, about completely losing control with another person like this before. With Mitch, it felt right, and so *good.*

And then, just as she had almost completely wiped away all thoughts of dead pirates, desperate ghosts, and the revenge of broken hearts, their kisses were interrupted by the distant sounds of cannons.

Mitch broke free from her embrace and poked his head up, as if he could somehow see through the darkness all around them.

In that frozen instant as they stopped and listened, Ella imagined hearing the distant pounding of ponies running scared on Ocracoke once again.

"What the *hell?*" Mitch whispered, dropping onto his back with a frustrated half-laugh. "You know, I don't think we're *ever* going to have peace and quiet while we're together."

Ella put her hand on his chest, savoring the touch of his warm skin and the hairs under her fingers. His heart was hammering almost as fast as the ponies' hooves were, and she hoped she had more than a little to do with that, more than the ponies' sudden stampede and the return of the cannons.

"Something's—" Mitch began, and then the cannons and the hoofbeats abruptly stopped. A single set of hooves clopped softly through the grass from what sounded like the other side of the dirt road. "Something's out there," he said.

"I think we have a guardian angel," Ella said. "I don't think we need to worry about anyone messing with us tonight."

Before covering herself and Mitch with the sleeping bag to ward off the cool breezes coming in off the water, Ella saw the faint hint of a glowing red light off to the north, close to the Coast Guard station.

"Make that a guardian *pony*," she said, snuggling closer to Mitch, completely unafraid now.

"Red-Eye," Mitch muttered before turning his attention

back to Ella. "I should have known."

Laughing, she zipped up the sleeping bag around them, and they began to slowly shed the rest of their clothes. She felt more drunk than she'd felt last night, drunker than at any other time in her life.

"Now," Ella said, taking Mitch's face in her hands so she could kiss him once more. "Where were we?"

Chapter Twenty-One

Ella woke just as the sun was lifting up from the Atlantic to the east, turning the sky purple with streaks of red. She blinked at the distant sun, and then looked at the face of the man sleeping next to her. The soreness in her back from sleeping on the ground with Mitch next to her faded when she glimpsed his peaceful face as he slept.

Trying not to move too much and risk waking Mitch, Ella looked at the island around her—dew covered the wild grass lining the airstrips, flickering in the sun, which was turning the sky a deep blue. The mosquitoes began to buzz slowly around her, but they were still too drowsy to mount an effective attack.

How did I ever end up here? she wondered, inhaling the cool morning air and listening to the distant crash of the Atlantic off to the east.

"Good morning," Mitch said from below her.

Ella jumped and instinctively pulled the sleeping bag tighter over her bare chest. Mitch laughed at first, but he didn't meet her gaze when she looked down at him.

I hope this isn't going to be weird, Ella thought.

"Good morning," she said at last.

A flash of uncertainty passed over Mitch's face as he looked from her and then peeked inside the sleeping bag back at himself. His grin was sheepish when he lifted his head again.

"So it wasn't a dream," he murmured, and with that Ella

relaxed. She slithered down next to him and rubbed his stubbly cheek.

"Nope," she said. "But that was some cannon fire, huh?"

Mitch didn't even bother answering with words, but with his lips on hers. She let herself relax into his warm, strong embrace. It felt so good to just let go, so good that the plane and the ghosts and the rest of the world could just wait a little bit longer.

"We can call and have someone get us on a boat if you want," Mitch said later, after they'd finally pried themselves out of the sleeping bag.

"No, that's okay," Ella said, pulling on her jeans. "I don't want to have to wait for anyone. Let's fly back."

"So you're over your fear of flying, just like that?" Mitch pushed Ella's shoes closer to her and tossed a balled-up sock at her.

She shrugged, trying to put on a brave face. "Not really. But we have some work to finish up, don't you think? No time to waste."

"You didn't seem to mind wasting the last twenty or thirty minutes," Mitch said, staring up at the sky as if his feelings had been hurt.

"I'm ignoring that remark," Ella said. "Still have the locket and chain?"

Mitch reached for the chain and the two pieces of the locket from under the blanket they'd used as a pillow last night. Ella was surprised they hadn't had nightmares with that under them all night, but her sleep had been deep, restful, and dreamless.

She glanced at the hand that had been holding the locket and chain yesterday as it heated up in Bonnet's presence. There was a faint outline of the locket, and a tiny, curving line across her palm from the chain, but there were no blisters as she had feared yesterday.

"Ella," Mitch croaked. "Look at this."

Ella stepped up next to Mitch as he held up the pieces of the locket to the growing sunlight. She froze. He wasn't holding up pieces of metal that had been chopped in two—this was a complete locket again, and it was attached to the chain as if the three pieces had never been separated.

She could see the distinct, jagged line where the two pieces of the locket had fused together. The tarnished black half that they'd found yesterday met the bright silver of the piece she had cleaned and carried with her.

"Amazing," Mitch said.

Ella pulled her gaze from the locket and chain. "Amazing? This is *impossible*, Mitch! What made this happen? I just don't believe—"

"Ella," Mitch said, touching her lips with a finger. "Just stop being a scientist and a researcher for a second. Just . . . *believe*."

"What?" Ella felt the world start to slip away from her, the past week of haunted shipwrecks, lighthouses, and cemeteries finally catching up to her.

"Just admit it's highly unlikely," Mitch said, setting the locket and chain in her hands. "Admit it's really improbable. Next to unbelievable. Just tell yourself it's really damn weird, and then move on. We can't get bogged down in little details like this. Not at this point. We're close to figuring it all out, I think."

Ella gave him one last incredulous look before stowing the locket and chain in her jeans pocket. It already felt warm to the touch, but not as searing and focused as the look in Mitch's eyes.

"I hope you're right," she said. "Because I've about

245

reached my quota of weirdness this week."

"I can't promise you more weird stuff won't happen," Mitch said. "But I can promise that I'll be right there with you during it."

Ella's shoulders relaxed at that, and she stood up straighter as a result. She squeezed Mitch's hand.

"Thanks," she said. "I needed that. You know, for a spacey guy, you're pretty well-grounded."

"Down to earth," Mitch said. "That's me. Grounded like a lightning rod."

He gave her a smile and a wink and left her to start prepping the small six-seat plane for the flight back to Ocracoke. Ella checked one last time to make sure they hadn't left anything behind, and then she climbed into the plane. Her breathing became more shallow the instant she was inside, the door closed behind her.

"Oh boy," she muttered. She got her seat belt on in the cockpit after only four tries. Mitch looked over at her, his face lined with worry.

"You're sure about this?" he asked her, and then looked down at her arms. She'd carried one of the sleeping bags into the cockpit with her, and she had it tight in her grip as if she needed an additional cushion.

Ella nodded, her mouth dry. "The flight will only last a couple minutes, right?"

"Be there before you know it. Just look straight ahead, and don't look down, and you'll be fine." Mitch touched her knee for a second. "Pretend you're going for a ride in your Escort. I'll bet that little car's bumpier than this plane ride would be. Just tell yourself it's just a quick trip on the interstate into Boston. Okay?"

"I'll try," Ella said, staring straight ahead as advised.

"Here we go."

Out of the corner of her eye, she watched as Mitch pushed the yoke of the controls forward, checking and double-checking his gauges as they built up speed. The end of the airstrip approached, with the blue waters of Pamlico Sound beyond it. She made herself look up and away from the huge expanse of water spreading out in front of them.

As they gained altitude, Mitch turned the plane. Ella could see the church and the cemetery where they'd first started looking yesterday. Like an explosion of wings and grass, the flocks of killer geese burst up and out of the marsh grass. She almost smiled at the memory of the geese nearly taking off both her and Mitch's heads, and then she remembered where she was. In a plane. She turned her gaze back to the blue sky.

Let this be over soon, she thought to herself. *Please let this be over soon.*

Mitch aimed the plane toward the east, and for a moment the morning sun hit the cockpit window like a supernova. Ella almost began hyperventilating. She fought the urge to grab for Mitch.

"It's okay," he said. "I can see. We're going to fly right over the shipwreck, Ella."

"I'll take your word for it," Ella said, her eyes jammed closed.

"You can almost see it, if you know where to look," Mitch said.

Ella cracked her eyes open a tiny bit. The brilliant sunlight had lessened enough for her to see the long strip of Ocracoke Island in front of them.

We're almost there, she thought, and relaxed her death grip on the sleeping bag a few notches. She risked a look down at the inlet below them, and Mitch was right—she *could* see something faint taking shape in the deep water below them.

She was tempted to point it out to Mitch when something flashed from down in the dark water. A heartbeat later, the plane gave a stomach-dropping lurch. The plane lost fifty feet of altitude in two seconds.

"Mitch!" Ella almost reached over to grab him before she stopped herself. She heard herself moaning in fear, and she slapped both hands over her mouth.

Mitch barely noticed; he was too busy fighting with the controls to the little plane. Ella's ears popped as Mitch pulled back on the yoke, trying to get the nose of the plane back up.

"It's okay," he said, his voice tight and hoarse. "We just hit a bad pocket of air. Hold on."

The plane leveled off for a few more seconds, and then the nose dipped again. They dropped another hundred feet. Ella couldn't stop herself; she glanced out the window and saw that they were directly over the shipwreck now. The sky was filled with smoke.

Is that us *making all that smoke?* she thought, watching Mitch pull back on the yoke again. The only response made by the plane was a coughing sound as the engine sputtered.

"Damn it!" he shouted. Somewhere in Ella's mind she thought she heard the taunting sounds of cannons. The blasting sounds drowned out the coughing engine of the plane.

Bonnet was down there, she realized. *This was the dead pirate's revenge for us walking away from him.*

"Hold on," Mitch said again. Ella could tell that the engine was now dead, and they were still about 300 feet above the water. "I think we can glide for a bit. If we keep the nose up, we could hit the water without—I'll shut up now."

Just like my nightmare, Ella thought. *All I need is two guys arguing, one defending logic, the other one . . .*

"Relax," Mitch said, and then he laughed at his own advice. "We're going to hit the water, but we'll be okay if we just relax."

"Just believe," Ella muttered, caught in the middle of her sleeping nightmare and her waking nightmare. "Just believe we'll be all right, Mitch."

She didn't know if he heard her or not, and at that point it didn't matter. All that was important was that Ella Simon—for the first time in a long, long time—wasn't fighting to control something she couldn't control.

For a handful of seconds that seemed to last forever, in complete silence, the water of Ocracoke Inlet grew closer and closer, filling the cockpit windows. Mitch reached out to touch Ella, and she grabbed his hand with both of hers.

"Hold onto me," he whispered as the plane dropped toward the water.

Chapter Twenty-Two

Not now, Ella thought in the last remaining instants before the nose of the plane struck the water. *Not now, not after we'd finally made sense of most of Caroline's story. And not after what I'm feeling for Mitch. It's not* fair.

And then she was thrown against her shoulder straps and the breath was knocked out of her. For a long moment she couldn't draw any air through her lungs.

The world went dark.

After what felt like hours, she opened her eyes, gulping for air. She'd been shocked awake by an image of sickly blue fire covering the inside of the plane and inching toward her and Mitch.

Stede Bonnet is here, her mind screamed, but when she looked outside, she saw only dark water covering the windows of the cockpit.

The impact hadn't been as bad as she'd expected, but the collision of plane and ocean had been louder than any cannons Ella could have imagined.

She reached for Mitch, who was trying to disentangle himself from the sleeping bag she'd been holding. Somehow the sleeping bag had flown out of her hands and wrapped itself around him when they crash-landed. When she touched Mitch's shoulder, she realized how badly she was shaking. Mitch gripped her hand and turned to her, eyes blazing.

She tried to say something, but she couldn't find her voice. Once she saw that she and Mitch had both made it through the landing in one piece, the full impact of what just happened hit her. A small whimpering sound escaped her lips, and the world began to spin.

"Are you okay?" Mitch whispered. "Ella?"

"I . . . We . . ." Ella couldn't get her mouth to work. The plane was bobbing up and down like *Cassiopeia* used to do, anchored to this very spot in the ocean.

"Just relax," Mitch said. "Let's get you out of your seat belt, okay? But first, show me that you're not hurt and can move your arms and legs, okay?"

Ella wiggled her fingers and kicked her legs, hitting the control panel with her right foot. She didn't smell gas, so she knew the plane wasn't in danger of catching fire or exploding—the blue fire she'd imagined earlier had just been another nightmare image from their underwater host, Stede Bonnet.

"I'm okay," Ella said at last. She undid her seat belt in one try. "Let's get out of this damn plane before it sinks."

She followed Mitch's gaze outside. He was frowning at all the smoke outside, even if it didn't seem to be coming from the plane.

"Okay," Mitch said. He undid his own harness and caught Ella when the plane rocked with a sudden wave. He held her for a long moment, and she could feel once again his runaway heartbeat. "All right," he said. "This thing has an inflatable raft. I'll call the Coast Guard and we'll be back at the Jolly Roger, kicking back a couple beers in no time."

Ella pushed away from him, nearly falling as the plane was rocked again by a wave. She thought she'd heard a dull thud somewhere outside it. Coming from under the water, possibly. Coming for *them*.

She touched the locket and chain in her jeans, not surprised that the silver was again growing warm against her leg.

"I think someone's here," she said. Before he could stop

her, Ella was staggering toward the door leading outside. She was pulling and swearing at it like a madwoman when Mitch called out to her.

"Ella!" he shouted. "Don't—"

But it was too late. She pulled open the door, her movements accompanied by another barrage of cannon fire. When the door was open, she squinted into the smoke-filled air outside. Bonnet had to be out there, she knew. But all she saw was the frothy, choppy water of the inlet, along with one of the wings of the plane floating past.

Mitch was behind her, a hand on her shoulder to try and pull her back, but another wave hit the plane with an explosive blast. Ella fell forward, through the doorway and into the roiling water just above the wrecked pirate ship, sixty-five feet below her.

She'd been able to suck in a big breath of air as she fell from the plane into the icy salt water, so she didn't have to surface immediately. But she was sinking impossibly fast, and the water was already turning her skin numb.

Ella opened her eyes and saw swirling lights far below her on the ocean floor. She stared down through the impossibly clear water at the lights, still sinking.

Instead of wondering how she was able to see all the way to the ocean floor or trying to figure out what sort of optical illusion this was, she simply stared at the place where the shipwreck had once been.

The pile of the ancient wreck had disappeared.

Rising slowly toward the surface as Ella continued sinking was the reassembled pirate ship. Somehow the wrecked pirate ship, covered in angry bluish-white fire, had pulled itself together.

Ella fought the urge to suck in a fatal breath of air as the ship continued inching its way up to the surface, while she kept sinking. Soon, they would meet.

As she dropped closer to it, she realized that the ship was truly magnificent. Even with its battle damage and tattered sails—even though the ship seemed to be on *fire*—the sheer size of the hull and the intricate workings of the sails were more beautiful than any re-created version Ella had seen in a museum. Three tall masts rose thirty feet above the deck, one of them almost within her reach, and a black flag featuring a skull and crossbones flew from the top. The flag rippled in the water as it rose, accompanied by strange moaning sounds.

Ten cannons lined the side of the ship, giving off smoke underwater as they fired off another round. The explosions knocked Ella into motion at last. She kicked and aimed herself upwards in the direction of what she hoped was where the broken plane now sat bobbing on the waves.

She burst out of the water, gasping for air. She clapped a hand over her mouth, trying to keep as quiet as possible. Bonnet would turn up soon, and she didn't want him finding her vulnerable and alone in the icy water. Smoke filled the air, along with the too-familiar beat of the cannons. Ella was shaking badly from the cold, and she wondered if she'd ever get warm again. She had to get out of the water.

She saw the plane barely ten yards away, but she couldn't see Mitch inside it. As she swam toward it, her gaze was drawn to the gaping hole in the fuselage of the plane. That hole was exactly the same as the hole she'd seen in *Cassie*'s hull just that morning.

Bonnet was responsible for all of this, she knew. As if on cue, she heard a man's voice.

"Ella!" the voice cried out, and she was relieved when

she recognized it as Mitch's, not a ghost's. "Where the hell are you?"

Mitch swam into view twenty feet away, facing away from her and getting ready to dive back down for her in another attempt. His face was red and his hair was plastered to his head.

"Mitch!" Ella shouted. She'd reached the plane, and she put her arm inside the open doorway to support herself.

Mitch spun around and looked at her with a huge expression of relief. Ella waved at him with a trembling hand and numb fingers, and then her chills went from bad to worse. Just behind Mitch, she saw something rise from the water like a dark cloud, close enough to touch.

The cloud took shape as Stede Bonnet. The dead pirate's beardless face was one step removed from a skull's head, and what hair he had left on his head was standing straight out like a pincushion. His yellow teeth were glistening with a vicious smile. Worms dropped from his dark coat and splashed into the water next to Mitch.

Mitch took one look behind him and froze where he was treading water. He looked straight at Ella, trying to ignore the pirates as they'd done yesterday to Bonnet. His efforts caused laughter to erupt not just from Bonnet's lifeless mouth, but many more. Behind the ghost pirate floated over a dozen glowing, nearly transparent apparitions. They glared at Ella as they raised their ancient pistols and cutlasses.

As additional translucent figures rose up from the surf, another wave of mad, triumphant laughter bubbled out of Bonnet's bruised throat, though the loop of the hangman's noose garbled the laughter into a horrifying sound.

Captain Bonnet, Ella realized, *had been busy recruiting last night while Mitch and I were having our fun on the island.*

The pirate ghosts, with their patched and tattered clothes, bandannas around their heads, looked much less substantial than Bonnet, as if they were uncertain about their place in this world. Below them, Mitch was doing his best to move closer to her, without *looking* like he was running from the pirates.

"Ella," Mitch called. "I don't know how much longer we're going to be able to keep *ignoring* these ghosts! Any ideas, professor?"

Ella pushed against the sense of fear holding her in place, unable to move. She reached inside the plane for her backpack, which she had wedged under the seats near the back of the plane.

"Please be in here," she whispered, half in and half out of the floating plane. She kept digging through it as the hum of cannon fire filled the air. The smell of smoke was everywhere now, making her dig even faster until she found what she'd been looking for. She grabbed the ancient pistol she'd found at the wreck site and tucked it into the back of her jeans. With the cold, rusty gun scratching her lower back, she turned to Mitch.

The sight of the pirates, now less transparent and growing more distinct with each passing moment, hovering closer over Mitch all alone in the water, was almost too much for Ella. She hoped she hadn't waited too long as she swam away from the plane. She reached him just as the first ghost pirate raised his sword above Mitch, who was still creeping toward the plane and resolutely ignoring the thirty pirates behind him.

"Caroline," Ella muttered, "this would be a good time for you to show yourself, girl."

"Boys," Bonnet said to his crew, "I'll handle this. Since there's a woman involved, I'll make this easy on both of you. You won't suffer for long."

The other pirates lowered their swords, and Ella felt a sudden weight on her shoulders, like an immense hand. She kicked and fought against the invisible grip, which made Bonnet laugh even harder. Mitch fought as well, but both of their struggling soon stopped. Ella couldn't move her arms or her legs anymore.

They were slowly being pushed under, and they were helpless to fight it.

As she sucked in one final, desperate breath of air, Ella saw a flash of blinding blue light cutting through the frothy waves as the rebuilt and burning *Revenge* broke through to the surface.

And then the waters closed over her.

Chapter Twenty-Three

Ella fought with all her might to reach out for Mitch through the icy water. Her arms felt weighted down, and she moved slower than a nightmare as she pulled him to her and wrapped her numb arms around him. Together they sank farther and farther from the surface. Her lungs burned and her eyes stung when she opened them, accompanying the sudden sharp stinging sensation that came from the pocket of her jeans. She was glad she was no longer alone now, at the end of it all.

But it can't end like this, she thought, trying to kick her legs and get back to the surface. She tried, but she couldn't fight it anymore. The last thing she did was pull Mitch close for a final kiss.

I love you, she tried to tell him with her eyes.

Ella kissed him even as her lungs began to ache for air and her ears throbbed from the pressure—they were surely twenty feet down now. Mitch's face was turning blue.

She pulled away from him, the strange pain in her leg still stinging her. The pain suddenly intensified until it was white-hot. Before she could open her mouth and inhale a lungful of water, Ella felt her eyes go wide. She remembered what was in her jeans pocket.

Forcing her heavy arms to move, she shoved her hand into the pocket of her pants and was rewarded with the searing heat of the locket she'd left there. Caroline's locket.

Luckily she'd been holding tight to it, because as soon as she pulled out the locket on its chain, glowing bright orange, it lifted both Ella and Mitch to the surface faster than a rescue line from the Coast Guard. Ella's ears popped, and her chest was starting to spasm due to a lack of air. They broke through the surface just as her lungs were about to give out on her.

Air, even though it was filled with smoke from the *Revenge*, had never tasted sweeter to Ella as she sucked in mouthful after mouthful. Mitch was doing the same next to her, while keeping her tight in his grip.

"Bonnet!" Ella shouted as soon as she had the breath to do so. "Stede Bonnet! Aren't you . . . forgetting something?"

Bonnet and his cronies were halfway to his risen ship of fire when they turned. Bonnet's skeletal jaw dropped in surprise, first as he saw Ella and Mitch, and then dropping even farther when he saw the glowing locket in Ella's hand.

"*Where?*" Bonnet hissed as he left his men and floated closer, moving dangerously fast. He touched his neck under the rotting rope of the noose, looking for the chain that had once rested there. "*Where* did you find *that?*"

"Dismiss your men," Ella said. "And we'll tell you all about it."

The locket was now too hot for Ella to hold onto, so she held it up by the chain. The water that had been on the locket and chain steamed off until the entire piece of jewelry was dry.

"Thieves!" Bonnet cried, gesturing at his unmoving men behind him. "Kill them!"

The chain was burning Ella's fingers, but she knew she couldn't let go of it now. The sight of the glowing locket seemed to be keeping Bonnet's men away from them.

Mitch tightened his grip on her. "I think his men recognized it from when Caroline wore it."

Now that she could breathe again, Ella was feeling the full impact of the emotions stored for decades inside the locket. A heaviness similar to Bonnet's spell that pushed them under the water was threatening to overwhelm her and make her sink again. But Mitch treaded water for both of them, keeping them afloat.

"What are you cowards waiting for?" Bonnet screamed at his men. "Attack! That's an order!"

"That's *it*," Ella said. With her free hand, she reached behind her and pulled free the ancient pistol she'd salvaged from the plane. She pushed it butt-first into Mitch's hand and moved the locket into her left hand.

"What—" Mitch said.

"Stede Bonnet," Ella said, ignoring Mitch and winding up as best she could to throw. *"Catch!"*

Ella launched the silver locket at Bonnet. Its glowing chain flew behind it like the orange tail of a kite, cutting through the smoke and unnatural darkness around the pirates. It hissed through the air like a snake until it came into contact with the suddenly solid hand of Stede Bonnet with a tiny slapping sound.

Bonnet gazed at the locket in his bony hand for a long moment. His weak chin began to tremble as he whispered Caroline's name. While he floated above the ocean, paralyzed with shock and guilt, his men began slipping away from him, heading back toward the blue flames of the resurrected *Revenge*.

"Mitch," Ella said, touching his arm. She was shivering badly now from the cold as her adrenaline began to wear off. "I think it's time for you to get *your* revenge now."

Mitch looked down at the ancient pistol Ella had pressed into his hand. He gave her a thoroughly confused look at first, his pale blue eyes wide. Then he raised the gun. Grimacing, he pointed it at Bonnet, but changed his mind. Ella nodded when Mitch looked away from Bonnet, across the inlet. They had both realized at the same time what Mitch's target was: *The Revenge.*

The cannons of the pirate ship had gone silent for a change, not wanting to fire at its crew returning to it after so many years away.

"This is for *Cassiopeia*," Mitch said and pulled the trigger of the pistol.

Ella heard the tiny click of the gun next to him, and for a split-second she felt foolish for believing such a thing would work. But the click was shortly followed by an enormous explosion on the ship a hundred yards away. The ancient, rusty gun had blasted a gaping hole into the hull, even though it had no bullets. Surely it was impossible, but that didn't stop Mitch from pulling the trigger two more times, dedicating each shot to his ruined boat.

Each shot resulted in a massive explosion on the ghost ship, which was smoking and fading out of existence with each passing second. The ghost pirates had also dissipated like smoke on the breeze.

Ella looked at *The Revenge* one last time, trying to memorize every detail, even though her mind kept telling her the ship wasn't really there. The real ship had to still be down below, in thousands of barnacle-encrusted pieces.

With a dazed look of triumph, Mitch lowered the pistol. As he did, the gun crumbled in his hand and spattered its remains into the ocean.

"I can't watch," Mitch said, averting his gaze as *The Revenge* sank for the final time. "Even if this one was haunted and trying to kill us, I can't stand to see another ship go down."

Ella gave him a reassuring squeeze before they both

turned their attention to the last remaining pirate.

Stede Bonnet hadn't even noticed the destruction of his ship or the departure of his men. He was still staring at the glowing orange locket.

"Caroline?" he whispered, his voice high and uncertain. He said her name as if remembering her for the first time.

Ella had caught her breath at last. "Yes," she said. "That was her locket. Your *wife's* locket."

"Caroline?" Bonnet said again, gripping the locket so tight in his fading hand that its silver edges poked through where his fingers should have been. He looked much less solid than he had just a minute earlier.

"She's been gone for so long," he said in a soft voice.

"Did you kill her?" Ella said. She moved closer to the pirate leader's ghost.

"Caroline," Bonnet repeated, the name cracking on his lips like the sound of a heart breaking. "You were only supposed to stay locked up for a day," he said. "As punishment for running away. But then we came under attack."

"You left her locked up?" Ella said, her voice growing louder. She couldn't stop herself, thinking of the awful death the young girl had surely suffered. "What were you thinking?"

Bonnet began to sink lower in the air. He lowered his hand and hung his head. "I wasn't thinking clearly. I get confused sometimes . . ." Bonnet pulled at his ghostly hair and touched the old bandage on his forehead.

"I thought I loved her," Bonnet whispered.

Ella froze in the middle of her interrogation of Stede Bonnet when she heard the sound behind him, coming from Portsmouth Island. The noise was like a mosquito in her ear at first, but then it grew in volume until she thought it was a piercing siren going off around her.

It was a girl's voice, one long wailing sound that never paused for breath.

"*Nooooo!*"

The wailing came from Caroline, whose ghostly orange-lit body flew in front of Mitch and Ella. She was still screaming.

"*No!*" Caroline shrieked. "You never loved me! Never!"

Bonnet stared at Caroline, his gaunt face filled with confusion. Her white wedding dress was lit up in a beautiful orange light, like the brilliant rays of the best sunset Ella had ever seen.

"But you're *dead,*" he whispered.

"So are you, you fool!" Caroline said. "You're just too thick-skulled to realize it."

"But how can you be here if you're dead? And who are these meddling people?"

"They're friends. They came to help me. They found *that* for me," she said, touching the locket in Bonnet's hand.

Bonnet flinched away from her, as if her touch caused him pain. Caroline plucked the locket from his hand and put it around her neck. With each passing second, she grew brighter as Bonnet's sickly blue light faded closer to darkness.

"Did you ever love me?" Caroline said.

"Caroline, I . . . I can't . . ."

"Did you?" Caroline raised her tiny hands into the air. Orange flames licked at her fingers.

Bonnet lowered his balding head. "Yes, once. When my mind was clear."

"You foolish, power-hungry man," Caroline hissed. "I loved you, too."

Bonnet reared up at her words, looking like a rat backed

into a corner, with the yellowed teeth to prove it. He lifted his sword while wiping tears from his ghostly face.

"What sort of spell are you casting on me?" Bonnet waved his sword at Ella and Mitch, who had been watching in silent awe. "Make her stop, you meddlers! I'll kill you all if you don't make her stop!"

"Now," a deep voice said from behind Mitch and Ella, "I don' think that'd be a good thing to be doin', ol' Stede me boy."

Next to Stede Bonnet, bringing with him the smell of burnt matches and gunpowder, the headless ghost of Blackbeard rose up from the water of the inlet.

"Oh no," Bonnet whimpered. He lowered his sword with a shaking hand.

"I've taken care of your men," Blackbeard said, walking slowly through the air toward Bonnet, a curved sword in his translucent hands. "They'll be restin' once again after ye stirred them from their eternal slumber. Ye'll be havin' to deal with them soon, old *friend*. My own dear *Judas!*"

With his final word, Blackbeard swung his ghostly sword at Bonnet, aiming for his head. Bonnet barely managed to get his own sword up in time.

"No!" Caroline shouted. "Don't send him away yet."

"Judas?" Ella said, looking at Mitch. "What did he mean by that?"

Blackbeard turned to Ella, and then to Caroline. "This man is a traitor," his deep voice boomed, "and he must go to the fires of hell for his transgressions. I will send him there, gladly."

"But there's another way," Caroline said in a small voice. She turned to Bonnet, whose ghostly image was fading in and out of sight. Bonnet cowered from Caroline and her headless friend.

"Stede Bonnet," Caroline said. "Will you beg forgiveness?"

Bonnet straightened up, lifting his chin even as a worm crawled down the tip of his nose. Ella could see, just for a moment, the nobility that the man had forgotten long ago. She understood why he was once called the "gentleman pirate."

"From you, my lady, and not from this beast, I beg forgiveness." Bonnet's head lowered the slightest bit. *"Caroline,"* he said. "I am so sorry we didn't save you. I loved you, and I still grieve your death, my lady, to this very day."

Caroline touched her locket and floated closer to Bonnet. The light she was giving off grew stronger, obscuring them both.

The orange glow turned bright as the sun, flickering a sickly blue for a moment, and then both of their colors blended into each other and turned to a pure, almost blinding white. When the light subsided, Caroline's face was radiant with happiness and relief.

"I forgive you," Caroline said.

An instant later, she and Bonnet slipped away with two tiny puffs of air.

"And I thank you, Miss Ella and Mister Mitch," Caroline's voice whispered in Ella's ears, leaving them treading water in the cold water of Ocracoke Inlet.

Ella stared at the empty space where the two ghosts had been floating an instant earlier.

Ghosts, she told herself. *They really had been ghosts.*

She shivered even harder, and not just because of the cold water soaking into her clothes. The smoke in the air blew away with one final gust of wind, and the sun burned bright and warm above them. The damaged plane was partially submerged next to them, and the distant brown smudge that was Ocracoke Island to the north was miles away.

In spite of all this, Ella stopped shivering and felt a warmth fill her, a heat that reminded her of the heat from Caroline's locket. It came from inside of her and was intensified by Mitch's touch next to her.

"Thank *you*," Ella whispered, and looked over at Mitch.

For everything, she added silently.

Chapter Twenty-Four

And then it was just Ella and Mitch—and Blackbeard's headless ghost—once again. Mitch slipped inside the half-submerged plane to pull out the inflatable raft for them to rest on while he radioed the Coast Guard. Outside, Ella was left alone with the ghost of Edward Teach.

"Well, um, thanks for stopping by, Mr. Teach, sir," Ella said, her teeth chattering from the cold water, but the air felt almost twenty degrees warmer without Bonnet hanging over them any longer. She could, however, still feel a small current of cold air coming off of the headless ghost of Blackbeard.

"My pleasure, lass," Blackbeard said, floating above her as Mitch dropped the raft into the water and Ella gladly climbed aboard. "Bonnet was stirrin' up the spirits somethin' fierce, but there was only so much I could do on me own."

"I'm just glad Caroline has found peace, after all this time." Ella saw Mitch at the window of the plane, checking to make sure she was safe, but she waved him off. The ghosts with evil intentions were no longer here.

"Thanks to the two of ye," Blackbeard said.

"Maybe," Ella said, distracted by the sight of what looked like a black pony trotting slowly down the beach at the tip of Ocracoke Island. The pony's eyes glowed red as it glared at Blackbeard.

"Well, I'd best be leaving," Blackbeard said, his floating body already fading. "Old Red-Eye's over there watching, and I don't need him coming out to fuss at me once again.

He's been a thorn in my side for a long time."

"But wait," Ella said as Red-Eye snorted at them from the distant beach. "What happened between you and Bonnet? How did he betray you? None of the history books said anything about that."

"Ah, lass, how d'ye think the Royal Navy was able to find me so easily on that day? 'Twas Bonnet, driven mad from the loss of his Caroline. Thinking he'd be pardoned for his pirating ways, he went to 'em and *told* 'em where to find me, the back-stabbin' bastard. But he got his re-wards—they hanged him for a brigand a month after my *Queen Anne* was sunk. Luckily we'd moved all our booty before that day."

"So Bonnet *was* responsible for your death?" Ella blinked salt water from her eyes. "We've had the story wrong for all these years."

"Let the books say what they want. I don't mind. I actually enjoy my evil pirate reputation. Impresses the ladies, y'know."

Mitch laughed next to her as he joined her on the raft with an armful of towels. The pirate gave them both a bow that showed Ella more of the wounds from his beheading than she really needed to see.

"Now then," Blackbeard said. "I must ask one last question of ye before I take me leave of ye. With all yer travelin' around these islands, did either of ye *see* it?"

"I'm sorry?" Ella said. "See what?"

Blackbeard pointed a big finger at the space where his head should have been.

"Oh." Ella looked over at Mitch. He shrugged as if to say, *Why not?* "Well, we may have seen something underwater out in Pamlico Sound. Where they named the channel after you."

A hissing sound came from Blackbeard's chest, as if the ghost was sucking in a sudden breath. "Tell me more, would ye? I *must* find it, before I can be findin' my own peace."

"Bonnet was holding your, um, well, your *head* while he was harassing us in the deepest part of the channel. The same place Mitch found the pistol. It looked like a battle had been fought there, long ago. He was trying to convince us to stop meddling."

"Ah, I knew from the moment I first saw ye, over on Hatteras, that ye were a good egg." Blackbeard's voice had grown lighter, and Ella thought she heard a deep sigh of relief come from his burly chest. "That's why I was dancing up there on that old house, ye know. I was glad to see ye."

"So that *was* you," Ella said. Mitch looked at her as if she'd lost her mind. "I'll explain later," she whispered to him.

"Aye," Blackbeard said with a chuckle. He was already starting to fade and shrink in size. Ella couldn't blame him—he wanted to be reunited with his head so he could rest, at last.

"Look in the deepest part of the channel," Mitch said. "I think Bonnet may have, um, sort of *dropped* your head when I tackled him."

"Ah, I see," Blackbeard said. "Now," he added in a rushed voice, giving them another headless bow, "I truly must bid you adieu."

"Wait!" Ella called, but the ghost had faded to a tiny glowing circle of white light. If it were dark, he would have looked like a bright white firefly. But in the light of day, with the smoke finally cleared from the inlet, Ella quickly lost sight of all that was left of Blackbeard's ghost. She had the impression his firefly glow had suddenly shot off toward the north, toward Teach's Hole Channel.

"My thanks to ye," Blackbeard's voice whispered in Ella's ears. "Now listen to this old pirate, and take good care of each other, will ye? Or I'll come haunt ye the rest of yer days, I swear to ye . . ."

After a minute of stunned silence, as Mitch and Ella waited, exhausted, for the Coast Guard to arrive, something began to bubble in the water next to them. Ella sat up straight on the raft, reaching for Mitch's hand. She was expecting the worst, so she was pleasantly surprised when, less than five feet from her, the now-familiar piece of the ship's hull from the cave below popped to the surface. It stuck straight up in the air for a moment before coming to rest on its flat side with a slapping sound. Somehow it had come loose from the cave that had held it for all these years.

Ella gasped. The chicken scratches and hash marks covering this side of the hull were the same as what she'd seen earlier, but now she could see so much more. Just like what she'd seen in her dream, she saw a wealth of scratched initials and dates. She saw Stede Bonnet's initials mixed in with "C.A." and a pair that looked like "C.A.B." along with notations from May and June of 1718.

In the middle of the wall was a metal plate proclaiming the name of the ship. This was, without a doubt, *The Revenge*.

"Dig deeper," Blackbeard's voice whispered again. "I couldn't let Bonnet or any of his thugs enjoy the booty we'd stored on this ship, so I've been hauntin' this ship ever since the day I lost me head."

"Thanks," Ella whispered.

"I trust," Blackbeard said in a fading voice, "that ye will know best what to do with what ye find down there."

269

And then Blackbeard's deep voice was drowned out by the rumble of the approaching Coast Guard rescue boat. With Mitch's help, Ella maneuvered the wall of the ship so it was hidden behind the half-sunken plane. She didn't want to have to explain that to anyone else just yet.

In the moments before the Coast Guard pulled up next to them, Ella felt something cool and small around her neck. She reached down and saw a shiny silver locket around her neck, of a similar design to Caroline's. She turned to Mitch, wondering how he'd been able to put that around her neck without her knowing it.

But he was on the other side of the raft, a couple feet away, and he was staring at something shiny and golden in his hand. Blackbeard had left a gift for Mitch as well: a pair of glistening, mint-condition gold doubloons.

Ella opened the locket and saw a faded painting of a young woman's face. Her pale complexion and radiant eyes were exactly like Caroline's, without the ghostly orange light illuminating them. The other half of the locket was even more pale, but Ella thought she could see a faint outline of the man Stede Bonnet once was, before his head wound and the madness that followed it.

She reached down to touch Caroline's painting, but before her finger made contact with the ancient paper, it dissolved, and the dust of it blew away on the wind. Bonnet's image also disintegrated, leaving both sides of the locket empty for its new owner to fill as she pleased.

With a smile, Ella let go of the locket. It rested against her chest with a reassuring weight. She took a deep breath of the salty air and felt a sense of peace fall over the water surrounding the shipwreck.

Their work here was done, in a sense, as far as Caroline and Stede Bonnet were concerned. But for her and Mitch, *their* work was just beginning, in more ways than one. Ella looked forward to that new challenge, with all of her heart.

The only logical action to take after the day Mitch and Ella had shared was to hit the Jolly Roger. After a change of clothes and a hot shower, of course. They agreed to meet at the restaurant as soon as possible.

With her hair damp and an incredible sense of lightness carrying her out her front door, Ella stopped when she heard a scrabbling sound coming from her new birdhouse. She peeked inside and saw bits of straw, grass, and paper inside the hole—the makings of a nest. She hurried down the front steps and up the road to Owen's produce stand. The old man was just setting up for the day, and Ella left him sputtering for words when she thanked him for everything and planted a big kiss on his cheek.

"You were right about those spirit fingerprints," she whispered. "But I think this will be a good year for your fruits and vegetables now."

Then she was off, almost jogging in her desire to get to the restaurant and see Mitch again. She waved at the occasional passing car and inhaled the salty air with relish. It was a good day to be alive, and a great day to be here, in Ocracoke, away from everything else.

Mitch was waiting for her outside, leaning on the worn railing. His welcoming smile electrified her, and then she was back in his arms again.

"Good thing it's noon," he said once they'd managed to let go of one another. He led her to a table where she saw his dad sitting with Melissa. "Otherwise we wouldn't be able to get served. North Carolina still has strict liquor laws on Sundays, and I *really* need a drink."

Ella nodded at him. She couldn't believe today was only

Sunday—so much had changed in the past week, she felt like she'd been in Ocracoke for months.

"Mind if we join you?" she said to Mitch's dad, reaching down to pet Barny, who was gnawing a bone next to the picnic table.

"Ella!" he said. "Please do, both of you."

Melissa walked up with a pitcher of beer for them, as if she'd been waiting for their arrival all day.

"Hi guys," she said, setting down the pitcher and mugs. She kept looking back and forth between Mitch and Ella.

Was it that obvious? Ella wondered. She was surprised when she realized that she didn't really mind.

"I can't stay and chat for too long," Melissa said, looking over at the crowd of tourists filling the restaurant. "We're slammed! And this was supposed to be my day off. Ben said that this morning's ferry brought hundreds of tourists to town. Crazy, isn't it?"

Ella only smiled. "No," she said. "Makes perfect sense to me. I mean, it's a beautiful day. Who wouldn't want to spend it here in Ocracoke?"

"Can't argue with that," Melissa said. She nodded knowingly at Mitch and Ella, winked, and hurried off to take orders from the next table full of customers.

"So will you be going out to do more research today," Mitch's dad asked, "or do you workaholics get to take Sundays off?"

Ella looked at Mitch, a smile crossing her face as she realized she could continue her stalled expedition at last. Dr. Bramlett would have quite a report waiting for him tomorrow morning, a much better report than the sketchy one she'd given him a few days ago. She thought about getting started on her work today, right after lunch. They could charter someone else's boat, get their gear, and be out there in an hour or two.

"What do you say, boss?" Mitch asked, his pale blue eyes blazing with intensity.

Ella glanced over at the empty space where *Cassiopeia* had once been docked. Ben must have called in help to get it moved while Mitch and Ella had been gone.

"You know," she said, "I think we'd be better off in Mitch's *new* boat. I think the, ah, grant money from the university we . . . earned should help cover the costs, don't you think?"

"Mitch!" his dad said. "Great news, son!"

"And anyway," Ella continued, "we've got plenty of time. Right, Mitch?"

Mitch's smile was big enough to wipe the last traces of sadness on his face left over from the loss of his boat.

That look, Ella decided, *was worth a hundred of Blackbeard's gold doubloons.*

When their drinks arrived, she took a glance around the busy restaurant. At the next table she saw the three elderly tourists who'd had the island to themselves just two days earlier, sitting at a table with a group of younger tourists.

One of the women was telling a ghost story about the sailors who lost their lives in the waters off Ocracoke. Ella listened for a moment and watched the awed expressions of their audience. She was about to turn away when, out of the blue, the old man at the other table smiled and tipped an imaginary hat at her. Ella had been expecting a scowl or even an obscene gesture. The old guy had surprised her again.

That just goes to show that you never know what's going to happen in life, she decided.

As they ate, she looked at Mitch's family around him, from his father at the table as well as Melissa rushing around the restaurant, seating yet another group of tourists. She wished her father could be here to share this meal with them; he would've loved it here in Ocracoke. She felt like he *was* here, in spirit.

Her gaze came to rest on Mitch once more, laughing at something his father had just said.

I have to trust my instincts, and trust that everything will work out, in the end. It was a philosophy she was getting get used to, quickly.

Mitch caught her gaze and set down his drink.

"You're looking awfully serious," he said with a smile that made her skin tingle. "Having second thoughts about not getting back to work?"

"Not at all. But starting tomorrow," she added, taking both of his hands in hers. She could almost see the air crackling with sparks as their eyes met. Ella couldn't resist—she leaned forward and kissed Mitch. "Tomorrow, we've got some serious work to do."

Yes, Ella decided. *I could* definitely *get used to life here in Ocracoke.*

About the Author

Julia C. Porter lives with her husband and son in Raleigh, North Carolina. She hopes to take another trip to Ocracoke Island soon. Visit her online at www.juliacporter. blogspot.com.